A LIFE OF DEATH
SACRIFICES

Book Three

WESTON KINCADE

Introduction
by
Scott Rhine

"A great YA story!"
~ John F.D. Taff, author of Little Deaths

For information about special discounts for bulk purchases, please contact Weston Kincade at wakincade@gmail.com or at http://kincadefiction.blogspot.com.
Book Design and Editing by Weston Kincade and Scott Rhine
Cover Art copyright © 2017 by Claudia McKinney at PhatPuppyArt
Partial stock photography by somadjinn.deviantart.com and depositphotos.com
The text for this book is set in Cambria.
Manufactured in the United States of America
Summary: Alex's ghostly visions can save lives. But can they stop a drug czar from disrupting the peace and harmony of Tranquil Heights?
For Alex Drummond trouble doesn't come knocking, it kicks down the door and raids the refrigerator. War is brewing between moonshiners and a murderous drug kingpin. Cremated human remains are appearing everywhere. And now Alex's family is in the middle of it all. To make matters worse, his son's powers rival his own... as does his stubborn nature. Choices will be made. Laws will be broken. And morality will be questioned. Will Alex's family survive the bloodshed?
Psychometric powers combine in this thrilling battle for survival in Weston Kincade's final book in the A Life of Death trilogy. The future of Alex's hometown is at stake... but sacrifices must be made. Step up and buy Sacrifices today.
ISBN 978-1546885030 (Print)

A LIFE OF DEATH
SACRIFICES

Alex's ghostly visions can save lives. But can they stop a drug czar from disrupting the peace and harmony of Tranquil Heights?

For Alex Drummond trouble doesn't come knocking, it kicks down the door and raids the refrigerator. War is brewing between moonshiners and a murderous drug kingpin. Cremated human remains are appearing everywhere. And now Alex's family is in the middle of it all. To make matters worse, his son's powers rival his own... as does his stubborn nature. Choices will be made. Laws will be broken. And morality will be questioned. Will Alex's family survive the bloodshed?

Psychometric powers combine in this thrilling battle for survival in Weston Kincade's final book in the A Life of Death trilogy. The future of Alex's hometown is at stake... but sacrifices must be made.

Acknowledgements

I would like to thank quite a few people who have helped *A Life of Death, Book Three* evolve into the trilogy it is today. If only my editor, Katy, could have seen it completed. Firstly, to the late, great Katy Sozaeva who helped make this trilogy what it has finally become. She will be missed, but her efforts will live on within this trilogy. I could not have flourished as a writer without her painstaking assistance. Also, the support and love of my wife, family, and friends is something I could not live without. A shout out to Tavis Potter, my friend and "brother from another mother," who has always been a personal inspiration and supporter when things looked bleak. Look Tavis, you made it into another of my books! Additionally, thanks go out to Roy Daily and Books of the Dead Press, who published the first two books in the *A Life of Death* trilogy back in 2013. The support and confidence he had in the series will always be remembered. Also, I would like to express my gratitude to fellow writer and the editor of *Sacrifices*, Scott Rhine. In addition, enormous thanks goes out to him for providing the personally written introduction to this book. An added note of thanks goes out to the man behind the story who was there when I needed his expertise on trains, Dan Wilburn, who also made his debut in this novel.

Personal Note

Tranquil Heights, the setting for the *A Life of Death* trilogy, is based on a mountain town I used to teach in, Abingdon, Virginia. Its unique beauty was certainly part of the inspiration for this story and the rest of the trilogy. Walking through the town after reading the novels, I'm sure you will recognize a few features; although, I did take some liberties.

Table of Contents

Introduction

Scott Rhine

Weston and I have been fans of each other's writing for six years. He has a gift for metaphor and cinemagraphic endings that will hang in your memory long after the book has been put down. I've watched him grow tremendously as a professional editor, but he doesn't have nearly the time to write that he wants. In the third installment of "A Life of Death", he pours himself into the story more than ever before. Whereas the first ALOD is a coming of age, this one is more of a passing of the baton to the next generation. His son, Jamie, has decided to follow in the family business of avenging those with no voice of their own—the dead. The backdrop comes from the sort of rural schools where Weston taught. The hero's frustration of knowing the culprit early on is palpable, but he has to build a case one brick at a time, or the villains will go unpunished. It's not dry police procedure because the pace continues to mount until the nail-biting finale. Unlike a TV series or movie, the main characters aren't guaranteed to survive until the next installment. All gloves are off in this bare-knuckle brawl. Alex is complex and haunted daily by his past failures. No flash-in-the-pan spree-killers, his enemies have survived for this long because they are careful and ruthless. Bodies mount at an increasing pace. Attempting to stay ahead of the tsunami takes its toll on him as he races to save more innocent lives. The clever drug-dealer hideout could have been something out of "Breaking Bad." The moonshiner fights reminded me of the old Patrick

Swayze movie "Next of Kin." I hope you enjoy the ride with sirens flashing. If you don't like the way Alex drives, then stay off the sidewalk.

-Scott Rhine
Author of Jezebel's Ladder

Bio:

Scott Rhine wanted to find a job that combined his love of reading with math problem solving, so he studied both short stories and computer languages. As a techno-gypsy, he worked on optimizing some of the fastest and largest supercomputers in the world. A couple of degrees, patents, and children later, at forty-eight, he still didn't know what he wanted to be when he grew up. When his third publication, "Doors to Eternity," hit #16 on the Amazon epic fantasy list, he decided to become a full-time author. Since then, each book of his "Jezebel's Ladder" series hit the high-tech science fiction top 100. His new medical thriller, "the K2 Virus," is his highest rated novel with the first 12 reviews ranking it five stars.

Humor is a part of every story he writes because people are funny, even when they don't think so. In the real world, something always goes wrong and people have flaws. If you can't laugh at yourself, someone is probably doing it for you. Strong female characters also play a major role in his stories because he's married to a beautiful PhD who can edit, break boards, and use a chainsaw.

Chapter 1

Adolescence

March 8th, 2012

SIX MONTHS AGO, I almost lost my wife and son to a deranged woman. The delusional lunatic chose to interpret her mother's lifelong work as though it were the product of an Egyptian-Lovecraftian romance, brought on by a mushroom-induced haze. My family was lucky. Paige escaped with minor burns, but Jamie... every time I look at my son I'm reminded of him standing atop the crossbeams spanning that vaulted ceiling, seconds from being hanged within an inferno. *How does a man live with the visible reminders of such an event? How does a son?*

Jamie's footsteps came bounding down the hall, each one thundering in the double-wide trailer like the giant trundling after Jack at the top of the beanstalk.

"Slow down!" I shouted.

Jamie appeared out of the dark hallway into the living room, a smile spreading across his narrow face. It was a shadow look, a grin hiding something subtle but ominous beneath the surface. He had never been a troublesome child, but now that he was fifteen it seemed as though his mischievous nature was revealing itself, like the terrible twos had somehow grown into a five-foot-eight Clark Kent lookalike with an undeniable desire to borrow the car.

Was I ever like that?

"Dad, give it up. It's not like I'm gonna bring the house down."

I frowned and shifted in my generic La-Z-Boy. Its faux-leather surface squeaked beneath my light-brown slacks. "You're giving me a headache, boy. Are you ready for school?"

Jamie rolled his eyes, and I couldn't help but notice the ankh branded into the center of his forehead. The black bangs curling down around it failed to hide the scar—a visible reminder of my failure. I hated Shelley Rayson for branding him like cattle. And I hated myself for allowing it to happen. As a homicide detective, it's my job to ensure everyone's safety, but what seems like yesterday, I was practically helpless.

"Fine, Dad. Don't have a cow. I'm ready." He trudged into the kitchen, his long, blue t-shirt attempting to hide his sagging jeans.

"Are you taking the bus?" I pulled the lever on the chair, and my footrest descended, rocking me up to my feet. I stretched, then powered off the television and the murmuring news reporter with the remote.

"Nah," he replied. Leaning over the counter separating the kitchen from the dining room, Jamie asked, "Mind if I take the car?"

"Yes, I mind. You don't have your license yet. You can't drive without an adult present." I buttoned the top of my shirt and hiked up my tie.

"Awwww, why you gotta be that way?"

"What, like a dad?" I replied, unable to help a slight smile. Jamie disappeared deeper into the kitchen, but his voice answered, "No, like a jerk."

"A jerk? I know you didn't just call me that." Striding into the kitchen, I gave Jamie a quizzical look.

My son's head was stuck inside the refrigerator as though searching for someplace to plant a flag, claiming it for his own.

"Jamie, we have rules in this house, and you know it."

He shrugged out of the refrigerator with a bagel in hand and a rolled-up tortilla peeking halfway out of his mouth. He mumbled something around it I couldn't make out, but his dark eyes still held an element of mischief.

"Do I need to tell your mother?"

At this, the look on his face dropped. He removed the excess tortilla from his mouth and swallowed the rest. "Sorry. I've just gotta get to school early today."

"Why's that?"

"A bunch of us are getting together this morning to plan something for this afternoon."

"That sounds nice. Anything I should be aware of?"

Jamie scowled. "No. I can take care of things myself. You don't always need to come to the rescue. It's just some boys ganging up on my friends. We're organizing a defense. They'll lay off soon enough."

Our small town of Tranquil Heights seemed to be getting more violent every year, but if the events of six months before had taught me anything, it was that I needed to trust Jamie. I couldn't handle everything myself. "Well, let me know if you need my help."

Jamie rushed through the kitchen and dining room. "I could use the car."

"Not that. Like I said, you're not old enough."

"That's not fair. Grandpa said he let you take the car out when you were fourteen."

The mention of Grandpa was a bit irritating. My father had been killed by a drunk driver before I entered high school. Our family was a little different than others. I frowned at Jamie. "Those were different times. Get your bag. We'll head out now. That should get you there in enough time."

"Is Mom already gone?"

"Yes. The hospital called her in at five this morning." I knew he could hear the agitation in my voice. I was sorry to have directed it at him, but children could often be irritants, especially those who could speak with your dead relatives. How was I to argue with my father when I couldn't talk with him without being flung into a deadly vision? And controlling those was practically impossible.

"But, Dad, it's embarrassing—"

I held up a finger. It worked almost as well as a mute button. "Do you have a car?"

His mouth clamped shut, and he shook his head.

"Do you have a license y—"

"I've got my learners," he interrupted, pulling the identification card out of his pocket and waving it between us as though I wasn't the one who took him to get it one week prior.

"Let me finish. Do you have a legitimate license yet?"

His head drooped.

"Pay for insurance?"

It dropped more.

"And did you not just insult the one person you wanted to do you a favor?"

His shoulders sagged, and he disappeared back into the hallway, heading for his room.

"That's what I thought. I'm taking you, and pull your pants up before I get the governor to outlaw sagging for indecent exposure. I taught you better than that."

"Awww, Dad," whined Jamie from the other room, but when he came back into view, his jeans were on right, if not a little askew. "Why can't you just lend me the car?"

"I'll tell you what. Wait nine more months, pass your test, get your license, and we'll see."

Jamie huffed but said nothing more as I locked up. We jumped into the old, unmarked police cruiser. The half-orb, rotating light sat on the dash, idle and unmoving like a turtle hiding from predators.

Hiding from my son, I thought with a chuckle. *Teenage angst will scare anyone.*

The engine revved and we drove down the street, heading for Madessa High School, my old stomping grounds. The drive would take fifteen minutes. We passed the old cemetery lined with large pines and a black, cast-iron fence. I stopped at a red light. Many family members were resting there. I even had a great-great uncle who we believed was buried in the mass grave of Confederate soldiers. A small fence enclosed the long rectangle of space within the cemetery. It was a grassy mound topped off by a large, stone cross. From the road that split the cemetery, I spotted the stone raven sitting atop the cross's arm. The bird stared down at the massive grave as though attempting to decipher identities. A few of the mass grave's inhabitants had their names chiseled into the wide square of weathered stone beneath the cross, but far more remained unaccounted for. So many lives lost and so much mystery shrouding their battlefield deaths saddened me.

"Dad, the light's green. Why do you have to stare at the cemetery all the time?" Jamie asked.

I hit the gas and caught up with traffic as we passed through the small, picturesque town. Classic red-brick homes towered along the sides of the narrow streets, white columns framing the frontages. "There's a lot of history in that cemetery."

"I know, but that don't mean you have to get caught up in it every time it comes into view."

"Doesn't, not don't," I corrected. "Maybe not, but we owe them more than a passing glimpse."

Jamie glared, then waved a hand. "I know. I know. But life goes on. There's so much more to the here and now. You can't forget about that."

For someone with even more paranormal ability than me, he often said things that made me wonder where he had acquired years of wisdom. The next moment, he'd be back to his old, teenage self. It was hard not to be drawn into the past. The world of the dead beckoned around every corner. Jamie somehow walked the fence between the two worlds better than I ever did. "You know, you surprise me."

Jamie grinned. "You shouldn't set your expectations so low and that won't happen near as often."

From anyone else I would have been hurt, but this was Jamie's sense of humor showing through. We both laughed. "But if I set them any higher, I'm not sure you could meet them," I replied with a grin.

Jamie's eyes widened as he looked at me from the passenger seat. "You didn't just insult me?"

We both laughed again. "All's fair in love and war... and parenting, or so they say."

A woman's voice squawked over the radio, "Car thirteen!"

I reached down, picked up the receiver, and clicked the handset. "Car thirteen here. What do you need, Taylor?" Taylor Hicks was our resident dispatcher on days. The Tranquil Heights Police Department wasn't large, but it had grown with the swelling population in our small community.

Taylor's bubbly voice echoed through the speakers, "I know it's early, Alex, but we found something on Mark's Row by the train tracks. You really need to take a look before the weather turns."

I glanced out the window at the vacant lot of waist-high grass whizzing by, the ancient, gnarled oaks and pines separating housing divisions, and then the new minimalls that just went up last summer. Above, gray clouds roiled across the skies, rolling over us and shrouding the sun's morning light as though Zeus himself had become irate. He was a father, so it was understandable. Thunder pealed in the distance. There was no need to ask what the situation was. The weather could destroy evidence. I was a homicide detective. It's what I did best. My abilities made me well-suited for such mysteries, no matter how much I hated enduring the visions. "How long?"

Dispatch replied, "Hector put up a tent, but the forecast is calling for high winds and sleet by lunch."

"On my way." Tossing the handheld microphone onto the center console, I asked Jamie, "You mind being a little late? I'll write you an excuse, but we need to get over to the scene ASAP."

Jamie gave a momentary frown but perked up. "Sure." He pulled out his cell phone and began punching a message in with his thumbs. "I'll have Donny get things organized this morning. So long as I'm there this afternoon, it shouldn't be a problem."

I shook my head. *Back to texting. Teenagers.*

Chapter 2

Lost Innocence

March 8th, 2012

I TURNED LEFT, exiting the main strip, and quickly entered farm and pasture land that could have been a scene from medieval England, just with more cows than sheep. The town's expansion hadn't reached here. We passed decrepit barns and houses that seemed willing to fall at the briefest touch; porch roofs slumped inward, and doors hung from the hinges. I turned right onto Mark's Row, an old road that had been paved some years back but not kept up. Barbed-wire fence lined each side of the narrow street along with tall, green weeds and plant life erupting after the fierce winter. The fields hadn't been tended in years, and everything was overgrown. Breaking up the vacant scene was a pair of police cruisers parked at the rise in the road, just before the train tracks. Their lights weren't flashing this far out, but I recognized the marked number on the back quarter panel of Hector's car.

We'd been partners for years and normally rode in the same vehicle, but when more area needed to be covered, the department had given him one of the old cruisers—number eight. He liked calling himself *"The Ocho"* when responding to dispatch. Taylor always got a good laugh out of it.

I pulled to a stop and opened the door to another peal of thunder.

"Mind if I help?" Jamie asked.

Normally children wandering around crime scenes was a big no-no. I glanced over at the last cruiser present—Theresa's. "Sure. Just remember to stay out of the way. Let me know if there's something you need to touch before you do. Officer Fuller won't throw a fit about you being here, but she's a bit by the book. Remember that."

Jamie threw off his seatbelt with a large grin and exited the car. "Don't forget Fluffy," he shouted.

I pulled the long, black trench coat he'd nicknamed out of the backseat and slipped it on along with my matching fedora. The overcoat was tattered and singed along the edges after our previous ordeals, but it was difficult to replace, like a comfortable pair of shoes that have been worn in. Besides, Fluffy and I had been through a lot. I approached the large, blue-topped tent between the white-and-brown cruisers. There weren't sides to the tent. It was more of a pavilion covering for weekend campers you might pick up at the local sports store, but we made do with what was available in rural Virginia. Hector was leaning over something, peering down at the ground between rectangular containers and a drink cooler while Theresa watched over his shoulder. If I didn't know better, I'd have thought they were trying to start a campfire, huddled as they were. Hector's beige sports jacket contrasted with Theresa's blue officer's uniform.

"So what do we have?" I asked. Just before stepping beneath the tent, a few raindrops spotted my shoulders and forehead.

Without glancing back, Hector replied, "Not much. The Meyers own this side of the road. Their son William reported it."

"Reported what?" Jamie asked.

I gave him a sidelong glance at the interruption, but Theresa smiled wide. "It's good to see you. Were you on your way to school?"

He nodded.

"Sorry to pull you away from your friends." She stepped over to Jamie and patted his cheek. "This is a little gruesome so you'll probably want to stay back."

"Okay," he mumbled without conviction.

He had no intention of following those instructions. He'd probably seen more death than Theresa in the last dozen years she'd spent on the force. *At least he's playing along.*

"Any footprints, tire tracks, some kind of DNA?" I asked.

"See for yourself," Hector said, rising to his full height of five feet eight inches. He waved at something on the ground. "This is all we found. It could've been here for a day or two. Thankfully it's in a gully. The sides sheltered the remains from the wind, but who knows how long ago it was dumped. We blocked it with everything we could until you got here. There isn't much." They had draped a clear sheet of plastic over the remains, but he pulled it back just enough for me to see a pile of chalky white dust.

I closed the distance between us, with Jamie inches away. The entire cone was no more than eight inches in diameter. However, a few larger chunks stood out amidst the rest. I squinted and knelt closer. Some particles had been blown into the surrounding grass, but who knew how much of the remains had been lost?

Hector used a specialized brush to knock some of the white sediment from one of the solid pieces. Silver glistened from the grooves of what now looked to be a filled tooth. Glancing at the others, they appeared to be more teeth and bone fragments from a cremation. It looked like dried clumps of white beach sand. "These have been here longer than a couple days, Hec."

My partner readjusted his knelt position to gaze closer at the remains. "What do you mean?"

I pointed at the sediment-like clumps. "These still contain some moisture. I think there was more here before, but when it rained last weekend some of the remains washed away. This is what's left. It absorbed the water. By now, the person responsible is probably long gone."

"We thought it might've been a fire," Officer Martinez explained. "Maybe a copycat killer like the one we found some months back."

I shook my head. "I don't think so. The location's not right. Fire can really damage bones and even destroy some, but these look to have been ground up and dumped here. There aren't any scorch marks from a fire or a pit. It's like someone just stopped their car, opened the door, and poured the cremated remains out like a soda that had gone flat. Plus, I doubt there's more than one copycat killer in Tranquil Heights. This is still a small town."

Hector gently lifted a fragile shred of bone from a small tray next to him. "This is the largest one we found. It's why the Meyers kid contacted us."

I held out my palm and readied myself for what was to come.

Hector set a bone from a human eye socket in my hand. It was smaller than normal, seemingly that of a child, and as soon as the pitted surface touched my skin, the long-familiar aroma of aged leather wafted to my nostrils. Darkness followed as though an inkwell had been poured into a swirling glass of water.

* * *

My vision lightened onto a blurred image that began to clear, revealing the decrepit front porch of an old house illuminated by moonlight. It looked huge. The wooden railing was at eye level, as if I had shrunk. The old, wooden boards beneath my black sneakers were painted gray but peeling, as though each step I might take could pull another layer off. I glanced up, inspecting the shattered glass in the front window, the splintered doorframe, and the looming door cracked open six inches. A look over my shoulder revealed a dark night, forest, and overgrown plants around the house. I took a couple strides off the porch, down the fractured stone steps. Vines grew over the two-story house as though nature had returned to claim it, a vengeful but possessive mother I wouldn't want to tangle with. I turned my attention back to the drooping porch roof. It looked ominous. Crickets chirped, an owl hooted a three-syllable mantra, and something scurried through the dark underbrush a few feet away. I swallowed the lump of fear that had crept into my throat.

"Stay out here," Momma had said.

This place looked as though nothing human had lived here for ages, but hissing voices echoed through the open door. One was Momma's. I didn't recognize the other. It was masculine.

For a moment, memories separated and I recognized my own distinct mental self. I'm Alex, not some kid, *I thought.* Keep it together. *It was always hard to distinguish between the victim's memories and my own, always a losing struggle for identity.*

The child's thoughts returned, overwhelming my own and pushing my consciousness to the back, leaving me an observer. Stay out here, *I silently repeated to myself.* Stay out here. Momma doesn't know. It's scary, too scary.

"Who-whooo-whooooo," sounded the owl again. I jumped. Something else shook the nearby bushes, and I gazed into the golden eyes of a creature sitting in the dark. It stared back, sending a shiver down my spine.

"Who's there?" I whispered. My voice was light, youthful, and a tremor ran through it.

Nothing but night sounds replied. The gold eyes closed and then opened, glaring at me. My knees shook, and my heart thundered in my small chest. A small baseball cap and shorts were hardly enough to protect me from whatever wildlife was out there. Something swept past my shin, stirring the hair on my right leg. I

jolted. Unable to remain still any longer, I ran back up the steps
toward the comfort of Momma's voice, but stopped at the door. Stay
out here. *"Momma?"*

The conversation inside continued, unwavering.

Something rattled from the depths of the overgrown front
lawn. I looked back, my eyes widened, and I dove through the
entryway. The house was dark with no lights, just dim moonlight
shining through the windows. The walls were skeletal and bare.
Sections had been ripped away, revealing boards and pipes beneath.
Sheetrock littered the ground. Each step crunched. I passed through
the remains of a doorway into a large room. The voices grew louder
the closer I got, but they weren't in this room. The sound of footsteps
echoed oddly as I crept into the kitchen. Metal pans hung from high
cabinets.

Momma leaned against the kitchen island with one hand, her
other massaging a thin man in a flannel shirt. "Please, just give me
some more. They always pay. I can sell more."

In the dark room the man stood shorter than Momma, but
his curly hair added a few inches of height.

Momma leaned closer to him. "I can make it worth your
while. Trust me."

"Momma?" I asked, stepping up and tugging at her jeans.

She jumped and turned her narrow features to stare down in
astonishment. "Tommy, what are you doin' here?"

"What the hell?" shouted her friend. He jumped back and ran
a frantic hand through his hair. It stood up around his head like

coiled vibrating springs, as though his appendages had just been attached to jumper cables. "You brought a freakin' kid?"

"I was scared," I whispered. "Something outside was watching me."

Momma gripped my shoulder in a shaking hand but turned her attention back to her friend. "I'm sorry. I didn't have a choice. There was nowhere to leave him. He doesn't know anything."

"Of course he doesn't know anything," the man shouted. "He's a kid."

"He won't tell anyone. I promise."

"He doesn't know to keep his mouth shut," her friend said.

Momma reached for his shirt, pulled him closer, and ran a hand down the front of his pants. "You know I can make it worth your while."

"Worth getting locked up for? I think not." He grabbed something off the counter next to him. It scraped across the countertop before vanishing into the shadows at his side. He leaned down closer to me, and his hair gave him the look of a demented clown. "You and I are gonna have a little talk."

I couldn't see his eyes, but something in his tone made the soles of my sneakers itch. I took a step back and then another.

"N-no, please don't," Momma pleaded.

"Come on back here, Tommy. You and I are gonna be friends."

Momma stepped in front of him, running her hands up and down his shirt. "Please don't. I'll sell it all. I won't take any. You won't have to worry."

"Was I talking to you, you damn junky?" He shoved her backward. "Do you think I care how much you sell... you who brought her child to a drug deal?" He shoved Momma harder. She tripped and fell on the dirt-strewn floor. Then he slashed her across the face with something clenched in his fist. The far window illuminated the long, rusty knife.

"Tommy run—"

He slammed it into her chest.

She gurgled.

My heart pounded like a humming bird's. Momma said to stay outside. My fault. *The soles of my sneakers itched more. I ran.* My fault. My fault.

Momma's angry friend pounded after me. I skidded over the boards and trash, almost falling. I turned into the hallway and up the stairs, leaping the steps that were missing or broken. Run, run, run. Almost at the top. *Over the lip of the second-floor's final step, a gust of wind fluttered a curtain in a far room where moonlight shone through the window. It beckoned to me like an otherworldly escape—until a hand clamped onto my ankle, jerking me backwards.*

"Get over here, you damn cockroach," the man shouted.

My chin slammed into the steps. As I tumbled downward, my forehead smacked into the railing. A blinding light broke my consciousness. My vision became vague, as though I had been thrust into a fog.

The man huffed and puffed. A strong hand gripped me around the waist and tucked me under one arm like a football.

Momma? Where are you?

"You've been a bad boy," said Momma's friend. "You're gonna have to suffer the consequences."

Momma? I'm sorry. *"Mom-ma?"*

"She can't help you anymore."

A shiver ran through my small body, but I couldn't understand why. My thoughts came slowly and were as hard to grasp as sludge. My... fault. My... fault.

Momma's friend clomped back into the first room I had entered. He set me on my feet and held me steady with a solid grip. "Tommy, I need you to stand still for a sec, okay?" *the man requested in a forced pleasant voice.* "Be quiet."

The world wouldn't stay still. The skittering I'd heard before sounded from the corner once more. I was having a difficult time standing. If not for Mommy's friend anchoring me in place, it would've been impossible. A wadded newspaper in the corner shuffled into the light amongst fast-food bags and other trash. I closed my eyes. My fault. My fault... but gotta accept the consequences, like Momma's friend said. *I forced my eyes open and stared at the dark corner. The same pair of golden eyes I'd seen outside peered from beneath the crumpled newspaper, looking at*

me. My knees trembled until a black nose and whiskers peeked out. A
bedraggled, gray-streaked cat emerged. "Meow?"

"Kitty," I said, raising a wavering hand toward it.

It hissed.

At that moment, the man reached around my head and slid
something sharp along my neck. It hurt. I couldn't breathe. Warm
fluid ran over my skin, down my neck and shirt. Kitty, why?

It hissed again.

No air... No words... My fault. My fault.

My legs gave way as Momma's friend whispered, "Good boy."

* * *

Another peal of thunder and the sound of sheets of rain
splattering against the cloth pavilion were the first things I heard.
As my vision cleared, I focused on the eye socket. Tommy's absent
eye seemed to be looking at me—calling to me. The words, *My*
fault, ran through my mind, repeating in his childish voice. A
shudder coursed down my spine. Now the vision was something I
possessed, a memory. It was difficult to discern between my
thoughts and those of the victim's whose death I was reliving. I
would now remember the events of Tommy's death until the day I
died. It was a blessing and a curse that haunted me daily. Every
victim was another memory almost indistinguishable from my
own.

"Yeah, it's getting pretty cold. That thunder gives me the willies, too," Officer Fuller added, rubbing my shoulder. "It's going to be one of those days."

"Don't I know it," I whispered, stretching my head to the left and then the right. My tensed neck cracked audibly, like a collection of snapping twigs. Paige hated the habit, but it relaxed my muscles and nerves.

Hector stared at me with knowing eyes from a foot away, where he still knelt. He'd grown accustomed to how I worked. After six years as my partner, we developed a relationship and got to know each other well—in some ways better than our wives. He was aware of my ability to relive people's murders; although, in the beginning he was skeptical, even after seeing the results. An ounce of that skepticism would probably never go away, but we trusted each other with our lives. He would take my secret to his grave rather than chance our supervisor, Lieutenant Tullings, finding out. They'd have me seeing a psychiatrist and probably drummed off the force. Science doesn't support my abilities, and neither does the justice system. I gave Hector a brief nod.

"Can I hold it?" Jamie whispered once Theresa had stepped to the edge of the pavilion tent.

Martinez's brows knitted. I ignored the look. He didn't know what Jamie was capable of, at least not yet. However, I was hesitant to agree knowing how brutally the boy and his mother were murdered. *Seeing such horrible things can't be good for a kid. Would I be a bad parent if I allowed it?* The ankh branded into the center of Jamie's forehead peeked out from under his curling bangs—a reminder of what he suffered and how he saved us all. *I have to give him a chance. He's capable of so much more than I give him credit, but Paige will kill me if she finds out.* "I'll take the heat if fingerprints turn up," I assured Hector. Turning my attention back to Jamie, I said, "Careful. Just hold it in your palm. It's a difficult one."

He nodded and held his hand out between us.

"Oh, and don't tell your mother."

He rolled his eyes. "Duh."

I sat the skull fragment in his palm, and a faraway look came into Jamie's eyes, much as I probably looked during my visions.

Hector watched my son, and his eyes widened, flitting back to me. "He can, too?"

I agreed silently. "Keep Theresa distracted, would you?"

My partner rose, and his knees popped. "I'm getting too old for all these *secretos*." His Mexican dialect slipped out. Hector strode toward Officer Fuller. I was barely into my midthirties, and he had just turned forty. Since then, every ache and pain was a result of *The Ocho* being "over the hill."

Chapter 3

The Search Begins

March 8th, 2012

JAMIE WAS SILENT after the vision, walking around looking at things. I began to question whether I'd done the right thing. Even in the car, he strapped himself in without being reminded and stared out the passenger window. The overgrown grass and barbed-wire fence whizzed past under his scrutiny.

Clearing my throat, I asked, "So, what did you think?"

Jamie turned to stare ahead at the glove compartment. "It's never easy seeing through their eyes."

Those were words I had said myself from time to time. "I know."

"I can't believe how cruel some people are... just because the guy was worried what a kid would say. Hell, most people wouldn't have listened to Tommy if he had tried to tell the world."

I was reminded of my own adolescence—a time when few people believed me, not even my mother. *Who would believe their own stepfather, or husband in her case, would have killed his first wife? Not many people. The drunk was a murderer, though. He'd admitted it.* I swallowed the lump in my throat. "I know," was all I could say again.

"And his mother... Why didn't she do more? She just kept trying to seduce the guy—I mean, come on!"

"That's something I've come to understand over the years, Jamie. It sounded like she was dealing for him and wanted to up the stakes."

Jamie quirked an eye at me as we passed from pasture and farmland back into residential Tranquil Heights. "It seems to me she had her hand in the cookie jar a bit too much."

I could not help but chuckle at his comparison. The stark innocence of a childlike action being equated to drug use was an unexpected contrast. Jamie was quite observant for a fifteen-year-old. "It'd make sense. Sometimes people develop a dependency on drugs. She was trying to get what she wanted and make more money at the same time. Honestly, most dealers I've encountered would have jumped at the deal... if not for this guy's paranoia."

Jamie nodded. "Probably. I just hate that Tommy had to go through that."

"You and me both. We still don't know how the boy wound up cremated."

Silence permeated the vehicle as I contemplated what might have happened. I turned up the street to Madessa High School. The new sign sat atop a low, red-brick foundation. It was digital and had a blue devil marching along, trying to stab the tail of a dancing goat that kept flipping and turning at the last second. "Skewer the Libsom Valley Goats!" scrolled by beneath the animation. Jamie groaned.

"What's wrong?"

He shook his head. "Nothing. I just hate basketball, and it's that time of year—March Madness."

I frowned. I'd never been much of a sporting type, but I wouldn't say I hated any. "Hate?"

Jamie rolled his eyes. "Fine, not hate. It's just annoying. Every time I get to school it's like, 'Hey, did you catch the game last night? That three-pointer at the buzzer was awesome.'" His imitation sounded like a modern version of Fred Flintstone.

I laughed as we came to a stop in traffic. "Okay, I get it, but you might want to keep your opinion to yourself. Who knows what some rabid fan might do if they overhear you at the wrong moment." With a grin, I grabbed my fedora from the backseat and plopped it onto his head. It slid over his forehead, reminding me of when he used to wear it before he could even walk.

Jamie raised his eyebrows, and they hid beneath the brim. "Good point." He paused for a moment as I turned into the circular drive at the front of the school. A tall, modern clock stood dark and sleek in the courtyard ahead, a waist-high, sandstone-enclosed flowerbed at its base. "You know, one thing I don't understand is why Tommy wouldn't talk to me."

I narrowed my eyes in thought and put the cruiser in park after pulling alongside the curb. "What do you mean?"

"Couldn't talk with Officer Fuller around, or she might think I had a few screws loose. I know Tommy was there with us because after the vision, I heard whimpering."

This was a part of Jamie's ability that differed from my own, the ability to hear and sometimes even see the ghosts of his victims. I could hear them on rare occasions, but to Jamie they were almost as real as flesh-and-blood people. "Could he have been scared or in pain?"

"I'm sure he was scared, and maybe something more than that." Jamie opened the car door and shouldered his half-full backpack, tossing the hat into the backseat. "I think he still feels like this is the consequence he deserves for disobeying his momma. See ya later." Jamie slammed the car door, bounced over the curb, and strode toward the school, the note I'd given him when we first got in the car gripped in his hand.

My fault... My fault, repeated in my mind. "Maybe you're right," I whispered. The sadness I felt for Tommy slipped deeper into my gut.

The ride back to the station was quiet and uneventful with only my thoughts to keep me company. *Who was this curly-haired murderer? What was Tommy's mother's name? Where was she? And the dealer?*

The brief look at the front of the house in the vision told me two things: one, that the place was run-down and no longer occupied, and two, that it was out in the wilderness. The only sounds I'd heard were that of nature, so it could be a mile or a hundred. Since I had nothing to go on beyond where the remains were dropped and a vague impression of what the killer looked like, I played with the idea of calling the department's sketch artist.

I passed through the old, brick station house's side door, patted a few uniformed officers on the back, and strolled through the sea of 1970s wooden desks we called Homicide HQ. By the time I reached mine, I'd changed my mind. I sat down in my leather chair. It was old and worn in places, with the stuffing showing through, but it was comfortable. It squeaked a greeting.

I couldn't help but frown. If I called in Jim Lint, our sketch artist, we could search the criminal database comparing the sketch to photos of past arrests. We could even work up a sketch of Tommy's mother for the NamUS database to see if anyone alerted the authorities about missing or unidentified people. Neither Jamie or I saw Tommy, but with his name and association, that would be added information to make the job so much easier. Unfortunately, I couldn't explain how I got the information. People didn't just buy into the paranormal; most would be skeptical. The likelihood that they would believe me, even if they went along with it and I solved the case, was minimal. The more likely result would be me getting kicked off the force, and that wouldn't help Tommy or my family. Not to mention, anyone else I might have been able to help in the future would lose their chance. Lieutenant Tullings sent me the hard ones even though he didn't know about my talents. He asked few questions unless it related to what could be proven in court. His leniency and confidence were hard to come by in a supervisor. If I were to tell him, he'd be obligated to assign me a therapist and relieve me of duty. It was just the way the world worked, and I had to operate within its strictures.

Dismissing the idea of calling the sketch artist, I scooted stacks of case files and reports aside, revealing my computer keyboard and flat-paneled monitor. They'd updated our computers recently, but as a state institution, the update replaced fifteen-year-old computers with five-year-old ones. They were fast enough for me, though. *I'll just have to do it the hard way.* I booted the computer and accessed the NamUS database. I punched in Tommy and some general details about age and US region. DNA analysis would give us the personal details I used if anyone asked, eventually. For the first search, I narrowed it to Tranquil Heights and guessed the missing date to be within the last month. Two boys around the age of eight appeared on the screen with school photos. I had no idea what Tommy looked like, but a brief search into each revealed their mothers' photos. One had died over a year ago. The other was still living, but neither looked like Tommy's mother.

This could take a while. I revised the search parameters and reduced the name to Tom. He could have been called Tommy as a nickname. Fifteen results appeared, but none were likely matches.

I revised the search again, extending the region to twenty-five miles and the surrounding counties. Over a hundred fifty results appeared on the screen. *This could take a very long while.* I rinsed out my coffee cup in the lounge and refilled it from the newly brewed pot.

Two hours passed, the seconds measured by clicks of my computer mouse and sips of coffee. Steam drifted from the mug, and the dark liquid cooled. It was astonishing how many people had gone missing and for so many different reasons. Each picture and missing-person report required that I scan it for unique details that might align with the little I knew, but nothing seemed to fit. It was like a jigsaw puzzle with missing pieces. Worse, this one had a timer. If this curly haired, paranoid drug dealer could destroy a body, there were more to come.

The next revision of the search parameters quadrupled my previous result totals, and my face sagged. Lunchtime had come and gone. This task might take days. My stomach grumbled, and my eyes itched as though some ungodly maid had taken a feather duster to them in her haste to clean the place. I rubbed them and refilled my cup for what had to be the tenth time. *How many pots of coffee have I made now? Three? Four?*

Returning to my desk, I found Hector sitting in my chair, swiveling back and forth with impatience. "Oh, there you are," he said when he looked up from my monitor. "From the bags under your eyes, it looks like you ain't had much luck."

I took another sip of coffee, hoping the caffeine would give me a little boost, at least enough to socialize through the mental haze. "Nope, no luck. You'd think knowing what I know would make this easy, but without pulling Jim in, we're at a standstill."

"We've had this conversation before," he replied, his Hispanic accent flavoring his words. "Tullings likes you, Alex, but his hands are tied. There'd be no way to explain things. It's like connecting dots, and we have to be able to document every step or else the bastard'll win. Remember that there's no double jeopardy."

"I know. I know. It just irks me sometimes."

"Anything I can do to help?" Hector rose from my chair and seated himself at the next desk—a much cleaner one. A faux-wood placard on his desk announced to visitors, Det. Hector Martinez.

Glancing back at my cluttered office desk, I wasn't sure where my nameplate had disappeared. Shaking my head, I took a seat and ran a hand through my dark, wavy hair. A minor headache seemed to be coming on. I loosened my tie. After so many hours of futile searching, it felt more like a noose after a witch trial. I contemplated wearing a tie more ornate than just striped blue. *At least I'd look pretty the day I really am hanged by it.* "I just don't know," I replied.

"Why don't I go old school. I can call the local county stations and see what they know. Maybe they've got some missing persons they haven't added to the database. You know how some of these small, backwoods towns can be. They try to solve it for the first six months before throwing things online."

I nodded. "Good idea. Add a tidbit about Tommy and his mother potentially being another victim—no certainties, though. Just say it was an anonymous tip when we started asking around."

"Will do."

Swiveling back to my computer screen, I resumed my search.

Hector paused for a second. "Couldn't we say the same thing to Jim?"

I paused, mouse icon hovering over another search result.

"No, it won't work."

"Yeah, it would."

"For the first time, but how many anonymous tips before people start getting suspicious. Word gets around. Once we do it, that will make it easier to do again. Best not to start. In another department and another city, it's not likely to come back and bite us in the butt, but Jim is a regular here."

Hector shrugged. "You're probably right."

I returned my attention to the screen. The lack of results was so distressing that I considered starting a new search, this time for the murderer. While I couldn't do much for the victim, or victims if there was more than just Tommy's cremated remains there, I could prevent future people from enduring the same fate— assuming the man did it again. I thought about going back to the remains, sifting through more bone shards. It might give me a different vision, one of Tommy's mother if she had been dumped with him. *But will knowing get me any closer to the killer? Probably not.* Besides, there weren't many bone shards left, and in my experience, fires destroyed both evidence and visions. It was lucky that the fragment of Tommy's orbital socket had contained a memory. Nothing else likely would.

Time is money. Without a clear look at the killer's face, it would be difficult. I had hoped to find a location to help narrow the

search since there would be too many arrest records and
photographs to go through manually.

Then my desk phone rang. I dug it out from under a pile of
paper. "Detective Drummond, Homicide."

"Mr. Drummond," a male voice on the other end replied,
"this is Mr. Cantril, the principal at Madessa High School."

The mention of the high school brought a flashback of Mr.
Larkin, the young administrator who tried to help me as a teen.
Adolescence hadn't been good to me, but during that final year, I'd
learned to look at the world differently. Besides, from what I'd
heard while attending college, Mr. Larkin moved on some years
later. "Yes, Mr. Cantril, How can I help you?"

"I'm sorry to bug you at work, but we've had a couple
problems with Jamie and his friends. Can you stop by? He's missed
his bus and will need a ride. First I'd like to go over some things
with you."

I let out a sigh. *What happened?* I would find out soon
enough, but my gut told me it had to do with the group of boys he'd
mentioned. *Things must've gotten out of hand.* "Sure, Mr. Cantril. I'll
be there soon."

"Thanks, Mr. Drummond."

I hung up and glanced at my desk clock. It had been a gift
from Jamie last Christmas. An old Civil War Confederate Soldier sat
atop an upright pocket watch with an expression somewhere
between consternation and constipation. In comparison to the
gray-clad soldier, the watch was the size of a boulder. *Come on,*

Jack, get it the rest of the way out, ol' buddy. You can do it! Between the soldier's legs, the hands of the clock ticked away. *Five till four.* I gathered my jacket from the back of my chair.

"Problems at school again?" asked Hector.

"Yeah."

"Did he say what about?"

I shook my head. "I'll find out in a few minutes. I'm guessing it's to do with something Jamie told me this morning."

"Well, have fun. I'll get on those calls."

"Sounds good." I headed for the car. Jamie had never been a troublemaker, but he was mischievous. At times that streak got him into trouble—nothing serious, but it got aggravating. However, I had a feeling this time was different. *What've you gotten yourself into this time, Jamie?*

Chapter 4

Overzealous Administration

March 8th, 2012

THE HALLWAYS OF Madessa High hadn't changed much aside from a few new coats of paint. They were white outlined in blue, the school colors. After school, the locker-strewn hallways were devoid of the childhood voices I remembered. Here and there a few students hurried past in cleats and sports uniforms, probably late for some after-school practice. I turned into the office. A boy Jamie's age sat in one of the wooden chairs lining the painted, cinder-block office wall. I nodded to him. "Donny, how'd I know you were involved in this?"

"Sorry, Mr. Drummond," he mumbled, staring at the floor.

I introduced myself to the young student filling in as a secretary, probably a junior or senior. She set aside her textbook and then rose, flicking her blonde hair over her shoulder as she approached the principal's office down the short hall. I followed, surprised at how short her green-and-black striped skirt was. A cheerleader would have blushed. The girl smiled as she gently knocked on the principal's open door.

"Yes, Cindy, come in," answered a pleasant tenor voice. The tone revealed a smile on the speaker's lips.

She strolled into the room, where a floor lamp lit the back of the office. She sashayed around the side of his desk with added flare, her attention directed at the youthful principal. He was barely thirty with a chiseled jaw, oval face and a GQ look. She laid a hand on his and leaned over to whisper in his ear. He smiled, nodded, and beckoned me into the office. Jamie sat in a low-back chair, tight-lipped and slouched. Opposite my son, Mr. Cantril stood up from behind his desk and extended a hand. I shook it and took the seat next to Jamie.

"Sit up straight," I hissed.

Jamie glared for a moment, but did as I asked without a word.

"Mr. Drummond, I'm sorry to pull you away from work. I'm sure you have more important things to deal with, but something happened that needs to be addressed."

"Just a murder investigation we're trying to solve before someone else becomes the next victim—nothing of importance," I replied, sarcasm caressing each word. I hated myself the second the words left my mouth. This man was just trying to do his job. I wasn't hiding my negative feelings about the place and its faculty from years before very well. Jamie glanced my way, and I caught sight of his scarred forehead. *I'm here for him, to find out who's at fault and what needs to be done,* I reminded myself.

The principal winced. A five-o'clock shadow and sunken look revealed that it had been a long day for him, too. "I... I'll make this short. Jamie, would you step outside with your friend so we can talk?"

Jamie left us, and Mr. Cantril got up to shut the door. "You don't mind, do you?"

"No. I'm sure you wouldn't have called if you didn't think it necessary. What's this about?"

After closing the door, Mr. Cantril half-sat on the rounded corner of his desk and folded his hands over his lap as he looked down on me. While I could tell the change in posture was meant to make this conversation seem more sociable, his choice to elevate himself automatically put me on edge. I stiffened but waited for him to answer.

"It seems Jamie and his friend Donny Pulin are trying to start a gang. Quite a few other students joined them this afternoon in a confrontation with another group, but it was clear who organized the charade."

At first, the absurdity of the claim evoked feelings of rage. I wanted to jump up, to shout and insult the man staring down at me like I was some troublesome student who had gotten out of line. I was back in this same office, feeling the emotions that overwhelmed me as an adolescent. When administrators finally believed me about my stepfather's abusive tendencies, their hands were tied when it came to doing something about it. I lidded the growing anger and considered his perspective. "What about this makes you think it's a charade?"

The question seemed to catch the principal off guard for the moment. "Well, they of course deny trying to form a gang." He folded one foot over the other while leaning on his desk, crossing his legs.

"I'd like to think I know my son. Jamie is a good kid. He's gotten into some mischief from time to time, but—"

"That's something else I noticed," Principal Cantril interrupted. He leaned over his desk and grabbed a manila folder, flipping it open. "It seems that in Jamie's first two years in high school, he's been quite the troublemaker: consistent tardiness, skipping classes, engaging in pranks on other students, and even a fight earlier this year."

My teeth clenched, grinding so loud I was surprised the principal didn't offer me a mouth guard. I did not like being interrupted, especially with accusations based solely on documents. Mr. Cantril had been hired midyear when the previous principal accepted a position in another district, so he hadn't dealt with Jamie in any of these instances. I flexed my fingers rather than follow my urges, which were pushing me to wring Mr. Cantril's scrawny neck like a cartoon ostrich. I wasn't a violent man at heart, but uneducated assumptions were evidence of an irresponsible and unreliable person. When those people are in charge of others, especially children, it is infuriating.

I stood up to my full height of five feet ten inches. While the lanky principal still had a few inches on me, I was more muscular. "Mr. Cantril, I know you haven't been here long, but there are a few things you should know," I explained, attempting to contain my contempt. "Firstly, I'd advise you to sit down. I won't be intimidated, especially by a presumptuous *ass* like yourself."

The principal's eyes widened and he stood up straighter, attempting to exercise his surplus height.

My eyes narrowed. "I'm waiting."

His jaw clenched as we stared back and forth. "I won't be bullied, Mr.—"

"That's Detective Drummond!" I shouted. "You'd best remember it and sit your butt down."

Cantril balked. "You can't speak to me this way!"

"The hell I can't. You accuse my son of being a troublemaker and trying to form a gang without the facts." Cantril tried to interject something, but I overrode him like a runaway steam train whose railroad engineer found a seductive harlot in his back pocket. "That tells me that not only were you a bad choice to run this school, but you've got a bad work ethic, too. If I did what you do, I'd wind up putting innocent people in prison. That wouldn't be good investigative work. You're supposed to be setting an example for these children. When you don't, what does that tell them?" He opened his mouth to speak, but I answered for him. "It tells them they can get through this world by half-assing it. How would you feel if I made a few assumptions from my limited knowledge of this office and what I've seen today?"

To this, Principal Cantril's brows knitted in confusion. "I d-don't know what you mean."

"Take a seat so we can talk like adults, and I'll explain." I waited for him to follow my instructions. He did, and I sat back down. "When I came in, I noticed your little secretary has on a skirt so short you can practically see her cheeks. I know for a fact your school policies have procedures for this. In my day, they would at least give the student a pair of sweaty gym shorts to put on. Now, I'm not sure if she's wearing panties because I was too embarrassed to look when she bent over. But I'm sure every person in this school, including yourself, could probably tell me. I also noticed that she smiled affectionately when she knocked on the door, as did you. I'm an astute observer. I couldn't help but notice how she caressed your hand and whispered in your ear rather than just speak from across the room. Either she had a secret to tell you, which I doubt, or she has a crush. Since we're both observant men, I'm sure you probably know this. Rather than have her work hours when other faculty are present and can vouch for the wellbeing of you and your student, you agreed to allow her to work after school—*in your office*—when you two might be the only ones here… alone."

During the explanation, Cantril's eyes slowly grew into orbs. By the end, he stammered, "H-h-how dare you! If I had known, I w-would have done just what you suggest."

"So you aren't very observant? Are you blind?"

"No!" he shouted.

"Then you *did* see. You *are* aware of what's going on. You just *chose* not to do anything about it?"

"I haven't had time!" He lowered his volume. "I was going to sit Cindy down and talk with her about it, but things have been hectic."

"So you see, if I were not a man after the truth, searching for certainty, I might jump to conclusions. I might arrest you right where you stand for child molestation, statutory rape, sexual misconduct, and countless other charges."

Principal Cantril erupted from his chair. "I did no such thing, and I won't stand for these accusations!"

I waved him down and calmed myself momentarily, leaning back in the chair and folding a leg over my knee. "Now, do you see the problem? I'm not going to arrest you because I personally think it's a case of childhood infatuation. I'm sure Cindy's a good girl, but I'd suggest you do something about the situation. Address her choice of attire, and make sure another faculty member is present when she's working. As a lead administrator, you should already know this. It's important, so don't put it off. Otherwise, things could happen, and you and I might not be seeing eye to eye on things anymore. In fact, it could warrant more research into your past and the goings-on here at Madessa High."

Mr. Cantril's eyes widened to milky orbs. Then he nodded. "I will."

"I trust Jamie. That doesn't mean everything he says or does is the gospel. He's skipped classes, which I've punished him for. I believe he's had notes for all of his tardies, which are mine and his mother's fault. We both work jobs that sometimes require immediate responses, leaving Jamie to either wait or come with us. The fight you so eloquently emphasized was self-defense. Mr.

Perkins, the previous principal, understood and explained it to me as soon as I walked into this office."

Mr. Cantril continued to listen.

"This situation today wasn't a charade, at least not on behalf of my son. Jamie actually told me a little about what was going on this morning before I dropped him off at school. You're right about one thing, though, gangs have been popping up within the school and the community. I've heard from some of the other officers about it and even dealt with gang-related homicides. I'm not sure if this group of boys ganging up on your students is technically a *gang*, but Jamie and some of his friends tried to help a student who was being bullied. Can we agree on that?"

It took a pregnant minute, but Mr. Cantril said, "Yes, that sounds about right."

"What have you done to the other group of boys involved?"

Principal Cantril smiled. "They've been suspended for three days, but I think you'll be surprised at what I have to tell you."

"Oh, why's that?" Adrenaline still pumped through my veins behind my calm demeanor, but this question was a surprise, more so because of Mr. Cantril's excited smile. It took a second to switch gears and await an answer.

"It was Jamie who started this fight."

"You sure you aren't jumping to conclusions again?"

The principal's grin broadened. "I'm sure. Did you see a scratch on Jamie?"

I thought back to when I'd walked in. "Nope."

"He's the only one who threw a punch."

"The only one? That can't be right."

Cantril rocked back in his chair with a laugh, clearly happy with having information I wasn't privy to. "I saw it with my own eyes—knocked another boy flat on his back, and he was a good head taller than your son. Don't get me wrong, Chase was asking for it. They had split the parking lot with the Reds on one side and Jamie's friends on the other. I thought we were going to have a brawl."

"The Reds?" I'd heard the name but couldn't remember where. I was pretty sure Cantril wasn't referring to the baseball team.

"That's our group of problem children. They're a wannabe gang that goes around wearing red clothes: shirts, shoes, pants, hats, whatever they can. They fancy themselves a part of the Bloods, but if we dropped the kids in one of those large, city neighborhoods where real gangs run around, they wouldn't survive ten minutes. It'll be fine. It's just a phase they're going through."

I frowned at this new tidbit of information. "You have an actual gang, and you called me in here accusing Jamie of starting one?"

Mr. Cantril shook his head. "No, they aren't a gang, just wannabes. I wanted to nip your son's attempt in the butt before it got too far along. It takes two to tango, you know, even if they're just kids trying to be something they aren't."

This new information sent my blood pressure through the roof. Steam would've been streaming out of my ears if I'd been in a Looney Tunes cartoon. Jamie might have thrown the first punch, but how could someone miss such an obvious problem while searching for it in others? There was no excuse. I clenched my fists. *Idiot!* "I don't know if you realize, but often it's the wannabes you really have to look out for. They want it so badly, for whatever reason, that they're willing to do things you'd never expect. It doesn't take two gangs to 'tango,' as you so eloquently put it. One of the things some gangs are doing is driving through the city at night with their headlights off. The first time someone flashes them, they turn around and speed after the helpful motorist. Then the gang initiates run the driver off the road and kill them."

At this, Cantril's smile vanished. His mouth dropped open. "That's just to get into a gang?"

"Yep, and to be recognized by a known group as your own gang would take a hell of a lot more. I suggest you take this more seriously. I've seen plenty of young boys arrested for theft, armed robbery, and even murder in our small town. The violence is growing. Learn to deal with it, or you'll have larger problems on your hands."

"I... I had no idea."

"Talk with Stanley, your school resource officer. He'll fill you in on these things and probably has some recommendations on how to handle them. He's been around the block a few years and did a few tours in the Middle East. The fact that Jamie and his friends stood up for themselves means they probably didn't think there was another option. You're failing to do your job."

"I will, but you still don't understand." His face turned stern. "Jamie and his friends were all wearing blue shirts, just like they were their own gang. Just keep him at home for a few days."

"I'm sure you're overreacting when it comes to Jamie. If he's suspended, I'll put him to work at the station. Think about what I said, though. The Reds could become more of a problem if something isn't done."

"I wish more of these kids could serve time at the station or working when they're suspended. They'll probably be left at home to play video games or run amuck on the streets. A lot of them get in trouble just so they *can* stay home."

"I know. You deal with your end and try to keep them on the straight and narrow. That includes maintaining your distance when these girls take a liking to you. These high-school girls may not look like children, but they don't know what they're doing. The laws are there for a reason. You could do more harm than you realize if you allowed something to happen."

The principal waved a hand and chuckled. "I'd never allow something like that. Don't worry." The principal stood as I did, extending his hand. "Thanks for coming."

Although I'd diffused the situation, something about Mr. Cantril unnerved me. I'd come to know the manipulative glint in some peoples' eyes, and the new principal was no choir boy. I half expected to become immersed in a vision of someone's gruesome murder when I touched him. "I hope not," I said, taking his hand before turning to leave.

"Oh, Mr.—I mean, Detective Drummond, would you mind taking Donny home? We couldn't get hold of his parents."

I nodded and left the office. A weight lifted from my shoulders with each step, and I found I could breathe easier. Shaking off the unsettling feeling, I ushered both boys to the car. They moped a few feet ahead of me in silence with slumped shoulders.

Chapter 5

School Safety

March 8th, 2012

ONCE WE PULLED into the vacant driveway of a run-down, blue trailer, Jamie got out and opened the back squad car door for his friend. The rear doors only opened from the outside.

Donny had been quiet for the entire ride. Through the metal grate separating the front seats from the back, I watched his bowed head in my rearview mirror. "I'm sorry you had to drive me, Mr. Drummond."

"It's okay. When will your parents be home?"

"Probably not till after dark."

I glanced at the trailer. Through one of the dingy kitchen windows, a yellow curtain with chicken prints was pulled back and a small face peeked through. "I see your little brother's home."

Donny followed my gaze. "Yeah. I'm sure he'll love telling Mom." As he stepped out of the car, it seemed like he was attempting to shrink rather than unfold himself.

I had noticed these characteristics before, but I never spent much time with Donny. Now I recognized feelings I'd grown up with: shame, regret, isolation, and what was worse—fear. My gut clenched as certainty clicked into place. The likelihood of abuse happening in this trailer home was more reliable than any auto guarantee you might see on television, even those commercials with a used-car salesman twirling around in a suit and pink tutu. In that moment, I knew what he went through each day. I didn't need to see bruises. I recognized what was going on behind the scenes in the Pulin family home. Unbuckling my seatbelt, I let the engine idle while I circled the rear end. "Jamie, why don't you drive home? Get in and adjust the mirrors. Give me a minute with your friend."

Donny appealed to him, begging with a silent look of uncertainty.

Jamie left us standing in the sunlit afternoon. The driver's-side door closed with a *thump*.

"It's okay, Donny," I joked to help him loosen up. "I'm not going to arrest you."

He let out a forced chuckle. "I know."

"I just wanted to ask if everything's all right?"

His eyes flitted away before he answered. "Aside from Mom and Dad grounding me for a decade when they find out, I'd say everything's fine."

"You sure?"

He agreed silently. I pulled a business card out of my breast pocket and handed it to him. He looked at it with intrigue but hesitated before taking it.

"If you need anything, you can always call me... day or night. Understand?"

"Yes, Mr. Drummond."

I gave his shoulder a friendly pat and slipped into the passenger's side of the car with a, "Take care of yourself."

Donny waved and disappeared up the steps and inside the decrepit trailer.

"What was that about?" Jamie asked, backing the car into the pothole-infested street and driving through the trailer park.

I considered telling Jamie what I knew was going on, but without solid proof or at least a vision, which could be too late, I didn't feel comfortable with the idea. Jamie's childhood had been different from both mine and Donny's. Jamie had dealt with more than his share of death, but abuse this close to home was a different matter. "Just checking up on Donny after today's fight."

Jamie laughed. "He wasn't even involved. I can't believe they suspended him, too."

My eyebrows rose. "Not at all?"

As Jamie pulled back onto First Street, heading home, he said, "Well maybe a little, but he didn't fight."

"From what I hear, you were the only one who did." I couldn't help the smile creeping onto my lips. "Laid him out with one punch—good job. I just hope it was for a good reason."

"It was," Jamie replied with enthusiasm. "They were picking on Marshawn. Chase said they were gonna take him out after school today and that if he ran, he was just avoiding the inevitable."

"So you and your friends stood up for him?"

"Not just my friends. All the local rednecks agreed. Chase and the Reds have been pickin' on people and beatin' them up for months. It's getting worse every day."

"Rednecks? You do realize they probably don't care much for being called that."

Jamie glanced my way with disbelief. "I just told you a gang is taking over the school, and you're more concerned with my language. What are you, a politically correct Nazi?"

"No, I just don't think they'd like it. It could cause problems for you."

"Well, it hasn't. All the farm boys at school call themselves 'rednecks.' Really, anyone who wears a large belt buckle, boots, or drives a truck with a lift falls into that description. It's a matter of pride for most kids who're called that, especially the guys with all three of those things."

I laughed. "Boy, how things have changed."

"Yep, they have, and the school isn't doing a damn thing about it."

I narrowed my gaze but chose not to interrupt him with a tirade on foul language. He knew, but his tone was evidence enough that he was emotional about this problem.

"You know what Mr. Cantril told me?" Jamie asked. He didn't wait for an answer. "He said our decision to all wear blue shirts was a gang symbol... a *gang* symbol. Can you believe it?"

"Gangs traditionally wear certain colors that they claim as their own, kind of like a country's flag. You should be careful."

"But Dad, most of our shirts were school shirts, from the baseball team, football team, basketball, and even gymnastics. It's the *school* color, remember? He threatened to ban students from wearing it."

I quirked an eye. "Seriously?"

"Yeah!"

I gave a subtle look at the speedometer. "Watch your speed."

Jamie's only acknowledgement was to slow to forty-five, the current speed limit.

"So what did you say?"

"It was hilarious," Jamie replied, slamming a palm on the steering wheel. "I reminded him that it was a school color, and we weren't just standing up to the Reds. We were also standing up *for* Madessa High School, something the administration didn't seem capable of. It shut him up."

A smile crept onto my lips. "I'm sure it did. He and I had a little talk, too. I have a feeling there might be a few changes soon, but for the next couple days, you'll be coming with me to the station house. It sounds like you were doing the right thing, though. Just try to stay under his radar."

Jamie seemed to gloss over the last half of what I said or simply didn't care. In the past, he'd actually enjoyed his time while on duty with me. "Don't I know it," he replied. "We heard you, Dad, at least some of what you said. Those walls are pretty thin." Jamie sent a friendly punch to my shoulder. "Good going! But I think you might have embarrassed Candice."

My eyes widened at that comment, and I clamped my mouth shut for the last few minutes of the drive.

Chapter 6

New Leads

March 9th, 2012

THE FOLLOWING MORNING, I stopped by the cemetery with Jamie snoring in the passenger's seat. It was a crisp morning. Large pine trees lined the border of the graveyard surrounded by a black, wrought-iron fence. Dew settled on the grass. While some was brown, spring could be seen in abundant green blades. I didn't make it here as often anymore and wished I could. However, I was certain my father understood.

At the end of one aisle of headstones, I found the pine tree I'd come to know so well over the years. The bark on the side nearest my father's grave was worn smooth by my constant company. Taking a seat beneath the great tree's bowing limbs, I stared at my father's headstone. A few birds squawked and called while a handful of ravens played around headstones a dozen feet away like kids on a playground. The wind whistled through the tree limbs above, and I stared at the flecked granite. The engraving my mother had helped me come up with read "In memory of a loving father taken too soon. We miss you, Terry, but will see you when we get home."

"Dad, what am I going to do with Jamie? He's getting into something beyond his control. I don't know what to do. I try to be a good father, but I can't help but think I might be screwing it up.

He's been through a lot already, more than any kid should, and he can't even drive yet." I was anxious; fear of the damage I might be doing by supporting Jamie's ability gripped me. At the same time, what would happen if I did the opposite? *Would that be worse?*

The wind grew, whispering through the trees like a chorus of ghosts struggling for a voice, but my father's was not discernable. Jamie once said that he spoke with my father, but I'd never had the privilege, not since that fateful day he took a drive to save a stranger and was killed by a drunk driver. Talking to him was something I'd longed to do for years, but at least Jamie knew his grandpa in some form.

Still no answer. The odd comfort of the peaceful cemetery descended on my shoulders. Leaves rustled. I stared at my father's tombstone, the name Terry Drummond chiseled into the stone like a constant reminder of his absence, my eyes pleading for answers that never came.

"I'll keep doing my best, just like I know you would. Love you, Dad. Miss you."

Getting up, I ran a hand over his headstone as I passed, heading back to the car where Jamie was waiting. *Someday,* I told myself.

* * *

At the station house, I put Jamie to work in the basement. It was vacant unless you counted the evidence cage in the back, metal racks full of brown, cardboard file boxes, and rectangular, foot-high windows periodically interrupting the top of the cinderblock walls. Since we had both seen the murderer's shadowed face, I decided to set aside the NamUS and pulled a few of the file boxes down onto long, fold-up tables. The moist smell of dirt mixed with long-abandoned cobwebs had assaulted us when we first came down the rickety stairs, but it didn't take long to grow accustomed to the smell. Long fluorescent lights with yellowing plastic covers illuminated the large room like a decades-old photograph. I slapped a file-box lid back on and slid it to the end of the table. It bumped against two more Jamie and I had already sifted through. Pulling another off the metal rack, I brought it to my table and pulled out a file. As I read, I plopped into the metal foldout chair.

"What do you think of this one?" I asked, holding up the slightly damp manila folder.

Jamie turned from a box at the table behind me and took the file. Opening it, he gave the report the briefest of glances and then tossed it onto the table in front of me. "Nah, the hair's not right."

"His hair could have changed."

"What about the amputated leg? Notice that in the report?"

I flipped the arrest file open once more and skimmed to the description, mumbling, "'Lacerated calf after a dog attack at six years old. Leg amputated.' I hadn't gotten that far." I stuffed the file into the section I'd already perused and slumped back into the chair, rubbing my eyes. "I need a break. Want some coffee?"

Jamie turned a disgusted look on me. "You've gotta be kidding. Unless it's Starbucks, I don't want it."

"Kids today," I muttered. Grabbing my orange college mug with the half-worn logo, I slogged up the brick-and-mortar steps. "Water then?"

"Yeah, that's fine."

I closed the basement door and inhaled. The air upstairs felt cleaner, less stuffy, like I'd just stepped out of prison after a ten-year stint with a roomy named Bubba who liked to cuddle. A few officers were around, but most were on patrol.

Hector walked by and slapped my shoulder. "There you are. Glad to see you're still human. Came up for a breather, I see."

I nodded, still absorbing the moment and enjoying the midday sunlight streaming through the windows of the old government building. "What time is it?"

"Almost noon."

That got my attention. "Really?"

"Yep. Any luck?"

I shook my head.

"Well, I've got some news."

"Great! Walk with me," I replied, heading for the lounge where an '80s coffee maker with stains adorning it from its first week of use was gurgling away. "I need caffeine."

"I just made another batch. Should wake you up."

"If I know you, you probably used as much coffee grounds as water."

Hector chortled. "It goes down strong and keeps you that way."

"If you can choke it down at all, Hec. You know, that stuff's like drinking sewage sludge when you make it." Still, I refilled my mug.

"It'll put hair on your chest. Get with the program, man. Women don't want those prefab beach boys anymore. Nowadays, girls are looking for mountain men with hair on their chests that can be braided like Pippi Longstocking."

The coffee was bad enough, but as his vision of chest hair being braided into red, horizontal pigtails blossomed in my mind, I about choked on the first hot gulp. "Where do you come up with these things?" I switched hands and shook off the spillage.

"No idea, but like I said, I've got news that'll cheer you up."

"Oh, what's that?" I grabbed a Styrofoam cup and filled it at the faucet for Jamie.

"Just got a call back from Wytheville. Rob, the guy I talked to yesterday, spoke with the guys in the precinct and thinks he has something for us."

The town was seventy miles away.

"They found some remains a few months back, but there was so little left that the body was just labeled John Doe. There was no evidence at the scene, at least none that could be traced. The scattered bones had been crushed to dust like ours, but left in a brown paper bag in a trashcan at the truck stop. It's so rural and old that there aren't any cameras on the pumps."

"That's not unusual for around here."

My partner nodded before continuing. "If not for the bag busting open due to some soggy trash, they'd never have found the bone remnants."

"Who discovered them?"

"The service worker. He probably wouldn't have noticed had one of the bones not been a finger segment. Even then, the only reason he knew the difference was because he was studying to be a mortician, or so the report says."

"So the wannabe mortician called it in?"

"Yeah, but not before pulling them out and trying to piece the chips and bone fragments together like a Goodwill jigsaw puzzle right in front of the store. The owner came out to see what was taking him so long and discovered the guy fiddling over it on the pavement."

Although I experienced death regularly when reliving murderous visions, I couldn't understand the clerk's morbid actions. I hated the visions but went through them to help people find justice—peace. Morticians just gave me the willies, especially kids with a desire to go that career route. "Weird." I headed toward the basement door.

"True, but without him, we wouldn't have caught this lead. So you want to head up that way?"

"That's over an hour one-way."

"I know, but how else are we gonna look at the evidence today?"

Hector opened the door, but I paused. "Evidence? I thought you said there was nothing linking them."

"There isn't, but they've still got John Doe in their evidence locker."

"All right," I replied. "Grab your keys and my coat. I'll let Junior know."

"You sure you don't want to bring him?" Hector's raised eyebrows told me what he was thinking.

"Around our people, it's one thing. We know who we can trust not to tell a jury a teenage boy was handling the evidence, but with strangers, that might arouse unwanted attention. It's not exactly standard police procedure."

"Yeah, you're right, I guess. I'll meet you at the car."

* * *

The ride to Wytheville was uneventful. Winding roads passed by with the hazy Blue Ridge Mountains visible in the distance. The blue hue made it evident where they got their name. The Wytheville police HQ also housed the fire department and other public safety groups. Their evidence room was in the back. We were escorted down by Officer Jenkins, the gentleman Hector had spoken with. We signed for John Doe, and a few minutes later the evidence clerk brought a Ziploc bag that looked almost identical to our remains. It was labeled with the temporary name and a brief description stating where they'd found it, just as Hector had relayed.

"Got a table where we can look at these?" I asked Officer Jenkins, a muscular man who looked to spend all his free time in the gym.

"Sure, in the next room." He opened the door into the narrow room with a long, wooden conference table spanning most of it. We pulled out two of the roller chairs and seated ourselves while Jenkins sat across from us. "What do you think you'll learn from this?"

"Honestly, we don't know. It may be that some bones were broken or crushed the same way. We might be able to make some comparisons and see if the victims underwent the same process," Hector answered. "Maybe we can match tool markings."

Officer Jenkins nodded.

I hadn't considered what Hec said, but he was onto something. I'd been so caught up in my own unique investigative techniques that I forgot about the standard processes technology afforded us. Opening the seal, I searched the white, sandy contents for the larger pieces. The finger bone and a few other pieces were still intact along with other fragments from larger bones. Some of the fluid that had leaked into the paper bag looked to have stained some of the remains purple in places. A feeling of dread settled in my stomach as I spotted a thin tendril of bone a couple inches in length. It looked more fragile than the others, but something about it beckoned to me. "You mind?" I asked, nodding to the bag.

"Not at all. If you can shed some light on whose remains these are, we'd be grateful. I'm sure their families have been worried sick. We found them before Christmas, so the families have been waitin' for months without word. We about gave up— no leads... nothin'."

Hector said, "We'll do our best."

Reaching in, my fingers caressed the bone, but nothing came. My gut unclenched, but it was less than fulfilling. It was unsettling to be wrong but not uncommon. Sometimes the search took longer. I plucked the bone from the bag and focused on the edges.

Officer Martinez pulled a magnifying glass from his sports coat and asked, "You mind?" He extended a waiting hand.

Handing it over, I knocked some of the dry remains within the bag aside, grasped the finger bone, then a few other fragments—not a glimpse. I clenched my teeth in aggravation. *So close, yet nothing? This can't be happening.*

As Hector examined one bone fragment through the magnifying glass, I began lining each of the pieces in front of him on the table until there seemed to be nothing more than sandy particles and small flakes too damaged to have been imbued with a memory. My hand dove into the bag, allowing the particles to slip through my fingers, but still no visions came—no smell of worn leather. "Are you sure this is all there was?"

Officer Jenkins folded his arms, his massive biceps flexing as he considered the question. "We've still got the paper bag, but there's nothin' in it."

At this, he gained every ounce of my attention. I tried to contain my impulse to shout enthusiastically. It was no guarantee, but it was something more. "Can I see it?"

"Sure." He rose from his seat. "Be right back."

A couple minutes later, Jenkins returned with another Ziploc bag. This one had a folded brown paper bag within its depths. He handed the evidence bag over, and I took it, barely able to contain my enthusiasm. "Did you have it checked for DNA?"

"Yes, but there was too much of everything on it. It was in the trash for a couple days before the clerk found it."

I peeled open the clear bag and withdrew the contents, still expecting a vision, but my heart plummeted. I unfolded the midsize brown bag. It had an assortment of stains all over it. The bottom was even torn and looked to have been soaked, then dried, but not before the contents escaped. *That must be how the clerk spotted what was inside.* I gripped the opening with both hands and pulled it wide to stare into the depths. The familiar odor of worn leather I'd expected before wafted up from its depths, and a tingle flowed from my fingers touching the insides of the bag. I slumped into my chair as my vision swirled to black.

Chapter 7

College Life

March 9th, 2012

I WAITED FOR the vision to replace the darkness, pacing my breathing. Instead of lights or other surroundings, a dim, brown surface appeared less than an inch in front of my eyes. Warm but frantic breath filtered around my face, caressing my cheeks. There was nothing to see, and even my own intake of air seemed to reverberate around my head. I couldn't move, and it felt as though my arms were bound behind me around a metal chair.

Why? Why me. What did I do? *"Scrub, don't do this!" I shouted. Something an inch wide looped around my neck and cinched tight, cutting off my air. "D-don't d-do this. I just c-came to resupply."*

A train whistle blew in the distance, long and hard like they do when traveling into small towns. "You shouldn't have come, Dizzy. I told you not to. Never! I come to you."

I recognized the voice speaking from less than a foot behind me. It was the same man who killed Tommy. Please, no. Please. *The paper bag crinkled as I tried to jerk away from the murderer, but the strap around my neck tightened. I couldn't talk or move. Pain suffused my throat as something pinched my neck like a buckle. I could feel the strength in the murderer's arm as he pulled on the* strap, crushing any hope of release. I struggled to scream but only croaked under the pressure.

"You've gotta learn, young man," the man hissed next to my ear, gripping even harder.

Visions of college friends came to mind: Frank, Emma, and even a lovely woman I called Betty. Others flitted past, but the names didn't seem important and didn't come with the visions. I remembered selling drugs to countless students out of a college dorm room.

My lungs began to burn, to cry out. Oxygen... I need oxygen. I opened my mouth wide, my tongue lolling. I tasted brown paper fibers. My chest felt as though it would burst. My heart hammered, thu-thudding *for everything it was worth until the beats began to slow. Ox-y-gen... need... air. With one last, subtle* thu-thump, *the dim, brown surface before my eyes dissipated, replaced by nothingness.*

* * *

When my eyes opened, I blinked away the fogginess. Both Officer Jenkins and my partner were staring at me. Jenkins hovered nearby. "Are you okay, Detective Drummond?"

The odor of worn leather was a dwindling memory, but the taste of the brown paper bag lingered on my tongue. I swallowed, trying to moisten my mouth. It felt like a desert. "Yes, fine," I finally muttered. "Just fainted."

Officer Jenkins looked to Martinez and back to me. "Yeah, that's what your friend said while you were out. You need a drink or anything?"

I nodded. "That would be good, if you don't mind. I'm parched."

Jenkins strode to the door. "I'll be right back. Don't you worry. You probably just need some sugar. One of the local guys has spells like that—a symptom of diabetes when his sugar gets low." He kept mumbling as he left the room, his voice echoing for a moment as he got farther away.

Martinez snickered. "Yeah, diabetes—that's it."

I smiled. "As good a reason as any, so long as he believes it."

"I take it we have another victim?"

My smile wavered as the memory of the vision came back to me. "Yep, unfortunately. We also have a nickname to go with the murderer."

"Really?" Martinez leaned closer, resting his elbow on the table near the bone shards. "What is it?"

"Scrub."

"Scrub? What? Is he a doctor or something?"

"That I don't know. This victim was male and fairly young, but not a child. His nickname was Dizzy. He was probably twenty, a college student, and a dealer."

"What school?"

I shook my head, sorting back through the vision, trying to bring something to mind that would place it, a memory of a building or sign. Nothing seemed important enough for the man to have recalled, though. "I've got nothing. He dealt drugs out of a dorm room and loved a young girl named Betty." Remembering her name summoned her face, smiling up from the rumpled Grateful Dead teddy-bear bedsheets I knew belonged to the victim. Miller and Bud Light bottles were strewn around the dim room, long candles sticking out of the tops. Wax from many uses had run over the sides of the labels like a collection of poor man's candle holders. It was my room—I mean his. He'd decorated as romantically as he could, and she lay on the bed gazing at him with adoration. In her eyes, the love she felt for me—or him, was clear. It was always like this—the difficulty of discerning between my memories and others from visions. Some from my oldest visions even seemed a part of me now, as if they were my own memories. I had learned to dismiss most visions of strangers and people I didn't know. It was easier that way. The best of friends and loved ones always left me with more than enough memories to draw from and tell the difference. The rest... well, they weren't important after their murderers had been brought to justice, at least not to my personal life. "I'd know his dorm room if I saw it, assuming it hasn't changed."

"How long ago was he killed?"

"No idea. There was a train whistle in the distance, but in these small towns those can be heard from miles away."

"And they come through every couple hours," Martinez said. "At least we've got more to go on than before. Did you get the victim's name?"

Before I could answer, Officer Jenkins stepped into the room trying to walk as quickly as possible without spilling a drop, as though he were walking on eggshells while trying to beat the best time for running a mile. "Here you go," he muttered, setting a well-used, green coffee mug in front of me. His shoulders seemed to slacken with relief as soon as the swells of dark soda sloshing within slowed. "Sorry about the dirty cup. It was the closest thing I could find."

"Thanks. I'm sure that'll help take the edge off." Attempting to hide the disgust at the coffee stains adhering to the lip of the mug, I took a swig.

Martinez swept the bones back into the evidence bag, and I resealed the paper bag within the Ziploc. Leaving them both on the table, Martinez stood and offered Jenkins a hand. "We really appreciate your help, Officer Jenkins."

The uniformed man shook. "Just call me Rob. I'm not sure how much help I was. Were you able to find anything? Is it even the same killer?"

"From the looks of it," I answered, "it's the same killer. We need to keep searching, but we'll let you know when we find more. I'd advise doing a DNA swab on the inside of that bag. You might find something worthwhile."

Jenkins gathered the two evidence bags. "I'll do that. Might take a week or two to get the results. If you need anything more or need to check these again, you know where I am. We'd be happy to help." He extended his free hand to me.

"Thanks." I hesitated at first but then took his hand. Thankfully, no visions came of it. So far as I could tell, Officer Jenkins was the genuine article, a local striving to keep his town safe. "I appreciate it," I added with relief. Past handshakes had given me insights I never wanted to know about. I had to accept my gift. Every day was a struggle, trying to do the right thing but fearing what I might see at the simplest touch.

On the way out, Jenkins dropped the evidence bags off with the officer assigned to the storage room and asked me, "You sure you're okay?"

"Yes, Rob, I'm sure." With that final reassurance, we made our way back out to the car. "Ready to visit some colleges?"

Martinez grinned and replied in a southern drawl, "Yes, Miss Daisy. I be drivin'."

His joke wasn't lost on me, but instead of laughing I feigned a scowl. "Thanks, Martinez. I appreciate it. Where's the love?" I slipped into the passenger's side and shut the door.

Martinez closed the driver's side, started the engine, and in a pretty good impression of Officer Jenkins asked, "You sure you're okay? Need me to take you to the hospital so the nurse can put a Band-Aid on your boo-boo? Maybe she'll give ya a lollypop if you smile real nice." He grinned.

I swatted his arm. "Shut up and drive, Hector. You know this truck stop where they found the victim's remains, right?"

"Yep," Martinez said, shifting the car into gear. "Not fifteen minutes from here."

"Good. We'll stop there, too. So what colleges are near that truck stop?" I asked as Hector pulled out onto the rural street of small-town Virginia. "I know there's Wytheville Community College."

"My niece Sarah lives around here. She went to WCC, and I know for a fact they don't have dorms. We'll probably need to go farther out to find larger schools. You sure it was a dorm room?"

I thought back to the vision. I wasn't sure. From the victim's memories, I remembered people coming in with backpacks, and it just made sense that it was a dorm room, but could it have been an apartment? There was no way to tell. I remembered a window and some trees outside but couldn't make out whether the buildings outside had been college housing, apartments, or simply storefronts. I doubted the last one, but we had very little to go on. "I really don't know. Emory and Henry is nearby, right?"

Hector raised an eyebrow. "It's close enough. Think it was a private school?"

I shook my head. "Radford or Tech?"

"Radford might be close enough. Tech's a little far, even with the bypass."

"Sounds good. Let's try the truck stop and Radford's campus offices. It's almost three o'clock now, and they'll probably shut their doors by four thirty seeing how it's a Friday."

"Sounds good." Hector stepped on the gas.

Chapter 8

Death and Fatherhood

March 9th, 2012

"THAT SECRETARY COULD'VE been a bit more helpful," Hector complained from the cruiser's passenger's seat as we left the registrar's building.

I maneuvered casually along I-81 with one hand on the wheel. The truck stop had been a bust. Dizzy's remains were just dropped there after the murder. "She did what she could. With so many students skipping classes, who can know who's really missing?"

"I just can't believe we've hit another wall on this investigation before it ever really got started."

"That's why we're here, Hec. If it were easy, they'd have no need for detectives. Hell, after the wacked-out Anubis killer, I'd think you'd expect this sort of thing."

"Yeah, but things just seem to be going from bad to worse—ground-up skeletons, come on!"

I phoned in to tell dispatch we were heading back to Tranquil Heights. Radios didn't always reach that far, especially in the mountains.

She updated us on the DNA tests. The lab had the whole team working on it. They confirmed there were two victims, one male child and an adult female, but their identities were still unknown and more tests were needed. The forensic scientists tested every piece they could in such a short time. Since I'd put in a rush order, it would cost the department, and the coffers were already severely depleted. I would hear about it from Lieutenant Tullings, but I owed the victims answers and to get their killer off the streets before more people were killed.

Taylor did cement one fact for us. "The DNA results were compared and proved a familial relationship between the two victims."

Hector shrugged. "At least we can be certain the second victim was Tommy's mother."

I had tried to remain optimistic about the possibility of finding her alive so we had a better chance of getting Scrub off the street. "Something about the remains is off. What did the other tests tell us? What kind of EZ Bake oven did the perp use?" I'd seen everything from bonfires to a pottery kiln. The heat and type of furnace would narrow the suspects.

Taylor replied, "Your gut was right. There were no signs of fulminant shock due to thermal stress."

"For us nonscientists?"

"The bodies weren't burned."

"How were they turned to ash?"

"No idea."

"Thanks, Taylor." After I hung up, I asked Hector, "Would you take the remains to Doug? He works late. Maybe he'll know how the bodies were cremated."

"Sure. Want me to leave you at the hospital?"

"Yeah. Paige should be working. I'll take her car."

* * *

We were about fifteen minutes from Tranquil Heights, the sun approaching the mountainous tree line in the distance. Clouds converged ahead. I put a second hand on the steering wheel and slowed the vehicle as we crested a large mountain covered in fog. The remaining light of day seemed to vanish, thrusting us into an unnatural haze. "Jeez, I hate this."

"The growing number of murderers in the area or the weather?" Hector joked.

"Both," I replied, leaning forward and squinting through the windshield. "I hate when it gets this way. I can hardly see a foot ahead of us. It's like—"

"Like some little señorita got her panties in a twist while you was steppin' out and clocked ya good, I know. Just keep an eye on the brake lights in front of you."

I sent Hector a flitting glare before lowering our speed further as red brake lights flared ahead then let up. "I am, but that wasn't what I was going to say. Maybe you're used to doing that, but I've never stepped out on Paige."

We both stared ahead for a few minutes. As the top of the mountainous highway began to slope downward, I applied the brake more, maintaining our distance between vehicles until the fog bank turned to wisps. The tension in my shoulders eased as we emerged into the open, the dwindling light of day appearing from nowhere. Tendrils of light shone through the cloud-covered sky like giant fingers.

Just when I'd relaxed enough to lean back in my seat, Taylor Hicks' voice crackled through the speakers. "Car thirteen, you back yet?" My fingers tightened into a white-knuckled grip. Her voice wasn't bubbly like usual.

Tearing one hand from the wheel, I grabbed the mic. "Car thirteen here. What do you need, dispatch?"

"We have a 217 at the high school. It's one of the students and isn't looking good—might become a 187 shortly. Principal Cantril requested you."

My stomach plummeted. *Jamie...?* After a moment's consideration, it occurred to me that Jamie should be at the precinct. "Is Jamie still there at the station?" From the sidelong look in Hector's eyes, I could tell I hadn't managed to hide a panicked undertone.

"He's fine, Alex—still going through files. It was another boy—potentially gang related."

Relief settled the twisting knots in my stomach, but my shoulders still held tight. This boy was assaulted and might not live through the night, or even the next hour. "Is the victim at the ER?"

"Yes. Officer Brightwell's headed back to the school now."

"We're ten minutes from the hospital."

The radio responded, "We have officers there. What about the principal?"

"I'll get to the high school when I can," I growled. "I wanna see the boy first, before..." I couldn't finish. Thoughts of Jamie and other boys his age lying lifeless in the morgue flashed before my eyes. I tried to maintain my focus on the road. "We're on our way." Adrenaline pumped through my veins, and I floored the gas pedal.

"10-4. I'll let them know."

As we crested the next mountain, the engine revved louder and we continued to accelerate. I maneuvered the car into the left lane. "Get the light," I ordered, my voice devoid of emotion.

Hector flicked the switch and colored lights whirled just outside the car windows. "Frickin' gangs. I can't believe this crap."

The lights and siren blared as we *whizzed* past cars.

* * *

At the hospital, Officer Martinez and I strode through the automatic double doors with determination etched on our faces. I carried a few large evidence bags along in case there were fingernail scrapings or foreign DNA on the kid's clothes. ER staff often cuts the pants or shirts off while working. Cops need every scrap of proof they can get. The first-floor nurse behind the front counter took one look at us and asked, "Here for the assaulted high schooler?"

I barely noticed her youthful complexion, dark eyelashes, or the sad set of her lips. I nodded. Tranquil Heights was still small enough to have a neighborly feel. Everyone in town knew your business as soon as it happened. This was a significant event, so of course everyone in the hospital was aware. I could feel the eyes of hospital staff gazing in our direction. Between the big city and rural communities like this, *privacy* had different meanings.

"He's under observation, Alex. Things don't look good."

It took a minute, but I recognized the tanned woman as one of Paige's co-workers I'd met at last year's Christmas party. "Sorry, Jenna. My mind's on other things."

She nodded, her shoulder-length, black hair waving with the movement. "I understand." She whispered, "You might want to get there quick."

"Anyone with him?" Hector asked.

"Yes, his father."

I'd have to put a name to a face and would soon speak with the boy's father, if not the victim himself—that is, if he could still speak at all. It pained me to ask, but I knew I needed to. "Who's the boy?"

"Jack Gardner's son, Cameron," she intoned. "They're in room 126, first floor."

The name sounded familiar and only took a moment to pry from my memory. I'd arrested him a couple times for drunk driving after he spent a long shift at the local coal mine and stopped off at a bar. He wasn't the best role model and wasn't home very often, but he worked hard to put food on the table. I tried to remember who his wife was but couldn't. Sometime in the past, the family had run into trouble—I knew that much. Turning to Hec, I asked, "You remember what happened to Jack's wife?"

Hector's brows scrunched in thought. "Didn't she die from cancer?"

"Right. That's it. The family's been through a lot already. Now there's this."

Hector mumbled, "There's nothing left of the family, or won't be soon. Whoever did this destroyed whatever Jack had left."

Cameron was Jack's only son. We both muttered our thanks and turned to the hospital doorway leading deeper into the building.

"Maybe we can find out who did this," I said as we strode through the hallway.

As we passed nurse stations, operating rooms, and sterile hallways, staff and patients gazed at us. The only person's attention I held was Paige's. She stood behind a nursing station counter watching me with depressed eyes. I gave her a nod but continued on. I'd visited the hospital often enough to know the layout, many times to visit Paige. *Labor and Delivery, fourth floor. One of the happiest days of my life.* I couldn't help the smile that came to my face just remembering holding Jamie for the first time.

However, some of the more troublesome memories of the hospital were from my childhood, like when my older stepbrother Frank had been killed in a car accident. Other work-related incidents had brought me to the hospital from time to time since then, but this was the first time I'd come knowing the child would die. I hated walking into a situation like this. I was a homicide detective. Most of my victims were dead. Sure they left living victims behind, family and such, but the dead spoke through visions and a few whispered words here and there. It was different.

The plaque next to a door labeled Room 113 passed by. Room 126 was half a dozen doors down and around the corner. I dreaded that turn. Just as we rounded it and paused in front of our destination, a closed door, Hector asked, "You good to do this on your own?"

"Yep, no worries." I handed him the squad car keys, and he dropped them in the pocket of his khakis.

"Okay. I'll bring Jamie by in a few." Hector patted my arm, turned, and strode away, his head bowed.

God, I hope this is the last time I have to walk into a situation like this.

Turning to the door, I gave it a brief knock and heard a grumbled, "What do ya need?" from the other side.

I slipped inside holding my fedora in my hand. The curtains were drawn, and only slivers of light from outside infiltrated the dark room. Every light was off except the glowing numbers and buttons on a machine in the middle of the room. It *beeped* and monitored Cameron's vitals, his heart rate fluttering on the display in a semiregular pattern.

A disheartened man I recognized as Jack sat slumped in a chair next to the bed. His clothes were rumpled, his shirt and jeans still covered in coal dust. Even his face was covered in grime except for the rounded circles around his eyes. His safety goggles gave him a raccoon look. One large, rough hand blackened with coal clasped Cameron's smaller one, but the boy didn't move or even acknowledge my entrance.

"Hey, Jack."

The whites of Jack Gardner's eyes seemed to narrow in the dim glow streaming through the sides of the window. "What are you doin' here?"

I held up a hand. "I know this isn't a good time, Jack, but I'm here to help you and your boy."

Cameron's father stood but did not release his hand. "He could've used your help hours ago, but where were you off gallivantin'? You off at a strip club, gettin' your jollies? Havin' a beer at Nelly's?"

My jaw clenched at the accusations, but I knew he was clutching at straws. His own guilt was eating away at his insides. He'd done all of those things instead of going home to be with his wife when she needed him—when she was bedridden. He'd gone out for drinks or a show with the boys instead of spending time with Cameron, and now the guilt and anger were the only things he could feel. He needed an outlet, somewhere to direct the anger. I suppressed my own hatred, my disgust at what this man had become. "Look, Jack, I'm here to help. You want to get the ones responsible, don't you? The ones that did this to Cameron?"

At this question, Jack's gaze turned back to his son and a tear slid down his cheek in a cleansing streak. Cameron seemed to be sleeping peacefully in the bed aside from the bruised face, arms, and bandaged features. Cameron's nose was obviously broken under the white wraps. His sandy hair had been cleaned, but even in the dim room I could tell clumps of blood remained. A sling covered his left arm, which lay on his stomach. He didn't even look to have hit his growth spurt. His face was rounded, cherublike. For an instant I was reminded of my stepsister Gloria the moment she left us, her six-year-old face upturned on the floor of my childhood trailer, blonde hair splayed wildly around her head—the result of the drunk's torment and outrage.

"You promise to get the bastard that done this?" he asked, his voice cracking.

"Yep, I'll do my best," I replied, wiping the tear from my own cheek. It always seemed to appear when I remember Glory.

Jack didn't look up again. He slumped into the chair, never taking his adoring gaze from Cameron's motionless body. The machine *beeped* and continued on like the march of a solitary drummer with one stick. Leaning against the wall, I could only watch through the shadowed room and sense the emotions passing from father to son.

Chapter 9

Apples and Trees

March 9th, 2012

JACK NEVER LEFT his son's side.

"Is he conscious?" I whispered over the rhythmic sound of the assistive breathing machine.

Jack let out a whispered, "No."

In the dim light filtering around the window curtains, Cameron's jacket caught my attention. In the streams of light that hit it lying across the chair back in the corner, the jacket's red outer layer appeared almost like felt. On light feet, I stepped to the corner where other chairs sat waiting for visitors that would never come. Slipping out of my overcoat, I laid it in the chair next to Cameron's. "Is this the one he was wearing?"

Jack was so entranced, he never looked up. A shaft of light illuminated part of a pin the size of a silver dollar attached to the jacket's chest. It was dark, worn, and old, but displayed the letters SC&C in tarnished, white letters. What looked to be an unrolled scroll seemed to flutter across the bottom half with the words *Sons of Coal*.

Having grown up in the area, I knew how much the coal companies were a part of life. They were the region's history, for better or worse. This pin was an antique from a lost time and company, a remnant from another era, but it spoke volumes about the silent relationship that existed between father and son. No matter their problems, they came together in times of trouble. Jack was there for Cameron. *Is it the destiny of every son to die early in this region?* In my lifetime there had been deaths in the mines, and many died tragically in the years prior. *Coal mines, collapses, and now gangs.* I shook my head and slid into the seat next to the jackets. *Sons of Coal* rattled through my brain as I stretched an arm over the chair back.

I unfolded an evidence bag to cover my actions. Touching the jacket gave me nothing, as expected. It looked new; although, I could swear I felt a shock and tingle as my finger slid along the soft surface. *Just static,* I told myself.

The machine continued to *beep*, marking time.

Glancing back at the occupied bed, sorrow filled my chest. There wasn't much I could do but wait. Principal Cantril was at the school with Officer Brightwell, but at the moment, that didn't seem important.

Just then, I could have sworn a young boy's voice mumbled, "So sorry, Pops."

My finger stilled. I realized my hand had drifted to the pin and had been massaging its curved edge. I waited, struggling through the silence to hear more.

"So sorry," came the voice once again, but it was so soft I wondered if I was imagining it.

A second later, the *beep* stuttered and stopped for an elongated moment, then chirped back to life. Another stutter-stop caused the alarms to blare, and Jack erupted from his seat, both coal-encrusted hands enveloping his son's smaller one. "No, Cam, don't leave me. You can't leave me," he pleaded, his gruff voice infused with heart-wrenching pain. "No, stay!"

In the midst of the electronic chaos and Jack's bellowing words, the youthful voice said, "It'll be okay, Pops. Don't worry," as it faded away.

From beneath my extended arm, the smell that had become so familiar over the years drifted to me, carrying me from the depressing scene just as two nurses and a doctor burst into the room.

* * *

"We'll catch you later, Cam," shouted Dexter, hefting his backpack full of sweaty baseball clothes. Dexter waved and put a leg over his Kawasaki.

A second friend named Tremaine adjusted the flat brim of his red baseball cap to ensure it angled off to the side. Black, tight curls hung out from beneath it, accentuating the chocolate skin of his face and neck while contrasting his red and black NFL jersey. I continued into the semivacant parking lot, the last light of day dwindling over the treetops and mountains looming in the distance. Tremaine's voice carried behind me. "We'll catch him tomorrow. You just wait." In a more subdued tone, he asked Dexter, "You sure this thing can hold two people?"

"Of course, Trey," Dexter replied. "I wouldn't give you a ride if it didn't."

I shook my head. How the hell did Tremaine even get into the Reds? Such a scaredy-cat.

A moment later, the motorcycle revved to life and sped onto the dark road with Dexter shouting at the thrill.

Someday I'll have one, too. Unlike Dexter's dad, Pops can't afford something like that, but I'll save up. At least I scored this jacket at the mall last month. *I ran a hand over the front, appreciating the red fabric's new feel. It even smelled nice. My fingers fumbled at the mining button for a moment.* The jacket was probably made in Taiwan or somethin', but free is free, right? *"Got the five-finger discount," I muttered with a smile. "Can't beat that."*

My sneakers scraped the school asphalt with each step. The high-pitched chirp of brown bats echoed overhead as they came out for an early feeding. Gotta keep the mosquitos down. Get to it, bats.

I shouldered my backpack on the right side but skipped a step when the sounds of nightlife were interrupted by something metal sliding across stone. I halted, glancing around. A few cars remained in the lot. One was an old, brown Chevelle belonging to Mary Jane, but she was nowhere around. Must have broken down again. *The few others scattered like distant stars across the parking lot must have belonged to teachers and staff.*

I cut across the lot at a diagonal toward the far corner. A few cars sped past on the street a dozen yards away, but after school hours few people took notice of school zones. I walked by an old Chevy truck with a lift, dreaming of the many things I could do with money. No cars that'll break down. I can just pay anyone to do my bidding. Talk about power. Someday.

"Hey, kid," a gruff voice said, interrupting my thoughts. "You's one of them Reds, right?"

I turned to find a tall, bearded fellow leaning against the truck. A few light poles dotted the parking lot, but the one over us was out, leaving this section drenched in shadow.

"Yeah, can't you see the colors?"

"Oh, that's right. Your little group of nitwits think wearin' colors makes ya a man," he retorted.

At that, my blood started to boil. No one makes fun of family. We're in it for life. *"Ya wanna make somethin' of it?"*

The old man snickered, tilted his head, and scratched at his scraggly, bearded chin for a moment. "I think I do."

The sound I'd heard before pierced the nighttime silence as he pulled a large, metal pipe from behind him. My eyes widened, but I fumbled in my jacket pocket until I grasped the hilt of my switchblade. Pulling it out, I tried to steady my nervous hand as it sprung to life, both three-and-a-half-inch blades locking into place. "If you wanna start somethin', I'll be sure to finish it." I winced at the trembling edge in my voice. Damn he's big, but the boys'll be proud of me after tonight. They might even let me in on the deals they've been runnin'. Then I'll get a taste of that money.

Light from the distant parking-lot lamps illuminated the side of the man's scraggly, grey hair as he took a step closer, hefting the pipe and spinning it once... then twice. "You ain't gonna squeal, pipsqueak?" he rumbled. "That little piece ain't gonna get ya far against me."

How old is this guy? What's his deal? *Before I could consider it further, three feet of heavy metal came arcing through the air. I ducked and dodged to the right, lunging and catching the old man's bicep with my blade. He yelped, twisted back, and took another swipe. I easily dodged it and couldn't help the grin creeping to my lips. "That all you got, old-timer?"*

He gave a hearty chuckle. "Ain't you full of yourself. You know, someone really oughtta taught you some manners. Maybe you wouldn't be in this mess."

I dove inside again, but this time the guy skipped back and brought the pipe down on my shoulder, sending me tumbling. I jumped back up and tried to lift my arm, but it refused to work, just sent a tingling sensation down from my aching shoulder. The grizzled, old man stood watching, the end of the pipe held against the asphalt. I could swear he was smiling.

Switching hands, I gripped the knife tighter and tried to shove the pain aside. "Good shot for an old fogey. You're a spry one."

"Kid, it don't take much to put down a varmint. I ain't that good, and you're about as durable as a house slipper."

"What, you wanna trade insults now? How about this, you're slobberin' ass is goin' down for the count. I'm gonna knock every tooth outta that rickety, old head, and use your skull for kickball."

"Just shut up." The old man took a step closer, emerging into a shaft of light from a distant lamp. The scraggly, wrinkled face was

somehow familiar. He followed up with another step faster than I'd seen him move yet.

The pipe came hurtling upward, cracking me on the chin before I could move. Pain blossomed in my jaw, my feet left the ground, and a variety of loose rocks jabbed my back and legs as though I'd landed on a bed of nails. A split-second later the stars overhead wiggled in the distance like off-colored fireflies. The back of my head felt warm and thick. "Wha' the hell?" I mumbled, unable to focus.

"Now, I hate to do this, kid, but you really oughtta pick your friends better." His large boot hammered into my gut, and I twisted onto my side, reaching up with my good arm and grabbing what I could.

"Cut that crap out," he hissed.

My skull rang as another swipe of the metal pipe rolled me over.

"Drug dealin' mother…," the voice mumbled through an audible fog that encapsulated my head. Another swift kick cracked my arm. A third and a fourth followed along with sporadic snippets of, "Son of a bitch… better watch himself… We'll whip all of… killin'…"

Each phrase was punctuated with another blow, but thankfully no more came from the pipe. A kick slammed into my nose and mouth, sending blood everywhere. I screamed, but it came out garbled. I wrapped my pained arms around his jean-covered leg, bellowing with everything I had in me. Twisting around it, I sunk my *teeth into his calf, biting down. Through the pants, I could tell some of my teeth had been knocked free, which enraged me further.*

Teeth be damned! Pain... he'll feel pain.

I bit down harder, fighting against the agony in my jaws, trying to rip through his jeans and into the muscles I felt within my grasp. He tried to jerk free, uttering a stream of obscenities, but I didn't let go. He jumped back, hopping on his good foot until he landed a whirlwind blow with the thick, metal pipe that sent me into a pitch-black void.

* * *

My vision cleared revealing Jack Gardner's anguished face over the shoulder of a burly male nurse ushering him out of the room. "The doctors are doing everything they can, Mr. Gardner," the man assured him. "Please wait outside."

The room was illuminated by overhead lights now, and it took a moment to focus in the midst of the chaos erupting mere feet away. The heart monitor blared in its long, drawn-out *beep* while another alarm blurted repeatedly. "Shut that damn thing off!" a white-coated doctor demanded from the group of medical professionals clustered around Cameron's bed.

Between their shuffling bodies and arms working at a frantic pace to bring Cameron back, I spotted his battered and bruised face. His eyelids were closed as if resting after an arduous journey, which I knew was exactly the case.

It'll be okay, Pops. Don't worry, I remembered Cameron whispering just before the vision. I knew now with certainty that it was his. There wouldn't be a return trip from his current voyage. Adrenaline coursed through my veins as my thoughts returned to the vision, the brutal beating, and the old, craggy face of the boy's attacker—one I recognized as Dillon McCullin.

I knew him from years before. The connection was infuriating and confusing. My thoughts returned to my own childhood. My stepfather, the drunk, tended to take his anger out on me and my mother. The beatings were vicious and memorable. He'd always used whatever was at hand but had a propensity for leaving heavy objects around the house. If nothing else, his fists, knees, and steel-toed work boots worked well enough. Dillon was his father, a stern mountain man who I'd rarely seen come down from the rural woods, let alone into town.

The apple never falls too far from the tree, but what could bring him out of the mountains? With any luck, Dillon's blood, sweat, and greasy hair would be all over Cameron's jacket. I stuffed it into the plastic bag, releasing the antique coal button. *It really will be okay, Cameron. I'll make sure of it.* Rising to my feet, I grabbed my overcoat, sidestepped the nearest nurse and exited past a teary-eyed Jack Gardner.

Chapter 10

Justice and Certainty

March 9th, 2012

WHEN I ROUNDED the hospital corner, I stopped by the nurses' station where Paige was scribbling on a patient's chart. Behind her, a large whiteboard advertised handwritten last names like Krager, Magis, and Tolly along with the hours, like a spreadsheet. I wasn't sure if they were doctors' names or patients, but I guessed the latter considering the times listed across the top and check marks according to various times and names. I struggled to work my jaw loose. "Hey, hon'. You doin' okay?"

She nodded. "Yeah, babe. How are you holding up?"

I shrugged. "The kid just passed." I paused, questioning my words. It was as though saying his name after the fact would cement the events in reality. *The kid...* I knew it was real—always was, but this boy could just as easily have been Jamie. Hell, I'd been through beatings almost as bad at his age. The difference was that I survived. "They're workin' on him, but he won't be comin' around. Can I get the car keys? I've gotta go see someone."

Paige's eyebrows came together, silently voicing the question behind them.

"It's important," I assured her.

Slapping the clipboard down on the counter, she grabbed my elbow and led me into a vacant patient room across the hall.

The lights were out and bed curtains drawn back. "What the hell do you mean he won't be coming back around?" she hissed. "Dr. Sageeden is one of our best, and he's been keeping tabs on Cameron. At the least, he'll buy the boy's father a little more time with him."

I shook my head. "He may be the best you've got, but he's not bringing Cameron back. Maybe he'll get his heart beating again, but Cameron said his farewells."

Paige didn't question it further. She knew better than anyone what I meant. Calming herself, she asked, "Did Jack hear?"

"No, I don't think so. He screamed and is pretty out of sorts. I'm afraid he'll never be the same after this—probably sink into the booze more than ever."

Paige gave a nod. "It's a shame, but after losing his wife and son, who could blame him?"

"I can," I replied with confidence. "I've pulled him over enough times for drunk driving to know what'll happen when his drinking gets worse. He'll get someone killed."

Paige's face softened, most certainly thinking back to my stepfather's rages. "Maybe, but you can't put him away for what he might do."

"I just hope I catch him before the worst happens. I'll do everything I can to get him into counseling or some kind of help. The judge'll side with me."

"I'll check up on him, Alex. We'll do what we can."

"Good. Now can I have the keys?"

"What's so important that you're going to leave me and Jamie stranded here?"

I paused at the mention of Jamie. "He's here?"

"Yeah, Hector dropped him off a few minutes ago. Will you please answer me?"

Licking my lips, I whispered, "I have to see a man about a pipe."

Paige's skepticism was etched in her face and eyes.

"It's the truth."

"I don't doubt that. Just tell me the whole truth."

"Honey, I would, but I don't want to worry you. I don't want to do this any more than you, but as you once told me, 'If I don't, who will speak for them?' Just know I'm taking precautions," I assured her. "I'm walking into this with my eyes open."

"So this is for Cameron Gardner?"

I nodded.

"He was beaten with a pipe?"

"Yes."

"I see. At least take Hector with you—promise me that."

"I will," I replied, caressing her cheek with my palm. Leaning in, I kissed her tender lips and remembered the first of many such kisses beneath the branches of that old pine. *Who would've thought the foot of my father's grave would bring us together?* "You'll find a ride?"

She gave me a worried grin but nodded.

I smiled and exited the room, conscious that she didn't immediately follow me back into the well-lit hospital hallway. *Gotta be hard on her knowing what I do.*

I made it down the hall, through the swinging hospital doors, and almost out the building before Jamie's voice reached me from the front hospital waiting room.

"Dad, where ya going?"

I stopped in front of the doors. They stood open, waiting. "I have some business to take care of. Did you find anything in the files today?"

"Some potentials we can check out in the system tomorrow, but where are you going tonight?" Jamie strode up. His eyes were eager, and I knew exactly why he was asking. He wanted to come.

"You know my work keeps me out late at times."

"Yeah, but I can help. No school tomorrow, as you know," he said, the words coming out with a slight laugh.

"Son, you need to stay here. What I've got to do is nothing you want to be involved in. It's too dangerous."

"But, Da-ad," he whined.

"No buts. You stay here. Mom and you will get a ride with one of her co-workers when she gets off later."

I turned to head out but stopped as he said, "That's not fair."

"Jamie, what did I say?" His jaw clenched, looking much like I did in the mirror sometimes. I lowered my voice and explained,

"Your help won't be worth anything if it gets you killed. I love you, son. Just stay here."

His gaze turned down to the tiled floor, and he stood quietly.

"If it'll make you feel better, I'll call Hec in, okay?"

He nodded.

Pulling out my cell phone, I flipped it open and strode through the waiting hospital doors just as they began to *beep* in irritation. The phone rang once, then twice as I walked onto the sidewalk before cutting out. I checked the display and saw that the signal had dropped off. I held up the phone like fan adjusting the TV antenna before the Super Bowl. I had to walk halfway around to the ambulance drop-off bay before the signal bars flashed back into place. Hitting redial, I stopped and waited for Hector to pick up. It rang and rang, eventually going to voicemail. I left a message and flipped the phone shut before unlocking Paige's green Subaru hatchback.

* * *

The hour-long drive through the winding mountain roads to Dillon McCullin's residence was grueling. The drive was one I was accustomed to having grown up in Southwest Virginia, but each passing second felt as though gravity were growing heavier and pressing on my shoulders. My ears popped while I adjusted to the altitude change.

As soon as I turned from pavement onto a dirt road that had more potholes than flat surface, I knew I was getting close. Rural roads are like carnival rides where the ticket price is paid in car repairs. Trees sped by in the headlights' periphery like they were attempting to stay out of the light. The dirt road had more twists and turns in it than a coiled snake suffering from a bellyache. By the time my headlights settled onto a ramshackle porch connected to an old log cabin, I was certain Dillon knew I'd come. His family home was deep in a gully between mountains, and my headlights were visible from miles away. Shifting the car into park, I turned off the engine and flipped open my cell phone. Hector still hadn't replied, and now any semblance of service I'd had was absent.

Leaving the headlights on, I took a deep breath of mountain air. It was crisp and probably 10 degrees cooler than Tranquil Heights. I patted the 9 mm cradled against my chest in my shoulder holster. Before I could pull the door handle, a shotgun resounded through the darkness. Buckshot ripped at the passenger's side doors and shattered the windows. Jerking the door open, I dove into the black night and huddled behind the back tire, positioning myself opposite the cabin.

Guess ol' Dillon isn't open to guests.

Training urged me to call for backup, but that would take far too long. They would also ask more questions than an amnesic psychiatrist. Another gunshot rang out, peppering the passenger's side once more.

Paige is gonna kill me.

Chapter 11

For the Better Good

March 9th, 2012

"THIS IS PRIVATE PROPERTY," shouted a gruff voice with a southern drawl. "Best get back in that car and turn the other way, or the next shot will be in your trespassin' *tuchus*."

"Dillon McCullin?" I shouted, waiting for his affirmation. I recognized his voice from the vision and the couple times I'd met him as a teenager, but I needed to be sure.

"Who's askin'?"

"The Tranquil Heights Police Department."

"Ah, hell! If I'd known that, I wouldn't have given a warnin' shot, piggy."

I ground my teeth. *Damn moonshiner!* They were some of the most paranoid locals around. "I'm not here for your shine, Dillon!" I shouted, pulling my pistol.

"Right, a little piggy comes to visit 'cause he just wants to say hullo, right? I know my rights. Get the hell off my property, copper."

"Damn it, Dillon—" but before I could say anything more, another shot rang out, peppering the side of the Subaru. Spinning over the hood of the car before he could get another shot off, I dashed into the overgrown shrubbery beside the cabin. The pump-action shotgun rang out as he cleared the shell. Then another roar tore through the bushes a step behind me. I rounded the bushes and the back corner of the house. This wasn't going to be easy.

The front screen door slammed and heavy footfalls reverberated inside the house, coming closer. I leaped the back porch banister, careful not to land too hard on the creaky, water-damaged floorboards. Sidling next to the back door, I waited for it to open. The screen door squeaked a moment later but only opened an inch. Another shotgun blast permeated the air, deafening me momentarily. The buckshot whizzed past, and the acrid scent of gunfire drifted to my nostrils. *Damn shiner's gonna kill me.*

"I know you're back there, piggy," shouted McCullin from less than a foot inside the door. "I ain't goin' nowhere, and you ain't either."

I steadied my breathing and waited for him to make a move. Seconds passed, turning to minutes. His heavy breathing was all I could hear. The chirps of nightlife had been silenced with the first gunshot, and now the dark night loomed around me like a snake, waiting to squeeze tight. Moonlight glinted off McCullin's wild, gray beard as he leaned into the screen door, peering out. *If I can see him, he can see me.*

Positioning the end of my pistol mere centimeters from the black shotgun barrel peeking through the cracked screen door, I pulled the trigger. His gun resounded as my bullet ricocheted off his barrel. Using the momentary surprise, I threw the door open and lunged inside, tackling the mountain man and hammering his fingers with my pistol butt. He yelped, and the shotgun hit the floor while we tumbled into the old living room filled with rustic, wooden furniture. The small dining table toppled as we struggled. His hand dwarfed mine and grasped my 9 mm. I held tight, struggling to pull it up as we stood opposite one another, but his strength was tremendous.

Dillon McCullin was larger than I remembered. I'd attributed the size difference to Cameron's youth in the vision, but that was only part of the cause. The man loomed over me, his bearded face grimacing as we fought. An oil lamp in the far corner of the room sent shadows stretching through the wood-paneled room. I threw a punch with my free hand, catching the older man in his midsection, but it was like hitting a tree trunk. *Jesus, what's this guy do for fun, wrestle steroid-popping alligators?*

A second thrust to his side was more effective. He winced. I followed with another and then a third. He bent lower with each one until the final punch caught him under the chin. The blow sent him crashing over the couch and onto the wooden floor, but his hold on my gun ripped it from my grasp. It sailed through the air, disappearing into the small corner kitchen. It rang against something metallic. Running after it, I pulled it from a sink full of wet dishes and soapy water. Dripping wet, I pivoted only to find Dillon scooping up the shotgun and leveling it.

"You don't want to do this, Dillon." We stood tensed, each of us aiming at the other, my pistol sopping wet, dripping over my hands and onto the floor.

He gave a grizzly smile. Blood seeped down his lip and bearded chin. "What do ya want, copper?" My ears were ringing, making his voice sound distant, as though the volume had been turned down to a whisper.

"Not this, Dillon. I just came to talk." Edging out of the kitchen corner, I sidestepped to the end of the couch. "Let's just put these down."

He chuckled. "Right—Wait, don't I know you?"

I wondered if I'd heard him right until I realized I'd stepped into the flickering light of the oil lamp. "Yeah, you do."

Dillon's glare intensified. "Can't be. Alex?"

I nodded. "That's right."

The huge mountain man growled like thunder rumbling in the distance. "Alex Drummond. I should've known. Couldn't stop with my boy and grandson. Now you're after me. Damn, I could have taken you out thirty times now, 'cept I was bein' nice... givin' ya a warnin' an' all that. Don't worry your little head, though. This one won't miss. I can shoot the tits off a tree rat at a hundred paces."

He took a step closer, and I raised my gun to his head. "I don't want to shoot you, McCullin, but I will."

"That piece of crap ain't enough," he said, closing the distance with another foot. His finger trembled on the shotgun trigger aimed at my chest. "You'll have to take me down with one shot, and I don't think you's got it in ya."

"Dillon, you know what Steve put me through. It wasn't like I had a choice. Don't make the same bad decision. You're smarter than that." I stepped around the far side of the couch, never taking my eyes off him.

"Go ahead. Take your shot, sonny. You'll only get one."

He ducked, and I fired. A split-second later he batted my pistol away with the end of his barrel. My heel slammed against his knee, throwing the large man off balance, and he tumbled atop me grappling for a handhold. Large, bulbous fingers wrapped around the wrist of my gun hand, clenching so tight I lost all control. The pistol tumbled to the floor while my free hand forced the end of his searing-hot shotgun away.

"You's gonna die now, Drummond," he growled, his tangled beard less than a foot from my face. The stench of rotting breath engulfed me. "You's mine." His words were flecked with malevolent joy and a bloody, red gash had appeared on his cheekbone.

I grazed him.

Flinging the shotgun away, his right hand circled my neck and clamped down, closing my windpipe. A second hand joined it, covering my entire neck. With my hands free, I felt for the guns but couldn't find them. The pain grew, and my face felt flush as though every breath not making its way into my lungs was building in my cheeks and forehead. I beat at his side and chest, even the crook of his elbow, but nothing seemed to budge the brute. My heart hammered while my lungs shriveled, screaming for air. Darkness swirled about my vision like a cascade of melting black-and-white oil paintings. He grinned, straddling me for better leverage, and a flash of his son Steve McCullin, seated in the same position when I was a teenager, came to mind.

The same malicious grin decorated his lips with an insanity bred from a lust for violence. His breath was filled with the stench of alcohol, and his eyes were glazed, a thick five-o'clock shadow adorning his face. I sputtered and choked under his overwhelming strength.

"Damnable kids cant's even call me Dad. You're worthless." A quick backhand from the younger version of Dillon McCullin accompanied his words. "Your mom was cursed with yous. Cursed. Gottas stop." Adjusting, he sent a knee to my groin for good measure, and I grimaced, pain infusing my gut and waist from the inside out. "Better for everyone."

His eyes glistened as his eyelids drooped. Then he slumped to the carpeted floor of my bedroom, unconscious. My vision was flecked with pain, and I could barely make out the bunk bed and picture of my real father and me roughhousing on the nightstand. Although I couldn't focus on it, I knew every one of his features: the crew-cut hair, smile, and gentle but strong arm circling my shoulders in a signature wrestling move. I even remember thinking, If only he was here, he'd never let this bastard do this to us.

An instant later, one sweet breath made its way into my lungs, then another and another. My vision cleared, revealing the older mountain man looming above as his fingers eased.

God help me.

As the *thudding* sound of my heartbeat slowed, I caught sight of a figure standing behind Dillon McCullin with a shotgun aimed at his back.

"I know you don't much need the front side anymore, gramps, but your asshole's going to itch somethin' awful if you move another muscle," the figure said.

Shock infused my face. *Jamie? No, it can't be.*

"You wouldn't. You'd hurt the poor little piggy," McCullin growled, but he let go and took a pained motion to stand.

"That's better. Now, mister, you'd best have a seat." Jamie motioned toward the only seat in the living room that hadn't been overturned.

Dillon McCullin took a step toward the cushioned chair, turned, and glared down at Jamie. "Who the hell are you?"

"Backup."

Dillon gave a hearty laugh. "Boy, you ain't no cop."

"Nope, better. I'm a cop's son—grew up learning to shoot, so don't push it." Glancing my way, he asked, "How you doin', Dad?"

At this, McCullin gave a boisterous laugh and fell into the large chair. "Oh, don't tell me you brought your son to do a man's work?"

I stood on shaky legs, regaining my composure, and stared down at the man who had once been my step-grandfather. Not grandpa. That name was reserved for a better man. "No, I didn't," I replied, sending a warning look to Jamie, "but you're going to answer a few questions."

"Oh, you wanna chitchat now—with ol' grandpa?"

At this, my son sent a questioning look my way.

"This is Dillon McCullin, Steve McCullin's father."

A look of hatred came over Jamie's face. I had never told him the details of my childhood, but he knew enough. The shotgun in his hand trembled, and I could see the fury seething in his eyes.

After picking up my pistol, I waved him down with a calming hand. "It's okay. I've got it now."

The look Jamie gave me was uncertain, but he lowered the gun.

"Dillon, why'd you kill Cameron?"

"Cameron? Who the hell's Cameron?"

I glared at him, but lowered my gun enough to ease the tension in the room. "The kid you murdered tonight."

The overturned couch creaked behind me as Jamie leaned against it. A quick look at his slack-jawed expression told me every word was a shock. *Get it together, Jamie. I don't know how you got here, but this is real life. In for a penny, in for a pound.*

Dillon's gaze dropped, and his smile vanished. "He's dead? I h-heard about a beating on the news."

"Yeah, of course he is, and don't give me that crap. I know you put him in the hospital. What'd you think would happen after taking a pipe to the kid?" As soon as the words were out of my mouth, I regretted them. At fifteen, Jamie had endured some of the same visions I had over the last year. I expected to hear a gasp or some other indication of surprise, but none came. My son stared at Dillon McCullin with grim determination. The added detail didn't seem to have fazed him.

The older man's hard gaze returned to mine. "I'm not sayin' I did nothin'. You ain't got no proof."

"Maybe not, but you and I both know I'm right."

The smug satisfaction in his eyes told me I was correct. The rumors about my abilities had gone around the region since I was a kid, and many of the Appalachian people were superstitious, more inclined to believe it than my own police force.

"Well, let's just speak theoretical like," Dillon answered. "How's that sound?"

I ground my teeth, hating these situations, but we were both limited by lack of evidence and knew it. "Fine."

"Theoretical like, let's just say that's what I was going for—not necessarily death, but to send a message."

The word "message" caught my attention, refocusing my thoughts. "A message to who?"

"The man behind these drugs, if you can even call someone selling crack, meth, and everything else to our kids a man."

"Wait, you mean to tell me you were trying to keep the neighborhood safe? I don't believe that. Dillon, you're just as bad."

"The hell I am!" the mountain man shouted, rising to his full six-and-a-half feet. I motioned back toward the chair with my pistol. Dillon glared but this time did as instructed. "These Reds are killin' our kids, Drummond. You know it better than anyone."

"Yeah, but that doesn't make you Mother Teresa," Jamie interrupted.

"Shinin' doesn't cost people their lives," he replied. "It's an age-old tradition, and we don't sell to kiddos."

I had to admit that he was right on that point. Shiners were a very reclusive group of mountain folk who dealt with family and friends. It wasn't about the money and getting them addicted young. "Then why go after Cameron?"

"'Cause they gave us an ultimatum—get out or die. They said it was their *turf* now. They didn't want nobody else dealin' in their parts, even if it was a couple old shiners like us."

"They saw you as a rival gang?"

"Nah, they would've given another gang more respect. What they don't realize is they're messin' with family tradition here. This ain't just a business. It's a way of life."

Things were beginning to make sense now, but I still had one question. "So why Cameron?"

"He's the one they sent to tell us—a damn kid of one of our own. Ain't got no sense. We had to send a message to whoever was makin' deals and givin' orders." Dillon shifted in his seat, obviously uncomfortable with what he'd done.

Something still didn't add up. "But you're not okay with this?" I asked.

McCullin glared at me. "Of course not. I did wha' had to be done, but he was still a kid."

Jamie perked up at this. "What had to be done? You're joking, right? You could've sent a message without killing him!"

Dillon nodded his hairy head somewhat off kilter. "Mayhaps. Like I said, I didn't mean ta go that far. I left him breathin', er... theoretical like."

He paused and looked at me until I nodded. Doing so was contrary to my very being, but there was no going back. I had to take a bit of my own medicine. *In for a penny, in for a pound.*

"Even so, what's the cost of one life if it saves others?" he continued. "No tellin' how bad things'll get for our kids if these Reds get more of a foothold and keep dealin'."

"Who's in charge?" I asked.

Dillon shook his head. "Don't know yet, but we're workin' on it. I'll tell you this. No one comes in ta our house an' tells us what ta do. That ain't how it's done. Now, Drummond, if you're really here for the kids, to save them, then you best get goin'. Work your end, and I'll work mine. If you come for my shine, you and me, we're gonna have a problem."

Jamie rose to his feet. "Are you threatening my dad?"

"Only if he don't know his place," Dillon replied unfazed. "Coppers stay well away from here for a reason."

"Yeah but, Dillon, you stepped into my stretch of the woods this time. I'll find the evidence I need to put you away." If the jacket didn't work, there might be fibers between Cameron's teeth. He'd go down. It was only a matter of when. If he did some of my work for me in the meantime, all the better.

Dillon rose to his feet again, but this time with what seemed like a genuine smile. "When you do, I'll be waitin'. We'll have us another li'l chat. Till then, you best be on your way. Just tuck your tail between your legs and skedaddle before things get worse."

Tilting my head to the side, my neck popped, easing the tension for the moment. "Drop the gun," I told Jamie. A look his way told me how much he hated doing it, but he emptied the shell. He left the gun on the overturned couch and marched out ahead of me, fists clenched at his sides. At the door I turned to Dillon, who still hadn't made a move for the shotgun. In fact, he was grinning at me. It was unnerving, but I holstered my pistol. "I'll be back for you, McCullin."

"You do that," he replied and closed the door behind me.

The walk back to the car was more difficult than the conversation had been. My nerves were on edge. To some extent, I could trust the shiners' actions. They were predictable but not necessarily to be taken at their word. McCullin was pure mountain man through and through, unlike his son, my ex-stepfather. As soon as I caught sight of the buckshot holes peppering one side of the Subaru, I was reminded of this. *I can shoot the tits off a tree rat at a hundred paces,* his earlier words repeated. *Yeah, you probably can. Those squirrels don't stand a chance.*

"Dad, are we really driving home in this?" Jamie asked. He stood next to the passenger's side door and waved a hand at the shattered windows and spiderwebbed windshield.

I rounded the car, passing in front of the one headlight still working, and got in. "Yes, we are. I'm just glad he went for the car instead of my head."

We might be able to add charges of assaulting an officer, I considered.

Jamie frowned, dusted the glass off his seat, and grabbed a towel from the trunk to sit on.

Puzzled, I asked, "How'd you know that was back there?"

Settling himself into the pockmarked side of the vehicle, he answered, "How you think I got here? Hid under the towel."

"Jamie, you can't..." but I couldn't say it. My words trailed off. Every bit of energy had been drained from my body. Starting the car, I put it in reverse and turned around in the yard. "Never mind. Just stay safe for now on."

Jamie smiled. "So, Dad, what are you gonna do about Mom's car? You know she's gonna kill you when she sees it."

The thought curdled my stomach. Trekking down the dirt driveway with the Subaru rattling and clunking with a periodic rhythm, I groaned, "I know."

Chapter 12

Sweet Dandy

March 9th, 2012

THE SUBARU RATTLING along the road for an hour almost disguised the vibrations of my cell phone. "Hello?"

"Detective Drummond," Taylor replied, "I've been trying to get hold of you."

"Just heading home. What do you need?"

"Brightwell's still waiting with Principal Cantril. Things have gotten pretty active down at the school, Drummond."

I groaned and took the next turn, altering direction. "I'll be there in a minute." Flipping the phone shut, I glanced at Jamie. His branded forehead rested on his seatbelt strap as wind buffeted his dark hair. "Jamie, you awake?"

"Yeah," he mumbled. "Work, right?"

"Yep. Seems like there's a ruckus down at the school."

Jamie brightened at the announcement. "Seriously? That's still goin' on? Can I help?"

I wasn't sure where he'd heard about it, but with his cell phone, Jamie kept up with news about as quickly as dispatch. I shook my head while keeping my eyes on the scattered, parked cars lining the main strip of Tranquil Heights. "No, you're going to stay in the car."

"But, Dad," Jamie whined.

"No buts. Stay in the car. This shouldn't take long. It's just some parents angry after what happened to Cameron. Officer Brightwell's been there all evening. The principal and I just need to chat."

"But I know the school."

I took a moment to glare at my son. "So do I. It may have been a while since I went there, but it isn't that different. Besides, I'm just going by the office."

Jamie frowned.

"You *will* stay in the car, or I'll take you home first."

Before Jamie could answer, we made the last turn and Madessa High School came into view. It was astounding. The only two uniforms in sight were keeping people away from the taped-off crime scene. Vehicles were packed into the remainder of the parking lot, the circular drop-off, and even lined the street. I spotted a group of adolescents wearing assorted hoodies and sagging pants trimmed in red. *This can't be good.* They looked angry, milling around the parking lot under a street lamp, screaming and yelling more than talking. Clusters of parents walked in and out of the school.

"I don't think you should wait any longer," Jamie said. "It's like a championship game or something." As we passed a green-and-brown camouflage hunting pick-up, he asked, "Do you think the PTA went on a recruiting mission in the Everglades?"

"It's just concerned parents." *And gang members.*

"Are you gonna tell them about Mr. McCullin?"

The mention of my former step-grandfather and the cough and rattle of the car's engine brought my thoughts to our current predicament. Rather than turning into the parking lot where everyone would see the vehicle's condition, I continued down the road. Around the next bend I parked alongside the road with the peppered side of the car facing the football field.

"So?" Jamie asked after a brief wait.

"No, son, I'm not. I don't have any proof at the moment."

"But—"

"No buts!" I lowered my voice and shut the car off as other voices filtered through the darkness and into the car through the shattered windows. "Of anyone, you should know why I can't. I don't like it any more than you, but we have to operate according to the law. I'll gather proof first."

Jamie's mouth snapped shut and he nodded.

"It's just the way the world works. Now, stay in the car. I don't even want that buckle undone."

In silent agreement, Jamie pulled out his phone and tapped away. I stepped into the crisp night, grabbed my worn duster out of the backseat, and headed for the lights illuminating the building in the distance.

Although not in the standard uniform, the town was still small enough that most people knew your name and profession, especially if you were in law enforcement. Some of the frustrated teenagers sat on the edge of a pick-up truck where the tailgate should have been but wasn't. Their voices calmed as I neared, but when they spotted me, one I recognized from Cameron's vision as Dexter shouted, "Yo, Mr. Drummond, what you gonna do about Cam?" He was still wearing the same black jeans and red, oversized t-shirt.

At first I continued toward the high school's front doors, but after a second thought I altered course, staring directly at the young hothead.

"Whacha gonna do, copper? 'Cause if you can't do nothin' I'll—"

"You'll what, Dexter?" I asked, stopping less than a foot away. I matched the boy in height and more than outweighed him in muscle. A whiff of alcohol drifted on his breath, and a hatred stemming from my own stepfather's murderous faults seeped to the surface. Adrenaline coursed through my veins. *He's just a kid,* I reminded myself. *He's hurting. His friend was killed.*

He hissed, "I'll cap the mofo myself," while closing the distance to within inches, close enough that I could count the freckles on his young nose.

Gritting my teeth, I said, "Dexter, you'd best take a step back and go home before you do something you'll regret."

"Yo, man, I don't regret nothin'. In fact, I ain't scared of nothin' either." With arms swinging wide, he spun and grabbed a whiskey bottle from behind a girl sitting on the truck bed. "See this, it's mine, and you can't do nothin' about it!" he shouted, holding it up.

As soon as he did, I took a large step forward and grabbed his extended wrist in one hand and his chin in my other, ensuring he looked directly into my eyes. An inch away from his face, I growled, "Dexter's not feeling so hot. I think your buddies should get you home before *I* do something *I* might regret."

Shuffling came from behind him, and in my peripheral vision I spotted a couple of his friends with hands lingering over their waists. The girl teetered, laughing as though drunk. Under their shirts, I was certain more than a few weapons could be found. *Unpredictable,* I reminded myself. *Wannabe gangsters can be even worse than a gang itself. They're unsure of themselves and can get trigger-happy, but maybe they don't know Cameron passed.* "Take him home. Cameron deserves your concern, not half-cocked anger running rampant." Turning, I let go of Dexter and strode toward the high school while listening for any movement behind me. I didn't want to pull my gun but would if necessary.

Instead of a gun cocking or even fast-moving footsteps, a different voice I remembered from the boy's earlier vision said, "He's dead. I got the tweet. There's nothing we can do here, just get revenge." The tone was deep, filled with grief, and when I turned around, I recognized Trey. He didn't look hesitant or scared, only determined. His chiseled jaw was set.

Crap, I was afraid of that. "Well, let me do my job. I'm good at it."

He harrumphed.

Ignoring it, I left them under the street lamp and passed into the well-lit school hallway, preparing myself to confront a less physical but just as intimidating group—distraught parents. This was one incident that had everyone on edge.

Inside, the hallways were bustling with parents. Stepping through the scattered attendants, the crowd grew denser the closer I got to the office and the auditorium across the hall. Through the window to the small principal's office, a mob was swarming around the counter. A rotund woman sat behind the counter fielding questions, trying to quiet the group. Principal Cantril was nowhere in sight.

Ducking into the auditorium where hundreds more parents were seated and milling about, my gaze was drawn to the woman standing on stage, a woman I was familiar with—Courtney Pulin, Jamie's friend's mother. Someone had flipped on the stage lights, but with no microphone, she shouted over the large group. Whatever she said thus far seemed to be riling the group up. "Cameron Gardner was a sophomore at Madessa High School," she continued. "I just received word that his brutal beating led to his death only moments ago. His father Jack is in the hospital right now crying over his son's lifeless body. Are we going to allow this sort of violence in our school?"

"No!" came the shouted chorus.

"The school should be doing something about this, something to protect our children, but where's Principal Cantril? I haven't seen him tonight. Have you?"

"No!"

"From the looks of things, Officer Brightwell thinks we're the ones to be feared." She pointed at the school resource officer who stood erect at the edge of the stage. I half expected him to shrink from her accusations, but the large ex-military man stood his ground, thumbs tucked into his black uniform belt. "Instead of trying to find the person responsible for this, Officer Brightwell's here supervising us. We're adults and parents. This is our community, our children. If they won't handle this, *we* will!"

A roar of voices followed, cheering her on. Shouts of hatred also flew from the crowd, directed at Officer Brightwell. He didn't say a word.

At least they're not making accusations of murder yet, but we've got to put a stop to this. I thought about speaking up myself but then thought better of it. While things had changed since my high school days—I was respected by some in the community—the rumors and skeptics still haunted me at times, much more so than any ghost I'd heard. I stepped back into the hallway and crossed into the crammed school office. Sideling through the throng of people, I didn't bother with the older secretary. Seeing me drift past and into the hallway leading to the principal's office, she seemed to consider stopping me. Her hand hung in the air, but whatever words were on her tongue never emerged. The attempt told me what I needed to know—Principal Cantril was present, probably hiding. *The coward.*

I strode down the dark hall and noticed a light emanating from under the closed door to Cantril's office. I didn't knock. Instead, I opened the door and closed it snugly behind me.

The interim principal sat behind his dark, wooden desk, an attempted façade failing to mask his fear. "It's about time you—"

"Cut the crap!" I interrupted, slamming a knuckled fist down on the desk.

He about jumped out of the faux-leather computer chair, his eyes darting to my tensed arm as I leaned over his desk, then back to my face.

I set my jaw, struggling to stifle the next words that entered my mind. My teeth ground, the sound echoing and seeming loud enough that it might have started a tremor in Japan. "You're hiding back here like a damned mouse while these parents are about ready to tear your school apart." I glared down at him. "You're a piece of work, you know that? Your elderly secretary has more balls than you."

Principal Cantril stammered, attempting to make excuses.

Another thump against the thick desk resounded in the small room, jostling his coat rack in the corner. A bowler hat reminiscent of the Wild West toppled to the tile floor. My gaze never wavered. "I'm not gonna do your job for you, mister, but I damn well won't let this town go to ruins. What are you goin' to do about it?"

"I... I... should probably have a word with them."

"You think?"

"Y-y-yes I do."

"Then what the hell have you been doing hiding in this office all night hounding my dispatch?" I tried not to scream.

"I... I sent Brightwell out to keep order."

After taking a deep breath and attempting to calm myself, his response infuriated me further. "I noticed," I growled. "That's a good man, ex-military. He'll try to stop a riot if need be, but this is your school, Cantril. Get it together!"

The principal nodded and rose unsteadily to his feet. Crossing the room, he opened the door with a shaky hand, paused to collect himself, then stepped outside. I followed, glowering at the sweat stain streaming down the back of his striped button-up. Seeing the bowler hat in my peripheral vision again, I took a split-second to grab it out from under his jacket. *He might be making a quick exit after all's said and done.* The instant I did, I regretted the decision. My tensed muscles deflated as the odor of aged leather drifted up to meet me. *What now?* I thought as my vision quickly melded with the black, inky cloud that prefaced a vision.

* * *

"Wha-what'd you do that for?" asked what had to be an elderly man's nasal voice. My vision grew to a light blur, and soon I could make out twilight beyond the walls of the school through the distant mountain forest. Snow topped the trees and coated the asphalt parking lot behind the school. I leaned back against a parked

car. My breath fogged in the crisp air as I continued speaking. "I'm just walkin' here."

A face I recognized from the group of Reds I'd encountered moments before in the school's front parking lot grew visible mere inches away, his arm extended toward my chest. Rather than look down, I could only stare straight ahead into the beady eyes of a boy no more than sixteen. His hair was so blond it was almost white, much paler than his olive skin. "Sorry, gramps, but you're times up," he said without sincerity.

With a jerk of his hand, I felt something long, round, and sharp pierce my chin, tear through my tongue, and up through the roof of my mouth. I snorted, feeling fluid flow through my nostrils and into and over my mouth. The familiar taste of iron-rich blood and piercing pain in my head overwhelmed my senses. Clawing at the young man with frail hands, I choked and coughed while tumbling to the ground.

Dandy, sweet Dandy... See you soon, *came unbidden thoughts accompanied by the memory of a woman posing in front of a '56 Chevy, her legs crossed beneath a bright-yellow sundress. Her bobbed hair and red lipstick were the cherry on top as I recognized her loving smile and knew it was meant just for me.* Ten long years, but it won't be much more now. *My vision began to dim as I stared at the fading back parking lot, reality pitched at 45 degrees from where I lay.*

"D-Deacon!" shouted the recognizable voice of Principal Cantril with a tremor. "What the h-hell?" His mouth hung open as he backed against the red, brick walls of the school. "How could you?"

The blond high schooler casually plucked my black bowler from the ground and strode toward the principal, a bulbous, bloody pen clutched in his other hand. Although the events began to blur, I could still make out a streak of what I guessed was my blood splattering the young boy's shirt, giving the black-and-white print of a tuxedo t-shirt a very morbid look. "Now, Cantril, you know I mean it." He plopped the hat onto the administrator's head. "I think you'd better wear this as a reminder of what'll happen if you try and stick your nose in our bus-y-ness." He drew out each syllable of the word intentionally. "If I see you leave school without it, I might just think you forgot our li'l discussion."

Mr. Cantril swallowed as if attempting to dislodge something stuck in his narrow throat—a frog, ostrich egg, or perhaps his damnable courage. The pansy! Then he nodded as darkness crept over my vision.

See you soon, darling.

* * *

Stumbling forward, I caught myself against Principal Cantril's office doorframe and shook off the vision. An itch just under my chin sent a chill through me. My mouth felt as though it had been stuffed with cotton balls. Well, that explains a lot. The Reds have him scared out of his gourd. What was that boy's name…?

Deacon... something. A second later it came to me. *Deacon Smotes, son of a local accountant in town, but who was the victim?* I couldn't come up with a name for that one, having no idea what the old man looked like besides the bowler hat I'd been wearing in the vision. I'd have to check into Dandy, his past love and likely his wife, but that was a question for another time. Dismissing it for the moment, I caught back up with the principal. He strode with his back rigid as he attempted to stand as tall as possible, overcompensating for his fear.

The crowd parted as he stepped into them, making way, but they shouted their protests. I followed behind as he passed into the auditorium. A discordant chorus of voices rose with his appearance. Each step up to the stage seemed to add weight onto the thin principal's shoulders.

I didn't envy him, but every man must step up and seize control when the world demands it. Those moments make the difference between a man and a child. Some people just don't grow up. I didn't have much faith in Cantril or his lecherous notions, but someone had to stem the tide of resentment in this school. Anger and violence flowed throughout the room on waves of air I could feel in my very bones. If things became any worse, someone would get hurt. I glanced at Officer Brightwell and gave him a nod, wondering for a moment whether to call for backup. *Have faith,* I reminded myself. *It'll take too long for backup to get here anyway.*

Courtney Pulin couldn't resist and shouted from the stage, "'Bout time you got here, Cantril! Get your tail out from between your legs."

The Madessa High School principal took the final step and glanced around the packed auditorium while I remained at the edge of the stage. Next to me, Brightwell had his arms crossed as he perused the rowdy crowd. I didn't have to tell him what to do. The man had been in far more dangerous situations in the Middle East than I could have imagined. My thoughts went to my father's dog tags hanging beneath my shirt, resting against my bare chest. For a moment they acted as a cold reminder of what so many people risk.

Unlike Mrs. Pulin who belted out her words across the large room, Cantril held up a hand as though to halt the audience while he retrieved a microphone from behind the burgundy stage curtain.

"How's this?" he asked, his voice echoing through the auditorium speakers. He emerged a moment later seeming a little more comfortable, as though the microphone itself gave him a grip on reality. He clutched it more like a drowning man would a life preserver while sharks circled. "Now let's settle down and have a seat. I have a few things to speak with you about."

A few rebellious voices echoed above the rest, perceived more clearly due to the quieting crowd.

"Come on. L-let's go," he continued, unable to help a small quake in his tone.

However, the crowd did as he asked. Even Mrs. Pulin stepped off the stage and took one of the plastic folding seats in the front row.

"Now, I know you're afraid for your children. Frankly, so am I."

Interesting start... Not sure it's the way I would have chosen.

Thankfully, Principal Cantril followed through with more stern composure than I expected after clearing his throat. "Every day I come to work scared that I might not be able to help them reach their potential. Life is full of challenges. Kids get into drugs, gangs, and so many things that feel out of this world. These are fears we all share, right?"

A few grumbles answered back, but many heads nodded.

"I still come. I do the best I can to help *your* children become the adults that will lead this world—and our small town—into the future. Though I can't stop everything, just as you can't. We try our best to make this world as safe as possible, but kids will make mistakes and learn from them. We just hope those mistakes are ones they can live with. Unfortunately, this isn't always the case."

More heads nodded, and a few voices jeered. Cantril plowed onward.

"I think we all know what happened here tonight. I received word that a student was on the school grounds after hours. For what reason, I don't know. What I do know is he was attacked." He gave the group a moment to absorb his acknowledgement. "Whatever the reason for this, I'm going to do everything I can to help bring the person responsible to justice. I've been speaking with the police and investigating the matter thoroughly. I'm sorry you had to wait, but that's why."

Hearing this, I felt as though a horse pill had somehow lodged in my throat. It was hard to swallow, but he sounded completely honest. *The guy could be a politician... or president.* I could taste stomach acid building in the back of my throat at the thought of getting roped into lies and excuses just to save Cantril's cowardly hide. *Politics at its best. I'll go to hell and back before I get involved in that crap.* I tried to swallow my disgust for the moment.

"They're searching for the murderer now. In our small town, this won't stand. I'll do everything I can to stop it, but please... please let the authorities handle it." Waving a hand toward me and Officer Brightwell, he stated, "Homicide Detective Drummond and Officer Brightwell have kept in touch with updates about tonight's events." He made a halfhearted motion for me to approach, but a slight shake of my head deterred him. "We'll keep you apprised," he said instead, turning back to the much calmer audience.

Seizing the moment to escape without getting pulled into the crosshairs of frustrated parents, I slapped Brightwell on the shoulder and muttered, "I think you've got this." Retiring to the backstage, I left through one of the school's side exits with Principal Cantril's bowler hat in hand. *There has to be some evidence that will tell me who the old man was.* His late wife's nickname fluttered through my mind again. *Dandy, sweet Dandy...*

Taking long strides out to my car where Jamie waited, my phone beeped. Pulling it out of my pocket, I saw that I had a voicemail and had missed a call from an unknown number. *It never ends.* Then I caught sight of the side of the Subaru peppered with shells. My shoulders slumped. The back of Jamie's head was visible in the passenger's side window, staring into his lap. In the dark, it was difficult to see his expression, but something in my gut told me my evening was far from over.

Chapter 13

Messages

March 9th, 2012

MY HEART POUNDED in my ears as I crept closer to the demolished side of the car, breath held and a lump forming in my throat thicker than a forty-layer mattress. "Jamie," I tried to say, but it only came out as a whisper. Swallowing, I tried again and took another heavy step. "Jamie, you okay?"

"D-D-Dad," he replied, his voice hollow and vacant.

Time sped back up as his voice permeated the darkness through the few remaining shards of the window. Closing the distance, I ran a hand along the back of my son's head. "You okay?" I asked, leaning in and staring into Jamie's downturned face. For a second the ankh branded into his forehead made me wince, but my gut told me something more was wrong.

"D-Dad, wh-wha' do I do?" He didn't look at me, just continued staring into his lap.

"What do you mean, Jamie?" I gave his head an affectionate pat. My gaze then followed his. In his lap sat something shadowed and somewhat hairy. As my eyes adjusted, I made out more features of the orblike object. A nose revealed itself amidst a shaggy head of hair. At this, my mouth drained, leaving it as dry as the Sahara Desert on a summer's day. Where a neck should have been was a bloody, jagged edge of ripped skin. "Son, where'd that come from?"

"Dad..., it's D-Donny."

Donny Pulin, son of the overzealous mother who had riled up so many people only minutes before and Jamie's best friend, was dead. Aside from the hollow shadows disguising Donny's eyes as some inhuman, pale object, the sight in Jamie's lap confirmed his words. *I saw him just a few hours ago... Jesus!* "H-how did this happen?"

"He... he's dead, Dad."

Nodding, I moved my hand to Jamie's shoulder and gave it a squeeze. "Yes, son, he is," I said in a somber tone.

Jamie's hands shook, hovering over the head. He seemed afraid to move, to even touch it. Blood was caked to one leg of his jeans.

"Don't touch it. I'll call it in." Standing upright, I flipped out my phone and hit the speed dial.

"Tranquil Heights Police Dispatch. How can I help you?" asked Sage Heathers, a part-time dispatcher. Taylor must have gotten off work.

I stared down at Jamie's shaking, bloody hand. "Sage, it's Alex Drummond. I've got a homicide on my hands... another one." I paused after using the common phrase and gave my head a shake. "Better send forensics and backup. We'll also need a coroner."

Sage's breath caught. Murder, while it happened, was not that common in Tranquil Heights, at least not in such a short span of time. The sound of her polished fingernails tapping at the keyboard echoed through the phone. "They're on their way, Alex. You all right?"

"Yeah," I replied, closing the phone and slipping it back into my coat pocket. "Jamie, sit tight if you can. I'm sorry, but there could still be evidence."

"I... I know, Dad. I get it."

"What happened? Did you see who did this?"

Jamie cracked an awkward smile, obviously attempting to make light of the situation. He finally looked up and met my gaze. "Define saw."

I nodded. "I see what you mean. Wait for a second."

Moving to the trunk, I opened it and pulled a black, plastic trash bag out of a container I kept for similar occasions, although I never thought something like this in particular would happen. I couldn't think or multitask, so I focused on one thing at a time. Briefly glimpsing grass and pavement through small holes in the trash bag, I grimaced. Closer inspection revealed an assortment of holes. Glancing at the back quarter panel of the car, I discovered similar holes in the Subaru. Shot from Dillon McCullin's gun must have penetrated the car and the bags, but it looked like only a few had thankfully. Grabbing another bag out, I double-bagged them, making sure the holes didn't line up. Then I grabbed a disposable latex glove and returned to the front passenger's side.

"Jamie, where exactly did you hide in the car?"

Jamie looked up at me. "The trunk of course."

Licking my lips, I carefully asked, "Are you sure you're okay? Nothing hit you?"

"Just a pellet or two, some bird shot from that old fogy's gun. No big deal. It just hit my arm. Felt like a pellet gun really. Must have lost most of its oomph going through the car."

I shook my head, muttering, "Your mother's really going to kill me."

He smiled, feeling more like his mischievous self with his mind on things other than his friend's decapitated head. "No worries. It'll be our little secret."

I pulled on the glove. "Ha! You think your mother won't find out? You have a lot to learn, sonny." Hesitating, I finally opened his car door. "Now, sit still." Using my gloved hand, I lifted the head off his lap and deposited it into the bag.

Jamie breathed a visible sigh of relief.

"I... I'm sorry, Jamie, sorry about Donny."

"Yeah, me too." He paused and turned, shifting both feet out of the car before meeting my gaze. "Dad, did you see what happened?"

I glanced at Donny's face peering up out of the bag. Jamie hadn't closed his friend's eyes, even while holding his head in his lap. "Uhh, not yet. One sec." The smell of blood drifted up from the bag. Reaching in with my ungloved hand, I closed his lids, hiding his brown eyes. The subtle scent of worn leather drifted to my nose, overwhelming everything else as my world turned to black.

* * *

"Hey, Chase," Trey yelled, "what you want us to do with this little bitch?"

From a few yards away, Chase's voice answered, "That little bitch is our meal ticket. Scrub said to make an example. We gotta send the cops a message. They're gettin' too close and need to lay off."

Their voices were the only things I could hear. In the dark, stray light emanating from below revealed folds in the burlap sack over my head but nothing more. "Wh-why are y'all doin' this? I never did anything."

The crunch of footsteps on dry grass approached.

"Take that damn thing off," Chase ordered. A second later, Trey jerked the sack revealing a clearing full of yellowed, dead grass, a blazing sun overhead, and the forest's edge a hundred yards away. "Now," Chase continued from just a few feet in front of me, "I can see those pitiful eyes. I'm surprised you ain't pissin' your pants."

"But I didn't—"

"The hell you didn't!" he interrupted. "You and Jamie went too far. That damn school gang you put together is more than enough reason. You ain't gonna stop us." After a pause he added, "And neither are the moonshiners or the cops. Jamie's dad and the shiners better back off or this'll happen to them and theirs."

"I'll tell him. I—"

"Yeah, you'll tell him somethin'. You're gonna pass along a message, but you won't have to remember it."

My eyes widened as what was coming dawned on Donny.
Run, Donny, run! *It was as though he heard me. I bolted before Trey*
could even get a hand on my shoulder. Legs pumping, I... I mean,
Donny headed for the woods at the edge of the clearing.

Laughing echoed behind me, Chase's laughter. "Look at that
chunky monkey go! You think there's anywhere you can hide?" There
were no sounds following, no footsteps, boots stomping, or anything.
It was strange, but Donny's thoughts simply repeated, Run away,
run, get away! They're out to kill me.

A second later a shot rang out. It felt like a million bees
embedded their stingers in my back and sent me skidding onto my
face in the dried grass and dirt, knocking the wind from my lungs.

"Nice shot, Deacon!" Chase said as he strolled up to my prone
form. This time an assortment of other footsteps accompanied him. "I
think that's the first time this little prick ever got any action." The
others laughed and chortled.

"Ahh, just a little bird shot. Ain't no permanent harm,"
Deacon replied, sounding disappointed.

It was a voice I recognized, not Donny but me. I searched my
mind for where I'd heard it before. Where...? Then I had it—the
bowler hat. Deacon was the boy who killed the elderly man and
controlled Principal Cantril.

I flipped over, feeling Donny's panic, pain blossoming in the
back of my thigh. Looming around me... us... him... were six teenage
boys, smiling and jeering. Each wore something red, be it a baseball

cap, shoes, or shirt. Chase squatted at my head and stared down at me. It appeared as though the world had flipped upside down.

"And now he's pissin' his pants," Chase chortled.

A moment later, I felt the warm liquid seeping down my legs and into my new wounds. I winced but bit my lip. "P-please don't."

Chase grinned like a wolf hovering over its prey, watching the pitiful final attempt at life and freedom. "The weak either die or get out of the way, little prick. Now it's your turn."

My eyes widened as Chase held a machete up I hadn't seen before. The world had certainly flipped in more ways than one. Doing right didn't always mean you survived. His dark eyes glittered with bloodlust as the blade dropped down. A jolt of searing pain, then nothing as it severed my neck. He grinned, gripped a handful of dark curls, and lifted me off the ground. Standing, Chase held me aloft for the others to see, the world jostling unsteadily as though I were at sea. A feeling of nausea took me momentarily, and I wondered morbidly how that would work considering nothing was left below the neck. As they looked at me, my dimming vision revealed vile emotions. Some reveled in the murder, while the shortest of the gang turned, bent, and lost his lunch. The last thing Donny saw were pieces of half-digested ham-and-cheese sandwich slopping onto the ground. Then the world vanished.

* * *

The nausea took hold like a lusting dog to a pant leg as my senses returned. Heat engulfed my throat, and I turned, emptying my stomach.

"Jamie," I muttered once my swirling vision and stomach had settled, "I'm sorry about Donny. If I'd never gotten involved, this might not have happened."

"Enough of that," he replied, still seated in the passenger's side, his feet resting on the pavement. "If you hadn't, others would've died in his place and he might still. Nothing you could do."

I nodded, wiped my sleeve across my face, and turned to look at my son. He was right, smarter than I gave him credit for and more mature than any boy his age. I felt another wave of bile rise in my throat, still imagining Donny's final events, but I pushed it down this time.

"I have a question though, what'd they do with his body?"

"I don't know, but I have a couple questions of my own. How'd they know I was onto them? And who's running this charade?"

"You don't think it's the guy with the frizzy hair anymore?"

"Probably, but who is he?"

Jamie shook his head. "Not sure. Couldn't they have read about the investigation in the papers?"

"No. Nothing's been released about it yet. There wasn't even a body or anyone claiming their loved ones were missing.

Nothing to report, yet. Do you know anyone who might've said something?"

"Nah. I've been checkin' the Twittersphere and Facebook but haven't seen anything about you, Dad. It's mainly complaints about the school and police force in general. Chase named you specifically… and the shiners."

That was true. Chase had meant this as a message for the shiners and the cops. It was a reply to the message the shiners sent by killing Cameron. Chase and whoever was pulling his strings wanted us to back off, as though this was some territorial gang fight over turf lines. It was like *Duck Dynasty* meets *Boys N the Hood*, and Jamie and I were stuck in the middle of it.

"That reminds me, how the hell did Donny's head get in your lap?"

Jamie didn't flinch at the mention of what had transpired only moments before. "I'm guessing it was one of the Reds. He wore a Santa Clause ski mask—you know, the ones with knitted, white beards and everything. Must have been lying in the back floorboard or somethin'. All I know is a little after you left to go to the school, he reaches up from behind me, puts a knife to my neck with one hand and drops Donny's head in my lap with his other. He said to tell you to back off or I'll be next. He left after that." Jamie's words were firm but without emotion.

Is he in shock? I wondered. *Probably.* Another doubt crept to mind about whether I was doing right by him in teaching him to use these abilities. Sirens echoed in the distance, growing closer by the second. They pulled me from my internal debate.

"Why didn't you text me or call?"

"'Cause the guy took my phone. Tossed it somewhere over in the woods."

I nodded and quietly said, "I'll go look for it as soon as backup arrives."

The old Jamie, the one I'd seen that very morning, would have had a smart retort waiting about me being a scaredy-cat, a pansy for worrying about him or some other lighthearted joke. We tended to banter like that; it was the kind of relationship we had, jesting with each other. It irritated me at times, but for the moment I missed it and wondered if it would return, because Jamie did not reply. That was far worse.

"We'll see if we can get some prints off it, too. Did you recognize his voice?"

"Maybe. Not sure."

Probably someone at his school. Damn kids playing at warlords. They were going to get themselves killed, and a ton of innocents alongside them. The shiners would strike back. Donny was a relation; distant, but to mountain folk blood is thicker than steel. They don't trust outsiders, so it means family means that much more to them.

As the spinning, colored lights illuminated the street, onlookers spilled from the school like gawking pigeons. I filled in the officers, borrowed a cruiser, and left to break the hearts of

Donny's family. Thankfully, Mrs. Pulin had already left after the town meeting. I headed for the trailer I'd visited earlier that day, trying not to step on my heart, which lay in the floorboard of the police cruiser.

I hate this part of the job.

Chapter 14

Normalcy

March 10th, 2012

BY THE TIME I got home the prior night with Jamie, Paige was nowhere to be seen. While it was quite late, it wasn't unusual for her to be called out at odd hours for emergencies. Once she was called into the emergency room for an umbrella some college kid got lodged up his anus on a dare, seriously. Don't ask how. However, this morning I was surprised to find her side of the bed made. She hadn't joined me at all. At first I panicked and sat up, worried something might have happened. She wasn't scheduled to work the nightshift. Then her voice echoed from the kitchen, plates rattling on the wooden dining room table as it was set for breakfast. For a change, Jamie's muffled voice replied back, his words indiscernible.

How late did I sleep? I glanced at the alarm clock I'd forgotten to set. It glowed 8:30. Grabbing a pair of shorts and a t-shirt, I dressed before joining them.

"Why'd you two let me sleep so long?" I asked, grabbing a seat at the table while the aroma of cooking bacon, eggs, waffles, and brewing coffee perked my interest. "Hec's gonna have my hide about coming in late."

Paige replied, "I would have, but Jamie stirred before you and told me how late you two were out. I thought you could use an extra hour. Hec will understand. It's Saturday anyway." She brought over a skillet of fresh bacon while Jamie finished laying out the meal.

"Weekends are the busiest. You know that. Quite a spread here though. Be careful, or I might get used to this... you cooking a hearty breakfast every morning." Honestly, I couldn't remember the last time we'd sat down to breakfast together before this week. Recently, it had gotten hard. Our schedules had us working such unusual hours that we were rarely together mornings. Normally it was first come, first served based on whatever you could find in the fridge, and with a growing teenage boy in the house, I never knew what I'd find.

Paige glowered, a small smile playing behind her dark, amber eyes. "Don't get too used to it, but I'm glad you like having me around."

They both took seats at the table and I grinned as a cardinal perched on the tree out back, visible through the sliding glass door opposite me. "We do," I said, spooning the dishes of food onto my plate. "Always love having you around. It's good to see that things can go on after such..." I couldn't say it, my thoughts going back to Donny's dismembered head and heartbroken parents. My grin vanished. Both his mother and father were there when I arrived, and neither kept it together when I told them. Whatever Donny was going through at home, they seemed to love him. It wasn't surprising; most parents love their kids, even those who abuse them.

"Such gruesome acts," Paige finished for me. "I know. The forensics crew was called in along with myself. They're short-staffed, and with Donny's body missing, they called me and Dr. Seller in. I assume you spoke with the Pulins?"

I nodded, turning my attention to my plate and shoveling a spoonful into my mouth. Unfortunately I could no longer smell or taste the wonderful meal Paige had cooked. It all tasted like ashes, dried, grimy bitterness spreading across my tongue. I gulped the food down, drank some orange juice, and tried more. It didn't help.

Looking over at Jamie, I was astonished to find him wolfing his eggs and sausage down as though he were in an eating competition for the newest iPad.

How does he do it?

"So what time did you get in?" I asked.

"About five thirty. Sun wasn't even up."

Jamie's fork paused midair, eggs falling back to the plate. Catching himself, he slowly returned to feeding the belly full of pigs that must reside in his stomach.

What made him stop? I wondered.

"Well I'm so glad you two like having me around because Hiram asked if I'd stay on with the forensics team until you close this case." Hiram Senai headed the forensics squad; although, for most of the team it was a part-time gig. Tranquil Heights was small enough that we couldn't afford a full-time team of forensic professionals, nor did we need one more often than not. However, with the population growing and violence on the rise, that was changing. They were getting called in more and more often, leaving Doug Trendle as the sole mortician in the department. "Hiram might have to choose between being coroner and head of the police force's forensics team soon. What will happen to Doug? He's a pretty quiet guy, not a leader."

"Oh really? Well, he should be fine. The slight pay raise won't hurt, and he'll learn to do what's needed. He's a good guy. Not like the morgue is all that difficult to manage anyway. It'll just take a little time, and the bodies aren't going anywhere."

"Yep," she said with that mischievous smile I still remembered from our teenage years, a smile she had passed along to Jamie. "He'll be fine. I know it's gruesome, but these are the only times I get to do what we did as kids. It allows me a little time outside the ER."

I licked my lips or tried to. My mouth felt drier with every spoonful, and this news made it worse. "Are you sure you want to do that?"

She leveled me with a look. This one left nothing dancing behind her eyes, only the sternness I knew was a part of her core. It was one of the many things I loved about her. She said, "Of course I do."

"You're good," I answered quickly. "There's no doubt about that. They could use you. I only ask because this one has me pretty well flummoxed. We're gettin' closer, but it's slow going." I tried to continue eating to put her at ease. "I'm only worried about your wellbeing."

"Will you be taking Jamie in today?" she asked.

"Probably not."

Jamie whined, "But why?"

This time we both glared at him. His mouth snapped shut.

I growled, "Do you have to ask?"

This piqued Paige's interest, noticeable from the slight tilt of her head. "What do you mean?"

Jamie glanced at me quickly, his eyes flitting back and forth between us.

"Do you want to tell her?" I asked, staring at my son.

He swallowed the large mouthful of eggs. They went down like a camel swallowing a porcupine, and his lack of voice when he tried to answer seemed just as fitting. "I...I..."

"Jamie was concerned about me when I left the hospital," I offered for him. "He rode along in the trunk."

Paige's eyes widened. "You didn't?" she almost shouted, glaring at our son.

His chin sunk to his chest, sending his gaze to his plate. It was empty. Avoiding her intimidating gaze, he began refilling his plate.

"Honestly, I'm glad he did," I added, interrupting the silent scrape of silverware on ceramic. "He saved my life." Saying it brought the memory of the shotgun cocking while Dillon McCullin hovered above, beating me, anger infusing his brown eyes in the shadowed room. I gulped, hesitant to add the next confession.

Paige's brown eyes stared back at me. "I went to confront Dillon McCullin."

Paige's fork clattered to her plate, and the white around her irises competed with the brief ghostly paleness of her skin. "You did what?" she shouted.

Licking my lips, I explained, "He beat Cameron to death."

She abruptly stood. "Did you arrest him?"

"Hon'," I said softly, motioning her back down with my fork as though in a half-hearted attempt at conducting an orchestra, "sit down. You know I couldn't, not based on what I know. I need proof."

"How did he take it?"

Thankfully, Jamie remained silent.

"How do you think? Like I said, Jamie saved my life."

Paige lowered herself back to her seat. "Then why don't you want to bring him back?"

"Umm..."

Jamie glared at me.

"Well, later that night one of the gang members dropped Donny's head in his lap while I was at the school meeting."

"What?" she screamed. "Those bastards! I'll kill them all." She slammed the table with her fist, her fork strangled within her grasp.

"Whoa, whoa, whoa. Let's not go that far. Yes, some may need it," I admitted, remembering those who decapitated Jamie's friend. I had to pause, soaking in the memory and summoning the right words. "But the courts will decide. Besides, like I told you, there's someone else behind this. Donny wasn't cremated. He was killed and sent to us as a message. If I don't back off, Jamie's next."

Surprisingly Paige took this information in stride, nodding in thought, her jaw clenched. "But you won't." It wasn't a question.

She cared about Jamie. I had no concerns about that, but we'd been through this before. I shook my head. "I can't. You know that. If I do, it'll only prompt others to do the same in the future."

"Yes, I know. And you can't leave him here."

I looked at her quizzically.

"I'm going with you, so who'd take care of Jamie?"

"With me?" I asked. "You aren't a doctor or a police officer."

"No, I'm a trained healthcare professional with two decades of experience helping you track down killers. That enough experience for you?"

I grimaced. "Sorry. I just thought you were working with forensics."

"I am, but you have a knack for stumbling upon remains." She smiled, the strain from our small debate ebbing from her shoulders. "And we learned something last night."

Looking over at Jamie, he smiled like a chipmunk, his cheeks bulging with breakfast. "Guess you're comin' too," I muttered. Turning my attention back to my wife, I asked, "But what could you have learned from Don... from a severed head?"

"More than you think. We found pieces of gravel in his hair."

My eyebrows rose. "And?"

"And it's a type of pea-gravel mix used at just a couple places in town. Hector tracked them down from the seller's records. Woke the landscaping owner right out of bed."

"So he was in one of those places that day."

"More specifically, his head was. How often do people lie down on gravel?"

"Not often. I get it. What locations?" I asked, taking another bite.

"The post office and a church day care called Blessed Children."

"So either he found religion in a church day care or he chose to lay down in the post office's front lawn after mailing a letter?"

Jamie chortled, almost choking on his breakfast.

Paige grinned sarcastically. "Funny, Alex."

"But really, his... head was—Wait, maybe Jamie shouldn't be here for this conversation."

Paige grimaced, giving Jamie a pitying look.

"Dad, I can handle it," Jamie responded. "I hate what happened, but I've dealt with murders. I've seen them. You know it. I can do what you do."

"I know, Jamie, but that doesn't make it easy. I've been dealing with these visions for years. It takes a toll."

"I get it. I do, Dad. It's not like this is my first rodeo." Jamie lifted his bangs, revealing the ankh branded into his forehead, and stared at me. "I know what can happen, and worse. What you don't seem to understand is that I also know what comes after. I speak to the dead, see them, and hear them. I speak with them every day: Grandpa, Donny, even Grandma and so many others. Do you know how long this ability's been in our family?"

This question stumped me. I'd been pondering it since I first learned that my father died while trying to help just one such person. When I first realized Jamie had the ability to relive these murders, too, it cemented my understanding. *But how far back does it go?* I wondered. "I don't know."

"Generations… dozens of them so far as I can tell. I've only talked to some of our distant relatives, but they all had the ability, the men and the women. It's been changing over the years though. Most had abilities like yours but more limited. Those that could told me about it. The older ghosts—the ones I've seen at least—lose themselves over time. I can't tell you how far back, where it started or how, but it's been going on for a long time. Who knows how many descendants share the ability?"

"S-seriously?" I'd never truly even considered the far-reaching potential. "I didn't realize—"

"But that's not why I brought it up. Dad, I deal with death every day. I see them walking around. I'm not afraid of death. I wanna bring them down, the Reds and that curly haired jackass. I'm not goin' anywhere."

Paige and I looked at Jamie with newfound respect, so much so that I didn't say anything about the interruption. He could have this one. "Jamie, you're right. Honestly you may be better prepared for this than I am, but I can't just ignore this ability. Neither can you. I understand. You saw the same vision I did. Donny wasn't killed in gravel." Turning to Paige, I asked, "So which place was he: mailing a letter or picking up his little brother from day care?"

"I'm not sure. Hector called to let me know when I was fixing breakfast. He was going to check out the day care first. If there's a chance this gang's been organizing things at a day care, we need to make sure the kids aren't around it."

"And you didn't tell me?" I demanded.

"I did... I am," she answered, her last statement dwindling.

* * *

After breakfast I grabbed my coat and fedora as we headed out the front door, a newfound urgency prompting me, when I felt a pull on my arm. Paige forged on, down the porch steps and toward the driveway as I turned to look at Jamie.

"You didn't tell her," he whispered. "What's she gonna—"

Paige's scream interrupted him, followed by, "Alex, what the hell did you do to my car?"

"She's going to do *that*," I answered, my shoulders slumping. "Guess we need to step up to the firing squad." Turning, I led the way to the vehicles.

Chapter 15

The Doghouse

March 10th, 2012

PAIGE SAID ONLY, "I can't believe you let him get involved in a shootout. He could've been killed," when we got into the car. The rest of the drive was filled with the rattle of a pellet-infested six-cylinder engine that sounded more like a horde of rodents was trying to gnaw its way out, wind and road noise seeping through holes scattered across the Subaru's side. An angry silence seemed to grow with every groan the car made. Even Jamie knew not to say a word. Paige would forgive me, but it would take some time.

At the station, I put Jamie back to checking old files that hadn't been digitized yet. I expected him to look defeated, ashamed after how angry Paige was that morning. Instead, a look of determination infused him as the task was set. He was becoming the kind of man who would never back down when he set his mind to something, especially if it meant finding his best friend's murderer. We both knew who had done the dastardly deed of decapitating Donny, but someone else was behind it. Chase was a problem child and would most certainly wind up in prison or dead, but he didn't have the smarts to pull this off. I believed Dillon when he said there was someone heading up the gang, dealing to the kids. It made sense, but the message intended for me left no doubt.

"There you are!" Hec crowed as soon as Paige and I strode into the office. "I've been looking for you all morning, Alex. Ahhh, the beautiful and glamorous Paige. What brings you to this grungy place?"

The few officers in the station that morning turned to stare. Most working the day shift were out on patrol, and the night shift had returned and gone home for the day.

"Hey, Hec. Sorry I'm late," I said, flinging my fedora onto the coat rack nearest my desk and shrugging out of my duster.

For a second Paige glared at my partner as though he had something to do with the prior night's events. "Hi, Hector," she grudgingly responded. "I'm here to help with any remains you find."

Hector laughed. "If you can call what we've found remains, I'm not sure how you can help. From what I can tell, it's all been pulverized—Oh, you mean Donny." His expression turned grave. Then he turned to me, pointing. "That reminds me, Alex. I discovered something about the ashes."

I nodded.

"They weren't ashes. They were dissolved in some acidic solution and then ground up in a machine. 'Pulverized'—that's the word Dr. Bryant used when I spoke with him this morning. They tested the remains, and that's what this guy's been doing. Evidently there are machines that can do this. You just drop the body in along with the ingredients and *voilà*, it makes you a remains cake with practically nothing to show for it."

It explained a lot, why I was still able to get some trace visions even though I shouldn't have been able to. *But where can one of these machines be found?*

Before I could ask, Paige chimed in. "What kind of acid?"

Grabbing a small notepad from his desk, Hector read, "Sodium hydroxide and heated water."

"Lye," she whispered. "It's an Alkaline Hydrolysis system."

"But how does that cremate remains?" I couldn't help but ask.

Shaking her head, Paige answered, "Some people call it biocremation because it uses lye and water and then crushes the remains. It's uncommon, very uncommon."

"Well, if we can find out where they have one of these hydrolysis systems, it could lead us right to that murdering bastard."

Hector put up a hand. "One step ahead of ya, partner. The doc said they're used by vets to cremate animal remains. It's supposed to be better for the environment than burning, but it's illegal in this state and most others to use them on people. In Ohio, churches objected to the disrespect of grampa being washed down the drain."

A child treated like an animal. I asked, "So we're looking for a veterinarian?"

"Seems likely," he said.

Sitting at my desk to scour the Internet, I pulled up all the local vets in the surrounding area. As expected, there were quite a few.

"Won't be any of the small ones," Paige suggested, staring over my shoulder. "Machinery like that's expensive. It'll be at one of the busy veterinary offices, the large ones."

Nodding, I pulled my own notepad out and recorded the few I knew dealt with large quantities and larger animals. In these rural parts there were still quite a few farmers, so vets were always in demand, especially those who dealt with farm animals. As I ripped the note off and stood, Paige snatched it out of my hand.

"I'll check these," she said brightly.

"You're not going alone," I announced, grabbing my hat and duster.

She scowled. "I'm not helpless, Alex."

Sighing inwardly, I lowered my voice. "I didn't say that, hon'. Hector and I always go together for a reason. Having a partner to back you up is *always* a good idea." She knew this. Hector had saved my life more times than I wanted to count, and I his. But with her emotions running high over the car and Jamie's involvement, it needed to be voiced.

"Hector can come with me!"

At this, Hector's bushy eyebrows rose in surprise like a deer in headlights. While we rarely argued or fought, especially in public, he had seen a few of those instances over the years and managed to stay out of the way. This statement brought him directly in line of oncoming traffic. "Uhmmm… sure," was all he managed to get out.

"There you have it. We'll be fine, and besides, don't you have to check out the day care and post office?"

Hector chimed in with a raised hand, "I already stopped off at the day care. He could've been there for a variety of reasons. Those kids were rolling around on the ground this mornin'. Parents and teachers alike were after them, some falling down and such, just tryin' to get them in the door so they could get to work. Is it just me, or are kids gettin' more rowdy?"

"What are you saying, Hec?" Paige asked.

"That it could've been the day care. He could've stopped off there for some reason, helping a friend with a sibling, or his killer could've. They might've dropped the head somewhere while picking up a wee one."

"Really?" I asked skeptically.

"Could've been a stopover for any reason. I interviewed the teachers but got nothin'."

Unwilling to give up, Paige threw out, "Then there's still the post office."

Both of us looked at her, skepticism clearly showing in our expressions. "Hector's right. They could've stopped off at the post office to send another message, one that could've been delivered legally, and many of the Reds don't have vehicles. Could be that they threw it behind the building in a sack while they went in or something. I really don't know, but it's seeming like the gravel link is less of a clue than this vet connection."

Paige clenched her teeth, fists balled at her sides. She growled, "Someone needs to check it out."

I understood her frustration. It was the one potential clue she had come up with, and we were dismissing it. "We will," I said. "We just need to go after our best leads first, and I don't like the idea of splitting up and sending one person alone. Not gonna happen. I hate that Hec checked out the day care alone already. If something had happened, I'd never have forgiven myself for sleeping in and…"

I stopped before I finished the statement, but it was too late. I'd already put my foot in my mouth. Paige had allowed me to sleep in and even taken the time to cook breakfast without having slept a wink last night. My mouth *clacked* shut. Paige's eyes seemed to swirl with anger hotter than an iron poker.

"Sorry," I muttered. "It was a very nice breakfast. I didn't mean anything by it. I just… He's my partner." I waved a hand at Hector.

Shaking her head, Paige stalked toward the front door. "We have more important things to do than deal with this. We'll discuss it later! You all coming?"

I was most certainly in the doghouse. Following after while trying to keep my head up, we were jolted to a stop by Officer Yost at the front desk, a young man in his second year on the force. "Mr. Martinez," he offered hesitantly, "there's a call for you."

"Hector's fine."

Officer Yost nodded and offered him the corded handset. We waited.

"Hello... Right... Oh really...? Okay... I'll be there this afternoon." Hector handed the phone back.

"So what's going on?" I asked.

"I think I'll have to rain check that trip to the vet's office." Answering my questioning look, he said, "There's another body... I mean remains. They think it's just the one, but it's hard to tell. It's in the same state, pulverized."

"Where at?"

"Radford. Some old fishermen found it on a back road to the New River. We're pretty lucky. If the killer had traveled down a quarter mile, he could've just dropped them in the river."

"He might have for all we know," I admitted. "No telling how many people this bastard's murdered, but this tells us one thing. He isn't from that neck of the woods, or he probably would've."

"Yep," Hector said. "So, I've gotta head out that way. It'll take nearly an hour and a half to get there. My connection over there's holding the site till I arrive."

"Renee?" I asked, knowing about their past relationship years before.

He nodded, trying to hide the stupid grin that always appeared at the mention of her. Hector was happily married to Delilah and had been for years. They'd never had children, and he'd taken to Jamie like one of his own. Renee was an old flame that would always hold a place in his heart.

Looking from Paige to my partner, I asked, "So how's this gonna work?"

"How's what gonna work?" Jamie chimed in from behind us.

Turning, I saw something I wouldn't have expected if not for the jubilant interest in his voice, a smile and curiosity dancing in his dark eyes. "We've got to split up, but it's nothing for you to worry about, Jamie. What's on your mind?"

He held an old manila folder out. Its color had been leeched from the years it spent boxed in the basement. "Found the curly haired guy," he whispered, happy to have accomplished his task.

"Really?" Paige and I both asked.

"Yeah, it's him, no hair... but the bulbous nose the size of a lightbulb, the beady, dark eyes. It's him."

Flipping open the file, the black and white photo that stared back was undoubtedly the attacker. At the time of this picture, his head was nearly shaved, the shirt collar of his prison jumpsuit clearly visible. It was a much younger version of him, but it was the same man from the boy's vision. "It's him. Name's Stanley Klein," I added, perusing the front page of his conviction notes.

"He goes by Scrub," Jamie added. He'd evidently read through the file. It didn't surprise me.

"So this is the guy, the killer?" Paige hissed, aware of prying ears in the department.

Even so, I took her elbow and escorted the group out, down the front concrete steps, and over to a picnic table under a maple tree where dispatch often took their lunches. It wasn't that time yet, so the area was vacant. Even the designated smokers' area, an upright ash receptacle some twenty feet away, was unoccupied at the moment. "Yes, it's the guy. We think he's the one behind the killings, based on the first vision. He's gotta be a part of it at least."

Paige's gaze grew hard. "Then what are we waiting for? Where is he?"

Jamie answered, "Not sure about right now, but according to the file they lost track of him years ago, after he was disabled on the job."

"Not too disabled if he's got a record after the fact," Hector added.

Jamie nodded. "Yeah, he wound up with a bum knee, but, get this, he was arrested just after the accident for indecent exposure."

I couldn't help the smirk that came to my lips at that revelation. In the picture, Stanley Klein looked wiry but fierce, a no-nonsense kind of guy. The image that came to mind now was of a hobbled man in his early thirties running down Tranquil Heights' populated streets with his pants around his ankles and one hand raised, all the while screaming at the top of his lungs. "He must have a few screws loose too then."

Jamie shook his head, uncertain. "Don't really know. The report doesn't mention much about it, just the charge. It's got more of his history."

"Then it looks like we have two, maybe three places to check," Hector interjected, "if we can find any trace of Stanley Klein, or Scrub as he probably still goes by."

"Man, when it rains, it pours. I think you're onto something," I added. "I'll look him up in the car. When was that arrest made, Jamie?" I had the file in hand, but Jamie could probably spout off the answer faster than it would take to open the file.

Living up to expectations, Jamie said, "June 8, 1990."

Grinning, I ruffled his hair. "Well done." To no one in particular, I asked, "You think he could be a truck driver?"

"That's just what I was thinking," said Hector. "He keeps dumping bodies up and down I-81, so it makes sense."

"I'd like to get a good look at the remains up in Radford, to… you know."

"Yeah," said Hec, "but you wouldn't want to leave the missus alone with a dirty ol' man like me, would ya?" He motioned to Paige with his eyes, hinting not so subtly. He was obviously uncomfortable being put in the middle of our little spat.

Grinning, I admitted, "You're right, you old lecher. Besides, Delilah wouldn't let me live it down."

Paige's eyebrows rose. "Delilah would do a hell of a lot more than that, to you and me both." Shifting her attention to Hec, she added, "I love your wife, but she'd tie his you know what in a bow and probably shave off a few of the incidentals." Winking at me and taking Hector's arm, she said, "Come to think of it, why don't you join me this time."

My partner's eyes widened into orbs that could have been launched into planetary orbit as he stared down at her. "Al, you must've messed up real bad."

We all laughed, and it lifted the burden that had weighed my shoulders down all morning. Now that Paige had gotten over her initial anger, her willingness to laugh, even at my expense, was a relief. However, she was right. Delilah would probably do worse than kill me for allowing an affair to happen, but that would never be. Hector and Paige were both too dedicated. It was then I noticed my red-cheeked son. *I guess the allusions weren't lost on him.*

Harrumphing, I said, "Don't you think we should get to work?"

It was then they noticed Jamie's expression, and the good-natured jesting ended. Paige dropped Hector's hand, and he said, "Tell you what, Al, I'll take Jamie. If we don't make it a common practice, word won't get around. Besides, we can dress him properly, right Jamie?" He slapped Jamie on the back. "You just need one of those black intern jackets."

I had to admit that it was a good idea. Plus, I'd just caught sight of the Subaru again and remembered the cause behind Paige's anger. I needed to address that as soon as possible and get a different ride. "Right, I'll get one. Be right back."

Running back inside, I spotted Rachel, our newest intern from Virginia Highlands Community College. True to form, she was wearing the thin, black jacket sporting Intern across the back and over the front left side. "Rachel, I need a couple things."

"Yes, sir."

"First, give me your jacket."

She looked stunned, as though I'd asked for her firstborn. Then her expression changed and a tear streamed down her cheek. "What did I do wrong, Detective Drummond?"

Oh God! "No, that's not what I meant. You're doing great. I just need to borrow it."

She sniffled. "You sure?"

"I am," I reassured her. I sometimes forgot how close in age she was to Jamie. Even though she would likely be entering a local police force in another year, being barely twenty, she still had a ways to go before she was emotionally prepared. *If a criminal insults her work ethic, how will she react?* I chastised myself for thinking such things. I wasn't a criminal. I was her superior. She would get there. She worked hard. That was enough for now. "You'll get it back, and I have something even more important I need taken care of." I handed her the Subaru keys. "Take my wife's car to the mechanic. The dealership down the street will work. Have them repair it."

"What should I tell them to fix?"

"Don't worry. You'll understand when you see it. It's the green one in the lot. Can you take care of that?"

She nodded, wiping away the tear with the sleeve of her jacket. Reminded of my first request, she slipped out of the jacket and handed it to me.

"Thanks."

Rachel nodded. Not saying another word, she strode toward the parking lot. I followed her and led Paige to my cruiser parked among the others in the side lot, while Jamie and Hector got into *The Ocho*.

Paige wasted no time logging onto my car's computer and looking up Stanley Klein. There was no trace of him for over twenty years, not since he got out of prison—no driver's license or permanent address. He'd disappeared before attending his first meeting with his parole officer up north in Richmond. They hadn't been able to find him and had given up. He'd simply vanished.

Chapter 16

Unforeseen Informants

March 10th, 2012

THE TRIP TO the veterinarian's office, while educational, got us no closer to the killer. Aside from an abundance of animals in need, their owners biding time in the waiting room, and vets so overloaded with patients that they would rather be giving themselves root canals, there wasn't a connection to Scrub, the Reds, or the shiners. From what we could tell, they were all simply going about their day. One of the vets took a few minutes to answer our questions, though. They weren't missing an Alkaline Hydrolysis machine but showed us theirs. It was a stainless-steel behemoth with a lid on top. The whole thing looked to be a good eight feet long and three wide. It could easily turn an adult to soup in two hours. If Scrub was using one of these, it required a lot of power, water, and space.

After grabbing fast food and heading back, Paige said, "So I've been thinking about your idea. This could be perfect for a trucker. With the amount of space in one of those trailers, a juiced-up power supply, and some storage tanks for the water, this could be how he's doing it."

Keeping my eyes on the road, I said simply, "Yep."

"But we can't call it in."

"Nope, not based on my visions."

She shook her head. "I don't know how you do it. This is killing me. He's probably out murdering more people right now, and we have leads but can't act on them."

"That about sums it up. Welcome to my life, doll."

A subtle smile crossed her lips at the reference to old gangster movies we'd watched together, but the implications bothered her too much for the nickname to break her troubled façade.

"Look, honey, we can do something. We follow up on our leads until we get proof. Then we take that to Lieutenant Tullings. He backs me up without too many questions so long as I can give a justifiable chain of events."

"I know," she said under her breath. "I just wish they were more open to your abilities."

"You and me both, but we have to operate within accepted practices. There's no real wiggle room if we don't want the killer to get off when it comes to court."

"So, what now?"

Before I could answer, my cell rang. Picking it up, I said, "Hello. Drummond."

One of the last voices I expected to hear rumbled in reply, "Alex, this is Dillon."

I was tempted to end the call immediately. The last thing I wanted, especially with Paige right beside me, was to talk to my step-grandfather.

As though reading my thoughts through the silence, he said, "Don't hang up."

"Why not?"

"'Cause I got somethin' for ya. I went outta my way on this, so yous best listen."

My jaw tightened, but logic took over. He hated talking to me as much as I did him. If he had rung me up, it was for a purpose. "Yeah, go on."

"I heard about somethin'. It seemed to me that it might tie in with yer killer. Out in Richland's Valley, there's an old family cemetery. One of our people spotted him about a year ago and took a potshot. He ran and never come back, but what he was doin's still left there."

"Where is this place?" I asked.

"I'll tell ya, but yous gotta promise me somethin' first."

"No promises, Dillon," I retorted.

"Promise or I ain't gonna tell ya squat."

I hesitated a moment. "Promise what?"

"That you'll keep the place quiet. No lookin' in the barn or bringin' in none of them other piggies yous befriended. The people there don't trust none of ya, and it took a hell of a lot to get 'em to agree ta this."

I wanted to ask what was in the barn, but I had a feeling I already knew—the family's homemade distillery. Dillon was throwing me a bone here. Whatever this was, it hadn't been brought to the attention of authorities over the last year because the family saw it as a local problem for the shiners. "Okay, I won't go pluggin' my nose into places it doesn't belong. I promise. And no strangers. Paige is with me, though," I replied, hating myself for agreeing, but we needed more to go on. Lives depended on it. "You've got my word."

"That'll be fine. The Picket's ol' place. I'll text ya the exact spot."

This surprised me. I didn't know many people his age who texted, but I had never really gotten to know the old mountain man. Hell, it surprised me that he even had a cell out in the backwoods. There was hardly any service out that way, yet another reason why I should listen. He probably had a heck of a time just trying to get a call out. "What am I lookin' for?"

"You'll know it when ya see it," he answered. "Just do your part, and mayhaps our next get-together will be a bit more cordial-like." Then he hung up.

Good to his word, a minute later, GPS coordinates appeared on my phone.

"Who was that?" asked Paige.

Grumbling, I told her. She was less than happy but remained silent as I passed along the new information. Paige plugged the coordinates into my Magellan, and we were off. The sun was just at its peak and starting to fall, its glare streaming through the windshield.

* * *

Thirty minutes later, we were pulling through an open cattle gate and parking at the entrance to a pasture. Old headstones peeked up over the hill to our right, a large barn that might once have been red downhill to our left. The sun glinted off parts of its rusted metal roof. A rundown singlewide trailer sat not far from it next to a decrepit farmhouse that leaned more than the Tower of Pisa. From this distance, it looked like a fire had taken half of the old home, leaving what was left to fall down. Without having to see them, I knew the Pickets would be peering through the singlewide's windows. At least I was driving my modern, unmarked cruiser and not *The Ocho* or, God forbid, a black-and-white. We didn't stand out as much this way.

Getting out, Paige and I trekked up the hill, evidence kits in hand. A rusted barbed-wire fence surrounded the small family plot, encompassing a dozen gravestones. The graves had sunk over the years, leaving deep, grass-covered impressions. One thing was for sure, mountain folk respected family. Even this small family cemetery had recently been mowed. Moving closer, I scanned the sunken graves and fence for anything that might stick out. Dillon had been vague. I didn't know what to expect but figured there wouldn't be a grasshopper playing a fiddle next to the spot. That would be too easy.

Opening a gate that could have been the entrance to a pigpen on any local farm, I stepped inside with Paige on my heels. Experience and training had prepared me for these sorts of scenes, but with a year of weathering, there could be little to nothing left.

Each grave looked intact. There was nothing to disturb them, only grass clippings littering the gravestones. Some were quite old with crosses and engravings that could barely be made out. The stones were chipped, porous material, and moss seeped out of the cracks. My gaze swept from one sunken resting spot to the next. A few of the graves were wealthy enough to have five-foot limestone slabs placed over the bodies, the engravings chiseled into them instead of headstones. These were far older and probably belonged to the founders of this area, those who blazed a trail into the wilderness, fought off Indian attacks, and cleared land. At the edge of one such grave in the corner of the cemetery, something caught my eye. White sediment mixed with moss had built up over the bottom third of the stone, ramping up to the grass lip. I hadn't noticed it at first because the moss coated larger chunks of what could be bone shards.

"What the hell?" I asked.

Paige noticed too and knelt over the spot. "Alex, there are tons here, some freshly ground up." She looked at me, her eyes holding sorrow in their depths.

"How recent?"

She shook her head. "Rain and wind probably blew a lot of this away. Most looks years old, yellowed and pitted with ground-in dirt, but this top layer is white as chalk. It has to be from the last few weeks."

My lips pressed together as I considered this. "With all the weather, how many bodies do you think there were?"

Paige stared at the layer of remains covering the bottom slab of stone. "Dozens, maybe more than a hundred."

Steel tacks plunged into my heart, one for every life lost. I couldn't breathe. "Good God!" came out as an exhale. I half-stumbled to the grassy lip. "Are you serious?" On closer inspection, bits of human teeth glinted like dirty alabaster among the pebbles and shards of bone. Reaching down for one partial molar, a waft of cured leather sifted through my brain.

* * *

Before the darkness drifted away, pain engulfed my head and jaw. Light slowly filtered into the room through scattered far windows, but it remained dim at the outskirts of my vision. Overhead, a bright light shone down as though a flying saucer were targeting me for abduction. Two meaty hands held both sides of my head, forcing it up straight. My eyes widened as Scrub's unkempt face hovered inches away. He smiled, his vicious eyes dancing with malice and glee.

I tasted something metallic but couldn't move my lips or mouth. They were held open... by something. What was it? I couldn't tell. Nothing was within my vision, nothing but his hateful eyes.

Adjusting something just below my chin, the mechanism ratcheted my mouth wider. Eyes bulging, I screamed.

"Yell all you want, Mica. It won't he-elp," he intoned, almost singing the last word. "So you told your family about our little proposition?"

I tried to shake my head adamantly but could hardly move. I whimpered as the memory of an elderly couple came to mind—Mica's grandparents.

I sat talking with them on the front porch in the memory, chatting and drinking iced tea with something more potent added to the mix. As the sun went down, I learned exactly what Scrub was referring to. As we talked into the night, I gloated about my new revenue stream. They didn't approve. What was more, they tried to talk me out of it. But it was too late. Once you were in, there was no getting out.

Scrub twisted the torture device yet again. The ancient metal plates grated against my lower and upper teeth, threatening to break them or snap my jaw. They dug into my gums, tearing soft tissue. I let out a bloodcurdling scream, but no one came to my rescue. The cavernous room had to be a warehouse, long abandoned from the looks of it.

"I told you to shop it around, not tell everyone you knew. Did you think they would be good customers?"

I tried to shake my head again, tried to talk, to explain. It came out in a jumbled mess of sounds.

Scrub shook his head. His curls were of medium length, giving him a fluffy helmetlike appearance. "Too many words, but nothing to say," he sang and cranked the medieval torture device again. Crack! My ears popped and pain blossomed in my jaw as though anesthetics had worn off midsurgery.

"Come on, Scrub," growled the brute holding my head. "Can we hurry it up? We're late."

The lunatic glared over my head. "You always have to ruin my fun."

Letting go of the device, he retrieved a pistol that had lain off to the side. He raised it above my head and fired. The resounding noise jolted me in my seat. Then he lowered it six inches, between my eyes. The next sound was just as thunderous. My brain screamed. Everything ended a second later in abrupt blackness.

* * *

As my vision returned and the immense pain of seconds before faded from memory, I tried my jaw. It worked. No pain.

Paige brought a finger down and almost touched the remains before stopping herself. "This is madness. It'll take the entire forensics team and at least a few officers to secure the scene and collect evidence."

"Don't I know it," I mumbled. "Damn." Considering what Dillon had said and how much evidence collecting would have to happen here, it would be impossible to keep my promise. I had to call someone in to help, but who? I couldn't call Theresa. She was a good officer, but I'd promised not to call in a stranger. It hit me like a rotten tree branch. *Fred's my only option.* I ground my teeth. Tensing at the sound echoing to my ears, I reminded myself that I wasn't in the vision anymore and returned to considering my only option. Fred had never been my favorite person, but he wasn't a bad man. He'd just never quite gotten over me putting his brother away for life. For a brief time I knew him as Uncle Fred. He even put the idea of joining the police force into my head when I was still in high school. That was before everything had gone down, and I discovered the truth about the stepfather I called the Drunk.

Memories of those days as a teenager haunted me momentarily, like they often did in my nightmares.

Paige said, "Th-this is insane," the words barely audible even in the stillness of this quaint hilltop. "W-we have to call in backup. We have to—"

Her words shook the remnants of my past away, and I shouted, "No!"

Stunned, Paige rocked back on her heels and stared at me. I never raised my voice to her.

"S-sorry, babe. I didn't mean to… Look, we can't call in backup. This lead was from McCullin, remember?"

She nodded, lips pursed, waiting for more.

Hooking my thumb behind me toward the rundown home, I said, "McCullin said the people here have known about this for a year and even ran the guy off some time back. He barely got their permission to bring us in. I can't call in an outsider."

"But there's far too much here," she exclaimed. "We can't wait. The weather has already destroyed almost every bit of evidence. I need everything here to catch this bastard!"

Nodding, I said, "I know. I know… but we can't."

Not to be deterred, Paige stood and shouted, "How can you take their side? More will die. This guy won't stop. You'll be responsible for anyone else who's murdered! It'll be on your head." Anger framed her beautiful features, overwhelming her confusion at my response. I was never this pigheaded.

I whispered, "I promised."

That stopped her tirade abruptly, but only temporarily. "You promised? You promised!"

I could only nod, feeling like a child who'd successfully stolen a lollypop, only to be caught with sticky, red hands by my mother.

Paige's voice rose another level and she strode toward me, barely missing the remains she was so adamant about saving. "You knew this was coming and promised not to call for backup? You knew we'd be working this site for days or even a week without Hector or anyone else? How could you agree to that? Are you mad?"

I started to nod again but caught the flaw in her statement. "That's not quite true. I'm not crazy, but I can't bring in an outsider." Her tendency for exaggeration was also clear in her statement, but I let it slide this time. It wouldn't take weeks if we worked diligently.

She stopped a foot away, glowering through narrowed eyes. "That's the same damn thing, Alex."

Giving her a quirky smile, I answered, "Not quite, like I said."

Furrowing her brows, Paige stared daggers.

"I know who to call. I don't like it, but I'm sure McCullin will be fine with it."

"Who?" she challenged.

I muttered under my breath, "Fred," not meeting her eyes. I'd run down thieves and murderers twice my size and won, been the lone man against overwhelming odds dozens of times, and never backed down. But Paige was different. She was a force of nature in her own right, one I never wanted to disappoint. And when her words reinforced my own guilt at agreeing to Dillon McCullin's piggybacked caveat, no man could stand her weighty gaze.

Her honey-brown eyes widened, shock and outrage battling for control. She had known Fred almost as long as I had and had been my rock during tumultuous seas as a teen.

Licking my lips, I gave her my best, most charming smile. "Love you!"

Chapter 17

Pinky and the Brain

March 10th, 2012

MY PHONE RANG just as we were depositing the last of the remains into labeled plastic evidence bags. Paige scribbled on the label while I took the call.

"Yeah, Hec. How's it going?"

"Dad, this is Jamie. Hec let me use his phone while he's driving." Jamie sounded enthusiastic. Even though he had just lost his best friend, helping with the search seemed to have energized him and taken his mind off the loss. "I've got you on speakerphone."

"Ahhh, good. So what'd you find, son?"

"What we expected, more visions. It's the same killer, Dad. Scrub did these too."

"How many were there?" I asked.

"Two at least, but there might be more."

Glancing at the load of evidence bagged and sitting in the open trunk of the unmarked squad car, I understood exactly what he meant. "Multiple bodies dumped together?"

"Yeah," Jamie replied solemnly, losing his energy momentarily as he flashed back to the visions.

"And were the ghosts any help?"

"Not much. They're talking, but it seems like no one ever sees this guy coming or going. He's either walking, or they're meeting him somewhere in town. You'd think someone would've seen the car or truck he was driving or somethin'. And there's no tellin' how long ago they were killed."

Jamie brought up a good point. How was Scrub getting around? Normally we could more easily track him down with a license plate number or make and model, but none of the visions I'd had ever showed him in a vehicle. "Think the trucker theory is still good?" I asked.

I could envision Jamie's shrug from his response. "Don't know... maybe. Nothin' points to it, but..."

I kicked at a mud hill sticking out of the wet ground and frowned. "But what, Jamie?"

"Well, it may be nothin', but the remains were found near train tracks."

"Hmmm..." Remains thus far had been found along roads primarily but near both train tracks and a river. In this part of Virginia that wasn't unusual. It just made it more difficult to determine the mode of travel. Train tracks had originally been laid along the same routes as rivers because that was the easiest way to pass through the mountains. Now even the roads run alongside both rivers and train tracks, hence the difficulty.

"So we basically just have the drop-point locations to go by," I stated, disheartened. "Since they all pretty much run alongside one another, could be any of them."

Jamie's voice deflated. "Pretty much, Dad."

"The refrigerated truck might be the best idea, especially if he's powering one of those hydrolysis machines in it," Hec supplied over the speakerphone.

"Yeah, but I've got a surprise for you," Jamie said, rejuvenated.

In the background, Hec's muffled voice said, "Now Jamie, remember what we talked about."

"I know, Uncle Hec, I know," Jamie responded, a hint of mischief in his voice.

"What was that?" I asked.

"Nothing," Jamie answered, far too innocently. "I'll tell you later. We'll be back in an hour or so."

"Y'all are still that far away?" I asked. "We've been working this site for hours. Hell, the sun's almost down. Y'all could've made it there and back twice by now."

"Dad, you can't rush perfection… Just let it go," Jamie added condescendingly. "We'll be back soon. Did you get a lead?"

Turning to gaze at the small graveyard around me and the sun setting over the tree-covered hillside, I dropped it. Jamie would tell me when he was ready. Plus, I trusted both of them, and there was far more to deal with at the moment. Fred had shown up, far from happy to be called in after working the night shift, but he understood the situation and pitched in sourly. Still, the job was about done. Fred was depositing the evidence camera into its bag and stowing it in the backseat of the car.

"Yeah, somethin' like that, Jamie. Drive safe, son."

"We will, Dad. Take care."

It took a little over an hour, but after the sun fell behind the trees we were finally loaded and ready to head back to headquarters. Page was practically jittery with excitement, looking forward to discovering whose bones were in our evidence bags. She fidgeted and couldn't stay still, but at least she seemed to have forgotten to be angry with me.

"Drop me off at the forensics lab, Alex. I can't wait till tomorrow to get started."

The lab was previously an old two-story school building from the early nineteenth century that had been closed rather than renovated. Since then the department had picked up the tab, refurnishing the first floor with new electrical and renovating whatever was needed. The incredible height of the building and arched doors lining the side had been restored, leaving visible proof of the building's origins, a carriage house. The second floor was left as storage. The old brick building, with its hand-crafted glass windows and brick façade, hunkered across the parking lot from the Tranquil Heights Police Department.

I nodded. It would be a late night for Paige, but that was normal. "I'll grab Jamie and take him home for dinner."

* * *

The following morning, I felt like I hadn't slept at all. Paige was facedown in bed, her breath coming out haggard through the covers. She probably snuck in during the early morning hours after being dropped off. Forcing my legs to work, I stumbled to the bathroom, showered and dressed, then opened the bedroom door to a new day. Jamie met my gaze as I adjusted the collar of my button-up. He sat at the dining room table, spoon in one hand, the other waving casually, mouth as full of Fruit Loops cereal as any chipmunk's.

"Hi, Dad," he got out once he'd swallowed a couple times.

"Hey son. You're up early. How's it goin' this mornin'?"

"Going great!" he intoned through another mouthful while I rummaged through the kitchen cabinets for my aluminum thermos. "Ya lookin' for this?"

I paused and glanced groggily at the thermos that regularly made my trip to work livable. Steam escaped from the twist-on lid as it sat on the dining room table. "Yeah, that's it."

"I made your mornin' brew," he admitted, finishing off the last of his bowl's contents with a slurp.

At this unorthodox admission of guilt, and the simple fact that he voluntarily did something for someone other than himself, one eyebrow rose in suspicion. "You can't have the car. It's at the shop. They said they could get to it in a day or two, but it won't be ready for weeks."

"Haha! You're funny, Dad. I don't need anything, really."

This response sent my dad alert off like a rocket, alarms blaring in my head as though it had been an unsanctioned nuclear launch. "Jamie, either Scrub is the devil risen and this is hell on earth, or you've got something up your sleeve."

Wiping his mouth on the sleeve of his long-sleeve yellow t-shirt, he grinned. It looked almost innocent except for the mischievous nature I knew hid behind it. "No, Da-ad," he countered with an added syllable. "I just want to get out there and kick this guy's butt." A look of determination settled on him. "He killed my friend. I'm coming to work with you again."

I couldn't help but think, *It's an embarrassment that it takes the murder of your best friend to wake your sense of responsibility, Jamie.* A second after the thought came to mind, shame filled me. Part of me continued to exclaim, "But it's true," and I couldn't shake the internal debate.

Seeing the ankh branded in the middle of Jamie's forehead, part of me wanted to refuse to allow him to come, to keep him home safe where vicious people couldn't get at him, but how well had that worked before? *Not well at all.* This conclusion silenced my fatherly concerns, at least for the moment. Having Jamie at police headquarters might be the safest place. Besides, his serious expression didn't look like it was up for negotiation. The notion of it was obviously illogical. Jamie had come to work with me countless times now, but Paige's concern over Jamie's presence during the encounter with Dillon McCullin echoed back to me, "I can't believe you let him get involved in a shootout. He could've been killed."

A look at my son's determined features made the decision as clear and picturesque as the most elegant stained-glass window. Jamie's mind was set, along with his notion of duty and justice. Grinding my teeth, I set my jaw, a mirror image of the way he looked. Grabbing my coffee, I said simply, "Let's go. Let your mom sleep a bit."

In the car, a neon-green sticky note adhered to the steering wheel. It read:

Do NOT leave without me!

—Mom

As soon as Jamie slid into the cruiser's passenger seat, he started to ask, "Why aren't we...," but then spotted me staring at the note, indecision weighing on me. "Dad?"

Paige was not always the best person to wake, especially if she hadn't slept much and you were already on her bad side, but there was one fortunate advantage to having kids. "Jamie, go wake your mother and tell her I'm waiting in the car."

"Really?" he asked.

"Really."

Jamie unbuckled, threw his practically empty backpack in the backseat, and went back inside the house. A few minutes later both of them came out. Paige had dressed hurriedly in jeans and a sweater, walking and attempting to tame her unruly curls. They jumped in the car, glaring at me.

Taking a sip of coffee, I declared, "And we're off!"

The drive to work started in silence, but Paige couldn't stay tightlipped for long, especially after the discovery she had made the night before. "You won't believe this, neither of you, but I was able to identify one of the bodies from yesterday's remains."

"Who was it?" Jamie asked, voicing my own question.

"Stanley Klein, AKA Scrub."

"But that's not possible!" Jamie exclaimed. "He did it. He murdered those people. I saw it—*We* saw it."

I nodded as we turned down a dirt road between tree-lined fields. "Yes, we saw the murders. There's no question about that, Jamie, but we don't have any idea when they occurred. Anything could've happened to Scrub between then and now, including being double-crossed. Anything could've happened."

"If only these damn visions came with timestamps," Jamie replied.

"Watch your language, Jamie," Paige interjected, "but you're right. That has got to drive you guys nuts."

We both nodded in silent unison.

"At least I can ask them afterwards... sometimes... if their ghosts hang around. I think Dad got the raw end of that hotdog."

"They speak to me in their own way, Jamie," I said. "It's suited me for nearly twenty years." However, I couldn't quite say how much a part of me wished I could shorten the conversation by speaking with victims' ghosts directly like Jamie. For me, waiting on visions to try and discover something is like playing charades with a mute, panic-stricken murder victim you can't see. A lot gets lost in the translation. Unfortunately, I never know how much. I can only work with the clues I glean from the traumatic memories.

Just then Paige noticed something. "Where are we going?"

"Well, our conversation yesterday got me thinking." When Paige gave me a quizzical look, I glanced back at our son. "Jamie and I were discussing possible types of transportation. I thought, 'What better person to ask than Dan?'"

Paige's confusion grew. "Dan who?"

I smiled, knowing Paige would love the old man's traditional values and work ethic. "An old friend I haven't seen in twenty-plus years. He knows a thing or twenty about trains."

For information on trains, old railroad tracks, and the historic geography of the region, most people would go to the local historical society or train depot, but that wasn't necessary for me. I knew just the right person to seek out, a friend of my father's who I hadn't seen since before my dad died. Dan—Mr. Wilburn, as I had been taught to call him as a young boy—had worked on the railroads in Virginia and West Virginia as a dispatcher for most of his life after World War II. That was where I was headed now.

When we arrived, we passed an enormous building covered in rusting corrugated metal sheets and came to a stop in front of an old two-story farmhouse. I jogged up wooden front steps that were clearly aged from the amount of paint peeling but had been repaired recently. Dan was never someone to leave things undone. While Dan was an early riser and would most certainly be up and around at eight in the morning, whether he would be home was an entirely different question. True to form, no one answered my knock at the door. Dan's wife had died some years back so I don't know who else I expected to answer it if he wasn't home—maybe his kids, but they were most certainly grown and out living their own lives. A glance at the workshop we'd passed a hundred yards down the dirt driveway told me he wasn't there either. The doors were closed and no smoke escaped the smokestack up top.

He could be anywhere, I concluded, *getting coffee, fishing, anywhere.* I could have put an APB out on Dan Wilburn, but that sort of abuse of power had never been acceptable in the Tranquil Heights Police Department if it wasn't an emergency. I had no idea whether Dan's knowledge would be of any help. No one knew trains better.

The side trip added the better part of an hour to our morning commute so I called Hec and let him know we'd be late. The rest of the drive carried on in silence, periodically interrupted by snores, as Paige and Jamie drifted back to sleep. Paige's forehead was glued to the passenger window. The sound of morning traffic, honking cars, and the city coming to life for another day woke her.

"So you think Dan will be able to enlighten you on which vehicle Scrub was using?" she asked as we pulled into the station parking lot.

"Maybe... at least whether it's likely he's using trains."

"Dad, why do you keep mentioning Scrub in the here and now, like he's still alive?" Jamie asked, having woken up too. "Mom said she found multiple bone fragments that were a DNA match to him. He's dead and gone, past tense."

Locking the car, I followed them up the precinct stairs and into the brick building. "What bones were they?" I couldn't help but ask.

"Well, to be completely honest, it's difficult to identify all of the bone fragments we found. Alkaline Hydrolysis really makes a mess of things, but some were phalanges, finger bones. Many were just bits and pieces, the last remnants after chemicals and compression. I was surprised to find enough uncompromised DNA to test, but there it was."

"So you're saying there's a possibility Scrub is still alive?"

Jamie guffawed. "Dad, give it up. He's gone."

"Then who dumped the more recent remains in Radford?" Hector asked, as the entire Drummond family tramped past his desk at the precinct.

"Do we know which remains were dumped first?" I asked, still trying to put together some form of timeline.

Paige shook her head. "No way to tell, not after everything that's happened to the bones, weathering and whatnot." She frowned.

"Could be anyone then," Hector offered, "even my Great Aunt Juanita, God rest her soul."

The added expression caught me off guard, and when I turned to look at my partner seated behind his desk, his face was turned up to the sky innocently, hands over his heart. The pose sent a chuckle coursing through my body like a hamster in a tube maze suffering from PTSD. I couldn't help the laughter that erupted, but it was joined by Jamie and Paige. It felt like the arguments from the past few days that had weighed me down so much fell away in that moment like discarded clothing. After the laughter died down, Hec looked at us so innocently—his cherubic expression contrasting heavily with the dark-black mustache squatting on his upper lip—that it almost set us off again. We finally breathed a sigh of relief. A few other officers shot curious glances our way at the outburst, but I was always considered the black sheep of the department, and for good reason. At least our small, tight-knit group could bring the murderers to justice... normally.

Giving into the assumption, I asked, "So Jamie, do you feel better knowing Scrub is gone?"

Jamie summoned a smile, but it was weak. "Yes and no. I'm really glad he's dead. The bastard can rot graveless for all eternity as far as I'm concerned."

"Understandable," I added, choosing to ignore his choice of words this time.

"What gets me, though, is who took out Scrub and what do they want?" Jamie questioned.

Hector agreed and it took me a minute to catch up. I would normally already be trundling down that train of thought. The question was so obvious, but it hadn't been this time. Either Hector's improvised acting skills had put me off momentarily or I was growing too dependent on my visions for the who-done-it.

"Maybe a partner in crime or apprentice?" Paige asked.

"Maybe," I answered, my mind churning over the options.

Paige added, "Unless the shiners got to him first."

"Possible, but I didn't get that impression from talking to Dillon. He is seen by many as one of the elders in the community, and it seemed like they were still coming to grips with it, like they thought they could avoid further bloodshed."

Paige interjected, "Oh and now you and McCullin are best buddies? You believe everything he says?"

I was happy to hear her sarcastic tone return after the last few days. It was contradictory, but in a constructive way—two members of the same team bantering—although she could never stop herself from jesting at my expense. It had returned to that of years before, when she used to help me track down murderers going all the way back to high school, including protecting my family from the Drunk, Dillon McCullin's son. It just took her time to forgive… if not forget. A grin crested my lips. *Time heals all wounds.*

"See, I'm right." She grinned back at me. "You and Dillon are in cahoots, trying to take over the world like Pinky and the Brain."

"You got me. I'm Brain. Nowhere to run, nowhere to hide. Guess I should hang up my shield now."

"Brain?" She questioned haughtily, her grin widening. "More like Pinky."

"Whatever you say, darlin'," I said with a chuckle.

Jamie chimed in with, "God you guys are cheesy when you make up. It's like watching the next worst show destined to be a hit, *Geek Romances*. Cover Fluffy's ears before you say anything else. The coat might commit *seppuku*. Then where would you be?"

Hector roared with laughter, put an arm around Jamie's shoulders, and walked him to the lounge. "Let's grab a cup of coffee, Jamie, and let the kids get it out of their systems."

"Sounds mighty fine, partner," my son replied in a very stilted Wild West impersonation.

As the two walked away, Hector said, "I still can't believe you named your father's jacket."

"It saved our lives. Was the least I could do after what it went through for us."

"And what am I," Hector asked as their voices faded, "chopped suey?"

When my attention returned to Paige, she was gazing into my eyes. Her anger was most certainly hidden deep inside, but it wasn't evident in her expression. "So, you forgive me?" I asked, crossing my arms and arching one eyebrow.

"Of course I do," she said, placing a hand on my forearm. "Let's not have a repeat showing though. Next time you go see McCullin, make sure you leave Jamie at home."

"It wasn't planned. I just—"

Paige didn't let the excuses continue. Instead she leaned in and kissed me gently, forgivingly, halting whatever words had been coursing through my mind. A few catcalls and whistles reverberated throughout the large room from other officers' desks and cubicles.

Paige blushed bright red but ignored them. "You know I wasn't joking about Dillon McCullin though, not entirely."

"What do you mean?"

"I mean, don't you think it's an interesting coincidence that the same man who raised your stepfather to be the Drunk we know and *love*." Sarcasm dripped from the emphasized word like deadly snake venom. "Out of nowhere comes up with the one lead to Scrub's remains? Isn't that a bit too much of a coincidence, Alex?"

In fact, it was. I just hadn't thought of it, but what could Dillon McCullin gain from putting us onto this information? For that matter, how could he have even known? I asked her as much.

"I... I don't know," she mumbled.

"And did he have a partner, or maybe an apprentice? When did these murders happens in relation to Scrub's death?"

"I... have no idea."

"So many things we still don't know. There may not even be a killer on the loose anymore, at least not one responsible for these murders."

Paige said, "Except for the gang and McCullin himself."

I nodded in thought. We still didn't know how Scrub got around or the majority of his operations, only that he dealt drugs using the Reds as his very own street gang, pushing even the shiners out of their territory. "Still far too many questions. I'm going to try Dan's once more this afternoon. Maybe he can shed some light on this whole mess."

"So, we're back where we started?" Paige asked.

"Yeah, we need to backtrack and see what we may have missed. Maybe I'll even be able to find some evidence to connect McCullin to Cameron's murder."

"How about I see what else I can find in the rest of the remains? I'd like to check out the last place with the pea gravel we found in Donny Pulin's hair too, the post office."

"Sounds good. Would you mind dropping off these letters?" I asked, reaching for a random pile of papers on my desk.

Paige glared at me, an ounce of humor hidden behind her face. "Post your own damn letters, Alex."

We both chuckled as Paige headed for the makeshift forensics lab. "Wait for me, and I'll take you to the post office, honey."

A lazy wave of her hand was Paige's only answer.

Chapter 18

Suspicion

March 11th, 2012

TURNING THE CRUISER out of town that afternoon, the small brick buildings turned to rolling hills and fenced-in pasture. Finally, Dan's dirt road appeared, and I veered left down it. Clouds of dust billowed from beneath my tires as I rumbled down the unmaintained road. The farmhouse appeared in a clearing ahead; a short distance away was the enormous metal garage that dwarfed most barns. The sight of it brought a smile to my lips along with a flood of pleasurable childhood memories. I don't have many memories with Dan—honestly, the man had scared me as a child— but I cherish the time I spent with my father, wherever we were. Dad and Dan went way back. They were both military but had served in different wars.

Stepping out, I first went for the garage. Dan had always been a tinkerer, and from the looks of the open metal sliding door that reached for the heavens, his habits hadn't changed. Peering in, I sang out, "Oh, Danny boy."

"I'm not your damn boy," echoed a gruff voice from inside the dimly lit garage.

I moved inside. In the light of hanging bulbs, an old 1930s roadster sat waiting for the day when it could be wheeled out into the sunshine. An original Ford Model T sat next to it, in far worse shape. Tools hung from the pegboard walls over makeshift two-by-four workbenches. Beyond the small workshop, shelves stretched into the darkness.

"Especially any boy of yours," Dan added, stepping out from an aisle of metal shelves. Car parts, boat components, and a multitude of motors littered the shelves. "Aren't ya a bit young to be singin' that?" A bit of gray stubble adorned Dan's jaw with matching hair on his head, cut short, reminiscent of his years in the service. Pulling a grungy, red bandanna out of his jeans pocket, Dan cleaned his glasses while staring at me.

I nodded. "Yeah, but you probably know why I had to greet you with it."

Dan gazed at me for a pregnant moment, then nodded with the certainty of all his ninety years. "You've got the looks of your father about you. I hate what happened. No man deserves to come home from war only to lose his life in a traffic accident, especially Terry."

The mention of my father sent me back to those years, before the Drunk, before my abilities, even before I was thirteen. As much as I had prepared myself for this meeting, my smile dropped.

"Sorry to bring up such things, boy. It was a bad time all around from what I heard."

I nodded, unable to speak momentarily. "Left me with all sorts of questions."

Dan tilted his head quizzically, a curious smile quirking the side of his mouth. "All sorts, I'm sure."

Something about his words hinted that there was more to this knowledgeable veteran than I could imagine, a knowing glint in his bright, green eyes. "You knew my father pretty well."

Taking a package of chewing tobacco out of his pocket, he inserted a wad under his lip. "Yes, sirree. I most certainly did," the man answered more clearly than I expected. "He was a good man, always trying to do what was right, to help others in need."

Even these words seemed to hint at something more, like an itch at the back of my neck. I couldn't help but wonder if he knew more than he was telling. But how do you ask someone you haven't seen in thirty years, and only remember from a few faded memories, about such a touchy topic as supernatural abilities—more specifically, mine?

Can I reveal such a thing? Should I? It might get me thrown off the force if he tells someone, or at least kicked out of Dan's home before I can inquire about the railroad tracks.

Something about the glint in Dan's knowing gaze and his curious posture assured me that I could trust him. "Look, I have questions about a case I'm working, but... but... I also..." I couldn't get the words out.

"Oh, do you?" he asked, straightening up, slipping his glasses on and smoothing out his wrinkled flannel button-up. "Well I'll be happy to help. Come on over and take a load off." Dan motioned to three bucket seats sitting on the cement floor that could have been from any 90s sedan. They sat circling an old wood-burning stove.

Following his lead, I took the bucket seat opposite him. Even though it wasn't very cold, the heat emanating from the stove quickly took off the chill in my bones.

"What can I do ya for?" he asked, reaching into a refrigerator that had probably been running nonstop since the 1940s and pulling out two beers.

The situation was eerily familiar. I remembered dangling my feet from a stool at the workbench as a boy while Dan and my dad sat chatting in this very spot. Nothing had changed in the garage in the thirty years since, and likely not much the thirty years before that. Popping the can of Bud Light, I took a sip without thinking or even considering that I was on duty.

"I... I don't know where to begin."

Dan sat up straighter. "Normally the beginning's as good a place as any," he said, taking a swig from his own can.

A loud clatter resounded from the back of the large building, from the depths of warehouse-like shelving. Another sound followed, of something heavy and metal falling to the cement floor.

"Damn cats," he grunted, lifting himself from the seat and striding toward where the sounds originated. "They won't stay out and damn near tear the place apart when I ain't lookin'."

The orneriness of Dan's reaction reminded me pleasantly of the few memories I could summon from this place. He'd always been that way, a hard worker with a phenomenal work ethic but little patience for fooling around. It had scared me at the time. I wasn't even in school yet. However, the characteristic was something Dad respected about him, a trait they shared and one that is lost on many youths today. I remembered talking to Dad about the old codger in the car one day as we headed home. I had asked something about why we had to come visit Dan. My father reassured me that Dan was a very good man and one of the most trustworthy he knew.

I got up and strode after Dan, down the aisles of used engine and machine parts. Various pieces stuck out of the shelves at odd angles. The dangers of this place reminded me of the first trip I took to a Civil War battlefield museum after my psychometry developed. Since then I learned to avoid touching unknown objects.

"Oh, there you are, Sibyl," Dan said, stopping halfway into the building. Lightbulbs hanging overhead cast shadows across everything, leaving the inner aisles themselves dark from the chest down. "You know you ain't supposed to be back here, girl." He leaned over and picked the calico cat up, settling its front paws on his shoulder as though it were a baby.

While Dan was a friendly chap, this affectionate action was in contrast to his stern demeanor and my childhood fears. He stroked Sibyl's back as he came toward me. All I could do was stare.

"Back the other way," he directed with a nod when he was only a foot in front of me. He paused, waiting. "Move your feet, turn around and head back, Drummond."

At the mention of my name, I could swear I heard a note in his voice catch like a troublesome thread, but I followed his directions. Avoiding the fender sticking out of the shelf, I was unfortunate enough that my hand brushed against what was left of a leather-wrapped steering wheel on the shelf behind me. The smell of aged leather, worn and true, wafted to me, sending my vision spiraling into nothingness.

* * *

Darkness was quickly scattered by the bright rays of light spilling out of the clear, blue sky. I tried to blink away the dim shadows of Dan's garage and adjust to my new surroundings. If not for the water droplets splashing across my face and the sound of waves crashing against the hull of a wooden motorboat as the engine revved, I would have thought I'd appeared in a tanning bed. Not this time, though.

As everything came into focus, trees swept past on the shoreline, wind buffeted my face over the boat's small windshield, and I shouted, "Wahoo! Yeah!" like a madman. I was on a river, a large one, probably in the early summer. Surprisingly, no thoughts came to me, only supreme delight, the thrill of the ride. "Yes, this is incredible."

I looked around the boat, searching for someone to share in the excitement. No one... not a soul. A momentary sadness seeped into my heart, but it was soon replaced. The river ahead drifted back into sight after a gentle bend. One hand gripping the steering wheel, I pushed the throttle hard, urging the boat for more speed, more buffeting wind, more spray slapping me like a refreshing coax from a giant elemental.

Throwing a fist into the air, I shouted, "Go. Go, Marianne, go!"

The boat's name came to me in that moment as soon as the words left my lips and were tossed backwards, tumbling through the air for the river animals to hear, for no one else was in sight.

Plowing through waves, my excitement grew as a large pier extending off to the right came into view. Its semicircle of wood decking was dotted with tables and diners. A restaurant stood behind them. Their chatter echoed across the river, audible even over the revving boat engine.

Yes! Public eyes, I thought. However, I could not fully understand the desire. This person's thoughts were hidden, overshadowed by the adrenaline and excitement.

"Yahoo! I'm going for it," I shouted to them.

Going for what? I wondered. But I'd soon find out.

People on the rounded pier began shouting and pointing. Individual words were lost, but this man was so charged that for the moment, I couldn't care less. The thrill was what it was all about: energy, excitement, and enthusiasm. I cheered myself on, shouting and screaming until I noticed something ahead. There were no more curves or bends in the river, no more trees lining either side. Ahead was only a cloud of mist hanging a hundred yards ahead where the river should be.

No, no, no. A waterfall. Stop… Stop!

Whoever's body I was in paid less attention to me than he did the diners watching the fiasco about to unfold before them. In fact, instead of lowering the throttle, he shouted for more, urging Marianne ahead like a jockey racing in the Kentucky Derby.

A hundred yards quickly became fifty, then twenty. I abruptly plunged through the mist and my stomach plummeted into my toes. My fingers clutched the steering wheel, struggling for all they were worth to keep me inside as gravity seemed to take a smoke break. Even time seemed to stand still but not the adrenaline coursing through my veins. It was an astounding feeling, terror battling with feverish excitement. If not for the fiercely contrasting emotions, I might have lost myself.

Suddenly time and gravity righted themselves as the boat crashed headlong into the river below. A thunderous crash resounded all around, and I was thrust into the steering wheel. Pain erupted in my midsection, and my breath fled. The boat splintered and was ripped apart. Water flooded in. Cold, undead hands seemed to grip me in a watery embrace, pulling me through the shattered wooden floor and into the depths below. A fire burned in my chest. My lungs wouldn't work, but I couldn't tell if it was from the impact, the lack of air, or maybe both. Thoughts were muddled.

No air… pain…, *was all I could manage.* No air… No… *I sucked in a breath and murky water flooded my throat and lungs. I tried to*

swallow, but it didn't help. Further confusion took hold. Swim...
Swim... The burning sensation spread. I struggled to kick my legs or
move my arms. Nothing responded as I thought it should. I struggled
to swim or even make headway. I'd been flipped, tossed, and turned in
the wreck. Right was left. Up was down. Air didn't exist. The burn
suffused my body, enveloping me until even my senses were dulled. I
gulped more. The last tingling sensation in my toes and fingertips
dwindled, replaced by spotted darkness—inky, swirling nothingness.

* * *

The dim aisle of Mr. Wilburn's workshop came into view as I stood panting, gasping for air. Dan stood a foot away, his free hand extended while the other supported the calico cat on his shoulder.

"You okay, boy?" he asked. His hand hovered six inches from my chest, but he made no move to touch me. However, his eyes held concern. "You look like you've seen a damn ghost."

"Yeah... you... could... say that." Something in the glint in the old man's eyes reinforced my earlier belief that he knew far more. "I... You...," but I couldn't quite say it. My breathing returned to normal, and we stood staring at one another in silence.

Seeing my discomfort, Dan gave a nod but said nothing.

Taking a deep breath, I blurted, "You know there was more to my father than most people thought, right?" It wasn't really a question.

Dan nodded again. His silence grew.

"And you know there is more to me?"

He nodded.

The quiet grated on my nerves. "Say something, damn it!"

Chapter 19

Revelations

March 11th, 2012

MR. WILBURN GRINNED and let out a breathy chuckle. "Hell, boy, I was wonderin' when you'd get around to sayin' somethin'. Yes, and there was somethin' special about your grandpa and his father before him. It's hereditary."

For an elongated second it was like an anvil had been lifted from my shoulders. But then it felt like the weight of thousands of lives descended on me. *My grandpa and great-grandpa too?* I had already concluded that the abilities were hereditary, passed on from father to son—that explained my abilities and Jamie's—but I had never considered how far back it went.

Dan chuckled, grabbed my shoulder, and steered me back to our improvised seats.

"Did you know them? My grandparents, I mean."

He shook his head. "Nah, just your pa. I take it Terry never got the chance to talk to you about this?"

I shook my head. "He died when I was thirteen. I didn't come into my abilities until I was a senior in high school."

We sat, and Mr. Wilburn placed the beer I had been drinking back into my hand. I was still in a fog. "I didn't know anyone knew. My mother didn't even know."

"God rest her soul," Dan intoned, momentarily ducking his head. "She was a good woman."

Mom and I hadn't gotten along for years after Dad's death, but that's a story for another time. We got over it. When she finally left this earth, I think she was able to leave without regrets. However, I had never been able to tell her about my gifts.

Seems Dad felt the same way, like she couldn't handle it. At least Paige can.

"Did Dad ever try to tell her?" I asked. I wasn't sure how much Dad let Dan in on this part of his life, but if he couldn't tell Mom, he had to have told someone. Anxiousness took hold of my legs after a few sips. Somehow I knew I had found my father's one confidant.

"Yes," Dan said. "He tried to tell her once, and it about drove them apart. Terry said they never mentioned it again and were able to move past it. Your pa kept it from her for you, I think. You were just a wee boy. I don't think he wanted to lose you."

Part of me wanted to disagree, to say he could have left and taken me with him, but even today Virginia isn't too fond of giving custody of children to fathers. Back then it was almost unheard-of.

"It was hard not having him around, especially when I learned the truth about myself."

"Hell son, I'm sure it was. I think he wanted to avoid that, but life doesn't always work out the way we want." Dan grabbed another beer and handed it to me.

I hadn't realized it, but I'd polished off my first. Taking the drink gratefully, I popped the top and said, "So, if you don't mind my asking, why didn't you find me? Tell me about things?"

Dan's lips formed a grim line, and for the first time he couldn't meet my eyes. "Boy, I'm ashamed to say it, but after Carrie began to go, I lost sight of quite a few things. I lost touch with most people and avoided the rest. Dementia's a difficult disease to cope with, even for a spouse. It was a dark time." He took a long drink.

"I was sorry to hear about her diagnosis," I muttered. "I don't know her well, but she was always the most reliable volunteer in our Toys for Tots program."

This brought a smile to Mr. Wilburn's lips. His face seemed to glow thinking about her. "She's always been a beaut'. Not another like her in all the world."

"I'm certain of it."

"Not too different than your own grandpa. Alzheimer's is a bad way to go."

This caught me unawares. It was true, before grandpa had died, he suffered from Alzheimer's for years, but why bring it up? "That's true."

"And the same for his pa, and your great-grandpa."

"What?" I had little to no information about my father's side of the family. "I thought you didn't know them."

"I didn't," Mr. Wilburn offered. "But I know what Terry told me. It's part of the gift, or linked somehow. Hell, it's probably got somethin' to do with all those visions you get, memories that aren't your own but will live with you for years to come."

"So I'll get Alzheimer's?" I asked in disbelief.

"More than likely," he answered, "according to your pa."

This new knowledge unsettled me more than knowing Dan had never tried to find me, to teach me what only he knew.

"Though, I did try to contact you once."

Shocked, I asked, "When?"

"I think you were fourteen or fifteen, livin' in that ol' trailer with the fake grass on the porch."

That was when we lived with the Drunk, a low point in my life, one of the lowest.

"Vivian shacked up with Dillon McCullin's boy, Steven," Dan continued. "Now *he* was a piece of work. He kicked me off the property just for askin' to see ya."

Remorsefully, I nodded. *If only one thing had gone differently, my whole life would've changed.* "Sounds like him."

"Hell, I don't suffer fools kindly. I wanted to beat the brute's head in. I was younger in those days, a bit brash, but that fool had it in his head for a fight. He was a young bull, and I was more than willin' to give him a whoopin, especially as drunk as he was. Somethin's gotta kill me, and I figured he might right then. We tussled but walked away when all was said and done. Each of us gave the other somethin' to remember." Dan held up a hand. "Now, don't get me wrong. I planned to go back, but I always figured you'd find your way here one day. Time just passed."

Understanding, I took another swig. It could not wash away the dirty memories of that time in my life, and a subtle taste lingered like rotten tomatoes. I drained the can. Dan handed me another.

"And here you are now." The old man grinned.

"Here I am," I mumbled weakly.

"A lot to take in, ain't it?"

"Yeah, it explains many things though."

Dan curiously supplied, "Like why your father died."

This stopped all thought, like the headlight of an oncoming train with my name plastered across the cattle catcher in neon. Dad was hit by a drunk driver late one night. "What do you mean?"

"You never wondered about that?"

I cautiously explained, "Vivian said he was hit by a logging truck," slipping back into my old way of calling my mother by name. "There were stories about him trying to save someone, but I never really knew what to believe. We got payments from the logging company when I was a kid, though."

"Yes, kinda," Dan replied, "but that's not the whole of it." He thought for a moment. "Makes sense that she wouldn't. Vivian didn't know the truth, but I thought she might have told ya some reason for him being out on that road so late, some story that might not have rung true."

I shook my head, more tuned in than any television viewer. "No, why?"

"Terry called me that night, left a message." Mr. Wilburn got up to his full six feet. "I've still got it somewhere."

He shuffled things around on the nearest workbench, then moved on to stacks of boxes hidden further beneath the benches. I sat in rapt attention, waiting. *Could he really? My father? After so many years?*

"Aha!" Dan exclaimed. "Damn, boy. Nearly thought I'd lost it." He lifted an old message machine out of a plastic carrying crate. "Hope it still works."

Pulling up the cord, Mr. Wilburn plugged it into an outlet over the workbench. I couldn't get up fast enough. Setting the machine on the bench, he said, "Let's just hope it's still good after so many years."

Dan pressed the Rewind button, and I stood next to him, looking down on the faux-wood machine the size of a large hardback novel.

Jamie probably wouldn't even know what something like this is, I thought giddily, like a kid unwrapping his first toy Christmas morning. The message machine clicked at the start of the tape and Dan pressed Play.

A fuzzy voice echoed through the speaker, but it was clear, my father's voice just as I remembered. "Hey, Danny boy, where are you? Remember that man we talked about a week or so ago? The one with the old jalopy that went off the cliff? Well, I worked it out. Get this: the killer's his boyfriend. Talk about something you'd keep under your hat. Here I thought it was the wife. Damn, I wish I got better information from these dreams. Wouldn't have taken me so long otherwise. I'm headed down there now. He lives in a small town called Freeze in the mountains. I looked on the map, and it's spelled F-R-I-E-S, like a burger and fries. I'm glad I thought to look, or I'd never have found it."

He laughed, something I thought I would never hear again, and it brought a grin to my lips.

My father finished with, "I'll keep you in the loop when I get back, Dan. See ya soon."

As my father's voice ended, Mr. Wilburn hit Stop. Tears streamed down my cheeks unbidden. I couldn't stop them, nor did I want to. I had no recordings of his voice or his laughter. The closest I'd ever felt was visiting his grave, which I did more often as a kid. This was the only recording I knew of. "C-can you play it again?"

Dan carefully unplugged the machine and handed it to me with a tenderness that told me the recording had been saved for more than just if I came around. My father had been Dan's friend. "That was the last I heard from your father."

Taking it gingerly and holding it to my chest, I said, "I'll make a recording at the station and bring this back to you."

Dan motioned as if to say "Not to worry" but stopped. "That would be great."

Looking into each other's eyes, we had a mutual understanding, a fondness for my father even after so many years. Without dust, the machine had been pulled out and listened to far more recently than Mr. Wilburn was likely to let on.

"Thank you."

The old man nodded and motioned to the seats. "I ain't as young and spry as I used to be. Hell, used to I'd have walloped that McCullin boy without breakin' a sweat. I'm wiry, ya know, strong, but age'll get ya when ya least expect it. I even thought to go after the truck driver who planted your father in the ground, but wasn't a week before it hit the news that he'd passed too. Been hit by a car if you can believe that. They didn't say who, but I looked into it. Got a few connections hangin' around even now. It was the woman— what was her name? Ah hell, the logging fella's wife. Talk about karma. If ya believe in that sort of thing." He guffawed good naturedly.

Something about this message made me wonder. "Did he call you every time he went out to investigate a murder?"

"No, not every time, but often enough. I kept tabs on him. Someone had to. He'd come home bruised and beaten up from time to time. Me or Carrie would stitch him up and send him on his way. When he didn't call, we figured he made it home safe and didn't need doctorin'. Wasn't till a few days later that we heard what happened."

"Do you have any other messages?"

Dan shook his head. "Always just recorded over them, but I couldn't bear to do it to this one." After a pause, he seemed to switch gears. "So boy, tell me, what'd you see a few minutes ago?"

The question tore my thoughts from my father unwillingly. I settled back into the makeshift seat and gently set the message machine on the paved floor. "A boat."

"Now tell me somethin' I don't know."

My eyes widened.

"I saw the steering wheel you touched," he explained. "I may be old, but I ain't dead."

"Some kid thrill riding a motorboat off an enormous waterfall. I don't think he made it." The word "think" made me grin. *Of course he didn't make it,* I told myself. *If he had, I wouldn't be reliving the scene.*

It seemed that Dan got the joke too because he chortled. "Good one, Alex. Who was it, did you see?"

I was getting the impression that this was the kind of conversation he and my father would have while I sat on the stool at the workbench. At the time I had no idea, but it felt real, like somehow Dad and I had switched places. Anticipation at the excitement of the story glinted behind Dan's eyes.

I shook my head. "I think I glimpsed blond hair flying in the wind, but it wasn't very long. Hard to tell." I took another swig, or tried to. I'd evidently finished another. By this point I felt a little lightheaded now that I was conscious of it. I did not drink often, a consequence of my childhood, but something about this put me at ease.

"Another?" Mr. Wilburn offered.

Exercising restraint, I said, "Nah, I'm on duty. Probably shouldn't have had any, but I'm glad I did."

"Loosened ya up, did it?" Dan grinned.

I nodded.

"Well so am I. You were too stiff. Walked in here with the weight of the world on your shoulders, a bit like your father before we met."

A small grin lifted my lips. "I'll take that as a compliment."

"You should." He handed me a Coke and lifted his beer. "Cheers!" I raised it, and he continued, "They call me Ema Dan, Victor Van, Esau I-saw, Jacob Wilburn."

We both practically rolled over laughing. I wasn't sure where the phrase originated, but it was evidently something else he and my father shared—a wonderful sense of humor.

"I can tell ya who it was."

"Who what was?" I asked, confused and a bit curious.

"The boatman."

"Ahh, right. Who was he?" There was no murder to investigate, simply stupidity, but sometimes that is enough.

"Yes sirree, 'twas Cecil Abraham. He went over Cumberland Falls in Kentucky. Didn't make it out—at least, not alive!" We both laughed shamelessly. "They said it was a part from his boat, the wheel I mean, but I didn't know for sure. The man's a bit of a folk hero in those parts, their very own Evel Knievel."

"Huh," was all I could say. I think that was the closest I had ever been to a supposed celebrity, even if just a local one. "Makes sense. There wasn't a fearful bone in his body."

"Truly?" Mr. Wilburn asked. "That fall's not all that deep. I'd have been scared of bottomin' out going that speed before I ever made it to the falls. There's a newspaper clippin' somewhere around here." He motioned around the workshop, beer in hand. He chortled again and took a drink, rocking back and forth in his seat, which looked to have been modified to do just that, his own version of a porch rocking chair.

I laughed. Now I understood more fully why Dad liked Dan so much. He was an easygoing guy, open to life.

"That reminds me," he said, "you mentioned something about a case you were workin'."

"Right."

As I sobered up, I told Mr. Wilburn about Scrub, the murders that were piling up, and everything Hector, Paige, Jamie, and I had turned up, including the Reds and shiners.

"Now that is quite somethin'."

"We can't figure out exactly how he's traveling, but I figured you'd know the train routes."

He nodded. "Yep, worked dispatch for Norfolk Southern for a long while."

"We figure he's probably in a refrigerated truck."

Dan asked, "What makes you think that?"

"Due to the size and power and water needs of the Alkaline Hydrolysis machine."

Shaking his head, Dan said, "Not necessarily. Could be a train. Hard to say though since the highways run along the same routes, like you said. Where did ya say you found the bodies again?" He pulled out a map that had yellowed over the years and unfolded it. This one was different from mine though. It had crisscrossing train routes that were color-coded.

"We found the ashes dumped here, here, and here," I said, pointing out the different drop points. "Even so far as Radford."

Rubbing his whiskered chin, Mr. Wilburn concluded, "Ain't been a train running along there for years. Besides, that damn bastard would have to pay off quite a few people—the engineer, brakeman, conductor, maybe even a few people up the chain from there—all to keep them quiet. Nah, not likely."

"Wait, there used to be, so there isn't any more?"

"Oh yeah, that's the Pocahontas line that runs that portion. Used to run the NS cargo trains pretty regular, but they closed it in the '90s. That's where I ran dispatch."

An odd thought came to mind. "Are the tracks still there?"

He nodded. "Yep."

"Still usable?"

Mr. Wilburn tilted his head in thought. "Theoretically, yes. Might need some tending here and there, but with no trains on them, they could be used from time to time. Don't tell me ya think this ex-con's got a whole train he's runnin'. That would take a lot of money, connections, and even then without proper maintenance, those tracks won't last forever. Not to mention, that would be pretty hard to miss."

He was right; that wasn't likely. It would've been much more likely Scrub had used a refrigerated freight truck. It wouldn't even have to be a full-size semi. "Do you mind if I hold onto this?" I asked. "My map doesn't have these old train routes."

Dan nodded and finished his beer. "That'd be fine."

"I appreciate it, Dan. You've been a great help, far more than you'll ever know."

"At my age, my best parts are what I've got up here." He pointed to his head.

We both laughed, for I knew how modest he was being. At over ninety years of age, the old codger would probably still give me a run for my money in a fistfight. Standing, I glanced at my watch and was surprised to find it was nearly five o'clock. We had been talking for nearly three hours. I had to get back to work. Paige wanted to go by the post office, and I'd told her to wait for me.

"Dan, I've gotta go, but I'll be back if that's alright. I'd love to talk more."

"Well hell, of course you can. You're always welcome here, boy, you and your family. I'd love to meet them, especially that boy of yours. Besides, you've got to get me back my tape." He stretched one leg at a time as he stood. They popped audibly.

Shaking hands, I made my way to the car and started the drive back to town. The visit had given me some information to think on about the case, but it revealed so much more that I would never forget. I tried Paige's office number at the forensics lab. No one answered. I'd have to catch up to her at the precinct, if she was still there.

Chapter 20

Ghostly Whispers

March 11th, 2012

THE FORTY-MINUTE TRIP back to the Tranquil Heights Police Station started fine. I pondered so many new revelations about my parents. Mr. Wilburn's insights set my mind ablaze about the decisions and actions that led to where I was in life, who I became: Dad's decision not to push Vivian about his abilities, to stay with her, and finally to venture down that small mountain road in search of a killer. He wasn't a homicide detective but still had the same problems I did with people's disbelief. And if Jamie's more well-developed psychic abilities were any indication of how the powers evolve over generations, Dad must have seen even less than me in his visions.

At least he had Dan, I told myself. *Without him, it might have driven him insane.*

That thought brought my family's inevitable demise due to Alzheimer's to the forefront of my mind. A shudder ran down my spine as I followed the windy dirt road back to the highway.

When does that start? I couldn't help but wonder. A frightening thought came to me. *Has it already? How would I even know? I could've already forgotten things, small things... maybe even large memories.*

The possibility was unsettling, but I told myself there was no indication of it. Ever since I had known my grandpa, he had suffered from Alzheimer's, so I always knew it was a possibility. Though having that confirmed as an inevitability would rock anyone's world.

I still have time, I reminded myself. *More importantly, I still have Paige and Jamie, even my stepsister Abby. Family.*

Part of me wondered if it was worth the cost. Logically, I knew it was. The people I was helping may already have died, but getting their murderers off the streets did more than bring solace to their families. It saved lives, the lives of future victims whose families would otherwise suffer over the loss of a loved one. My final years of sanity were a worthwhile sacrifice.

Plus, it's not like I can change it. No sense crying over spilt milk.

During the last half of the trip, my thoughts turned to Scrub and the case. I felt like I had made little to no headway, and my inner detective chided me for the loss of time. A few times I glanced at the folded map lying on the passenger seat. Something about it tickled the back of my neck like a cat batting repeatedly at a hanging string. It wasn't a vision or anything supernatural, but my detective sense kept going off, subtle alarm bells the size of finger cymbals. There was something more to this, something I had missed while talking to Dan: a clue, hint, or message. Paige would hate me for delaying our visit to the post office, especially since they would be closed even with extended hours, but I had to look.

Pulling onto the shoulder of the highway, I unfolded the map across the steering wheel and looked at the points where Scrub had dropped bodies, or what was left of them. I went over everything again as cars *whizzed* past. Dan had been right. The Pocahontas line ran not far from every one of them, as did I-81. Ten minutes passed. I stared like Galileo struggling to discern the complexity of the planets... until the itch seemed to sooth upon one specific conclusion.

Scanning the Tranquil Heights area for the post office, my heart thudded in my chest, slowly increasing tempo as though in time with The Velvet Underground's "Heroin". Finding the small, insignificant dot that represented a government post office, my eyes widened. I flung open the glove compartment and grabbed the street map from within, unfolding it and comparing the two, one clutched in each hand. There was an old train depot for the Pocahontas line. It had been closed ages ago, probably when the line itself was shut down, but what gripped my heart in that moment was its proximity. Train tracks passed right behind the post office. Opposite it was the old depot. Like pieces of a puzzle, things began falling into place; the pea gravel from Donny Pulin's hair, the post office, the train depot, and every location the ashes had been found. It seemed impossible—unthinkable—but somehow Scrub had pulled it off. He was using the abandoned train route. Dan was right, even though we'd both doubted it.

How many people are in on this? How did no one notice?

There were still countless questions, but the key to it all was here.

"But Scrub's dead," Jamie's voice echoed, as though he were sitting in the passenger seat. "He's dead. Mom found his body."

"Maybe, but who's still committing these murders?" I asked the silence.

Nothing responded... until a voice I almost didn't recognize whispered, "Hurry, Alex. For Tommy."

I jumped, spinning around in my seat, but no one was there. Memories of running from Scrub, the enormous adult, passed through my mind like a reel-to-reel on fast-forward. The rickety steps creaked through my mind. My heart raced. Scrub's voice echoed after me... after Tommy, and I knew this ordeal wasn't over. Flipping open my cell, I tried Paige again. Nothing. No answer but voicemail.

"Paige, call me back ASAP!"

Ending the call, I cursed myself for not getting the new number to the renovated forensics lab.

Paige wouldn't go to the post office on her own, would she?

I knew the answer immediately. Paige was a headstrong woman. That was one of the very things I loved about her. Yes, when she didn't hear from me, she would. But she was smart. She would have taken one of her forensics team members. Shoving the transmission into gear, I flicked on my siren and lights. The engine roared as I sped into traffic.

Please God, keep her safe.

I raised dispatch on the radio and asked, "Taylor, is Paige still at the precinct?"

"Hiya, Alex. No, she isn't." Sensing the urgency in my voice, she asked, "Something wrong?"

"Maybe. Can you call over to the lab and find out for sure? I've got a bad feeling."

"Oh no, not again, Alex. Hold just one sec."

I listened while weaving through traffic, siren blaring. Taylor's conversation with the person on the other line was muted and one-sided, but still audible. Before she hung up and returned to me, I knew.

My heart hammered against my chest and nausea engulfed me as she said, "I'm sorry, Alex. Paige and Dr. Senai left without you half an hour ago so they could interview the postal employees."

Swallowing the lump that appeared in my throat, I said, Dispatch all units to the post office on Elm and Third."

Tommy's mother's voice whispered once more next to my ear, "Hurry!" There was pained insistence in her voice.

"This isn't going to be pretty, but I'm on my way, Taylor," I added, slamming my foot down and jolting the car onto the shoulder.

Little did Taylor or I realize, but Jamie stood listening in the hallway, just outside of dispatch. And he had heard everything.

Chapter 21

Hurry Up and Wait

March 11th, 2012

SWERVING TO TAKE the closest exit to Elm, I sped down the ramp. I was only ten minutes away—five at this rate. A phone call later, and Hector was on the line.

"Hec, we got problems."

"What do you mean? Where?"

"Scrub was usin' the old abandoned Pocahontas line to dump the bodies. Don't ask me how, but he was. I'm sure of it."

"Okay... that sounds like good news. You're onto—"

"The old depot's right behind the post office on Elm and Third," I interrupted.

"*Jesus Christo!*" he intoned. "That's where—"

"I know. I'm ten minutes out, maybe five if I take the sidewalks. You still at the station?"

"Not for long." The sound of shuffling movements rubbing against the phone's mic filtered through the speaker. "Be there in five." The call ended.

Dropping the cell back in my pocket, I gripped the steering wheel, white-knuckled. Each turn and inattentive driver that delayed my progress made me grimace. At one light where traffic was backed up for evening mass at a local church, my prediction came true. I couldn't budge.

"Hurry," the ghost's voice hissed. "Soon… too late."

Pulling onto the sidewalk, I honked repeatedly, nearly shoving pedestrians out of the way. I passed under store awnings, tore through a café sign advertising buy-one-get-one-free desserts, then took out the front legs of a table. An overweight author sat in front of a bookstore autographing books. The author fell backward in his chair, and people jumped out of the way as the table crumpled against the car's weight. A book landed on my windshield, titled *A Life of Death*.

The way I feel every day!

Jumping the curb and flooring it through the intersection, cars squealed to a stop to avoid me as though the flashing red light and blaring siren weren't enough notice. Flicking the wipers on, the paperback fluttered into the air in my rearview mirror like a dying bird and plummeted to the ground.

Someone could've died, my conscience scolded.

Thinking of Paige, I answered sternly, "But not today," and drove on.

* * *

I skidded to a halt in the pea gravel just as a voice came over the radio. "Code 9-9-9," echoed to all cars from an unsteady female voice. I recognized it—Rachel, the intern I'd spoken to just the day before. "Code… God, what's the color…?" Suddenly remembering, she shouted, "Code Purple. Officer down. Shots fired. 10-1, 10-1, 10-1!" We're stuck in the post office. One civilian."

Gunshots reverberated through the air. Two cruisers were already parked catty-corner in the lot, doors flung wide, uniformed officers ducking behind them. The forensics van was parked meticulously inside the yellow lines just in front of the post-office entrance. It and the Honda Civic parked opposite were the only civilized remnants in this chaos. Officers exchanged gunfire with adolescents dressed in red shirts and jeans. Some even had red bandanas wrapped over their heads. They huddled on the tracks behind random train cars, firing at us. Fortunately, pistols weren't very accurate at that range. This seemed mainly about containment and stalling for the outnumbered police. One of them radioed for backup in more measured tones.

An assortment of tracks separated the post office from the old train depot. More gunfire resounded across the landscape from the depot itself.

Jeeze, what did Paige get herself into?

I ducked low, peering out and trying to make out what was happening. I had been in gunfights before, but something seemed different about this one. Bullets pinged off the cruiser, but they seemed scattered and random, as though they weren't intentionally directed at me. Teens wearing an assortment of red darted between trains while local mountain folk chased them down. Watching the events unfold, I spotted Dexter and Trey huddled in front of two rusty metal barrels that might once have been used to transport goods or fuel. The two gang members were clearly visible to the police officers, trying to hide from shooters at the depot. They popped up and around the cans, firing wildly. Bearded mountain men and their wives scrambled around, rifles and shotguns in hand. The officers seemed at a loss for who to shoot. We were like the odd men out. No one loved or hated us.

Wow, talk about timing. Everything seems to have erupted at once.

I pulled on a department jacket with big, white letters so my own people wouldn't mistake me for a dealer. No time to dig my vest or the riot gun out of the trunk. I did, however, pocket my spare clip from the console, which I normally used for the shooting range. Leaping out of the car, I ducked and ran for the front door to the post office, pistol in hand. Judging from Rachel's unsteady voice earlier, I was likely to get blasted if I didn't give warning. Using my portable radio, I reported, "Post office, I'm coming inside. Don't shoot."

"G-got it," came her response, "Ten-Four."

"Clearing the hallway," Officer Brightwell replied audibly as soon as I entered through the double doors. "These little bastards are getting a hell of a lot more than detention."

He was ten feet away, a teenage girl clad in a red t-shirt two sizes too small facedown at his feet. Brightwell zip-tied her arms and legs in quick motions, then quickly joined me at the inner door to the customer service department.

I mumbled, "Are our people pinned in here?"

He nodded and silently counted down on three fingers before kicking in the door, his gun directed into the room.

Brightwell smiled through the event, acting with a fervor he probably didn't get to exercise as a school resource officer and hadn't since his military days.

Just don't let it get you killed, I told him silently, hoping for the best. *Or me.* Brightwell was a good cop. The last thing we wanted was to hear another 9-9-9 call. One officer shot was enough. We rushed into the room, checking every corner and behind the counters. Nothing. No one living at least. A post-office employee dressed in her uniform blues lay still behind the counter. A quick check for a pulse told me all I needed to know.

Looking my way, Officer Brightwell softly asked, "Morgue, not ambulance?"

I nodded and straightened. The customer-service room was riddled with bullet holes and overturned advertising stands.

"In here, Detective Drummond," came Rachel's weak voice from the package sorting and delivery room.

Stepping through the swinging doors, I was astonished to find Dr. Senai lying on his back, a pool of blood growing beneath him. His eyes were closed, and his normally tan skin was pale. Rachel had his head propped in her lap, fingers combing through the doctor's jet-black hair as she sat on the floor, legs crossed. Her other hand held a white cloth to her side. Dr. Senai still wore his dark blue forensics jacket and was taking shallow gasps.

I wanted to shout for Paige, to scream her name, but I had to take care of the threat first. I also wasn't sure I could bear seeing her dying on the ground like Dr. Senai. "The shooter?" I hissed.

Rachel pointed to a back office. Through the open office door, I made out an assortment of desk materials, papers, and a lamp scattered across the floor. On the desk lay a teenage boy with a shaved head and red jogging suit. His bloody t-shirt had been sliced away and now hung over the sides of the desk like a red and green tablecloth. His torso was bared. Paige leaned over him, assessing his gunshot wound. Her patient didn't move.

Breathing a sigh of relief, I warily stepped into the office, pistol aimed low but ready for anything. "He gonna be okay?" I asked, not really caring considering the gunshots still being exchanged outside.

"Better than that one," she intoned without raising her head.

Chase, the leader of the Reds and the man behind Donny Pulin's decapitation, hung backward limply, half inside the room and half out. The large indoor window separating the sorting room from the office had been broken by his body. Large glass shards skewered Chase's abdomen and stomach, pinning him in place. The three gunshots to the slain boy's chest had probably sent him through the window.

"Yeah, he's not going anywhere. You know you've got two patients waiting out there, right?"

After wrapping the boy's wound and tying a strip from his pants around his midsection to maintain pressure, Paige nodded. She grabbed her portable toolkit, which resembled a 1930s doctor's bag, and packed everything back inside.

"He okay where he's at?" I asked.

Paige looked at me for the first time since I'd walked through the door. The depths of her honey-brown eyes I loved so much were pierced with sorrow... and something more.

"Are you okay?"

She nodded, but said, "No."

Confused, I took a step closer and gazed into her eyes. They kept shifting to the body and away as though attempting to avoid him, but she had worked on patients for years, victims and murderers. A look at the sleeping patient told more. Both wrists were handcuffed, one to a metal drawer handle and the other to a heavy office chair next to the desk. A 9 mm sat on an end table next to the office door. A lava lamp stood atop the table, unfazed by the chaos. Paige's clothes were bloody, but aside from bruises and scrapes, she didn't appear to be physically harmed. "What's wrong?" I holstered my weapon.

"I swore to do no harm, Alex," Paige muttered. "I'm supposed to help people."

Blood spatters on the floor and wall told me the key shots had come from in here.

"You did this?" I was both surprised and ashamed at the disbelief in my tone.

"And Rachel... but I killed him, maybe both of them."

Paige didn't carry a firearm and neither did interns or Dr. Senai. The guy on the table had to be one of the assailants. The ladies had overpowered one of them, taken a gun, and defended themselves. I was relieved and impressed. Paige had always been intelligent and headstrong, but this time the true scrapper in her had come out.

"Honey, you had to. I'm just glad you're safe. I'm so sorry I wasn't here with you." Taking her shaking form in my arms, I pulled her close. "You are the strongest woman I know, Paige. You had to."

"But the Nightingale Pledge," she explained into my shirt.

She was close to tears, but before the flood sheds opened, she gently pushed me away. Paige licked her lips and straightened. "Compartmentalize, Paige," she whispered. "Save it for later. Hiram needs you." After a deep breath, she lifted her satchel, squared her shoulders, and strode toward the sorting room where two patients waited.

I smiled as she walked away, proud and brimming with love for the woman. I was a wreck after my first shooting, and it had been nothing like this. I took possession of the weapon so the prisoner couldn't use it against anyone else and tucked it behind my back, then quickly zip-tied the sleeping patient's legs just in case he woke up. Paige had obviously dosed him with something, but I had no idea what or how much.

"Rachel, the ambulances should be arriving shortly," I said. "Listen for them."

She acknowledged the order without a sound. Paige was already kneeling over Dr. Senai, his shirt cut apart, revealing a knife wound.

"Was that the only civilian here?" I pointed toward the deceased employee in the customer-services department. "No one else? No customers?"

Rachel pointed at the back door. A neon Exit sign hung over it. "As soon as we secured the post office, we sent them out the back."

"The gunfight outside hadn't started yet?"

She shook her head.

The girl appeared to need a reason to chin-up. She had taken a bullet protecting my wife. I didn't know the details, but that certainly put her in my good graces. I grinned. "Good job." The witnesses would need to be tracked down and interviewed, but they were safe for now.

"Thanks, Detective Drummond."

"And Alex will do for now on, okay?"

She nodded, a smile playing at the corners of her pained lips.

Brightwell urgently motioned me over to a window at the far side of the room. Gunfire continued to echo outside. He stood to the side of the window, peering out at the battle raging but staying out of view. I took the other side.

"What do you see?" I asked.

"Looks like the Reds and moonshiners are fighting it out. Turf warfare. Who would've thought? It's not like the black market for shine is something gangs normally get in on, but maybe the Reds are behind the flood of drugs into the school."

"I think you're right. They must have been the ones to cut off Donny Pulin's head."

"I wondered who pissed in Dillon McCullin's Cheerios." Officer Brightwell indicated the train nearest the depot where a large giant of a man in a flannel shirt strode into battle.

"The bastard," I mumbled.

"I know you don't care for the man, Drummond," he said with concern, "but he ain't so bad. My family's known his since they settled this area."

I glared at the school resource officer for a moment before letting the look slide from my face. He didn't know what I'd been through as a child, what the Drunk had done, the beatings I took, the abuse. However, he should know about Dillon's son's murder conviction.

"Does that statement include his son, Steve?"

The ex-marine paused for a moment. "Of course not." Changing the subject, he asked, "What should we do? There has to be at least thirty combatants between the two groups. I only see five of us, counting you and me."

Lieutenant Tullings didn't seem to have made it here yet. He would have led the charge, but with our small numbers there was no way the Reds and shiners would listen to us, not while trying to kill each other.

"First, I think you should bring that bound girl in here so we can watch her. No sense letting her get away."

He moved to do as I asked. While he was gone, I dialed Hector but only got his voicemail. It didn't worry me as much as my unanswered call to Paige earlier, for he could be hidden somewhere. More than likely his phone was off, but something didn't sit right. A minute later Brightwell returned dragging a screaming girl by the feet.

"Shove her in the corner and slap some duct tape on her."

He grinned as he worked, saying, "Sure, boss. Silence is golden..."

"But duct tape is silver," I finished. The saying had practically become a motto in the precinct.

When he joined me back at the window, I asked, "Have you seen Hector?"

Brightwell shook his head. "No, but his car is parked across the tracks." He pointed.

Squinting, I made out *The Ocho*. It was parked behind a collection of beat-up trucks, blocking them in. *That can't be good.* I hit Redial on my phone and listened as it went to voicemail yet again. "Where are you, Hec?"

I didn't even realize I had voiced the question aloud until Brightwell answered, "No idea. Haven't heard a peep from him, but it can't be good."

"Well aren't you just a geyser of good news," I complained.

The muscle-bound officer shrugged. "That wasn't in the job description."

Shaking my head, I turned my attention back to the outside world. Hec was out there somewhere. I scanned the trains: freight cars, coal transports, and even a few cabooses.

"Wait," Brightwell said, interrupting my thoughts, "isn't that your Subaru coming in? I don't know how you tore that thing up so badly, but you're like an evil penny. Bad luck follows you everywhere."

I would have glared at him, but he was right. Coming into the parking lot was the Subaru Rachel had supposedly dropped off at the mechanic's. "Rachel, who's got my car?"

"It's at the—shop," she responded, taking in a sharp breath as Paige dabbed antisceptic on her gunshot wound. Dr. Senai seemed to be breathing a little better, at least from this distance. He appeared to be unconscious, hopefully sleeping through the pain.

My attention returned to the parking lot and my car—well, Paige's—which had come to a stop near the entrance next to the closest train. The passenger door opened and a young Clark Kent lookalike ducked out, running behind the train, making a beeline for something. He was too far away, but I knew I would see an ankh branded into the middle of his forehead. *Jamie, what the hell are you doing here?*

"Shit!"

"Ain't that...?" Officer Brightwell asked without having to finish.

I just nodded, head bowed.

"Damn, you are the unluckiest SOB I know."

"Don't sugarcoat it, Stan." I responded dryly. "Just tell me how you really feel."

"Hey P—"

I clamped a hand over his mouth. "Are you nuts?" I growled. "Keep quiet about it or you'll get my wife killed. I'll go get him."

Realization dawned on Stanley Brightwell a second later. A mother's love would draw her into that deadly hornet's nest. He glanced at Paige, then back to me. Our eyes met. Seeing there was no room for discussion, he gave a slight nod. "I'll keep 'em safe here."

Turning, I sprinted for the door. "Gotta go, honey. Take care of them. I'm leaving Officer Brightwell here with you."

She agreed silently, bandaging the wound until Rachel could get to the hospital. As I left, Paige had her lie back and shoved cleaning towels under her head.

Chapter 22

Mercy

March 11th, 2012

STEPPING INTO THE setting sunlight amidst so much chaos was against every instinct I had. Like firemen running into burning buildings when everyone else is running out, part of me silently screamed, *This is insanity*. But the more dominant instinct, that of a father, suppressed all else, with an added curse of, *What the hell are you thinking, Jamie?*

I drew my sidearm again. Dodging from obstacle to obstacle, I encountered Trey first, the large Red who'd been drinking a bit too much in the high school parking lot the night of Cameron's murder. We spotted each other at the same time between two trains. We both hesitated, unsure of the other's intentions.

"Drop it!" I finally announced.

This fiasco was going to end one way or another, even if I had to take it down one participant at a time. Innocent people would die if I did nothing, and thus far little to nothing had been done.

In answer, Trey fired and jumped between freight cars. He didn't aim, like he really didn't care to shoot me, only frighten me away. I hadn't taken the shot. *And it could cost someone's life,* my conscience replied, *like Jamie's.*

I hated that it had come to this. These were kids led astray by Scrub's fanatical desire to be a drug lord. Many of these kids I had watched grow up.

"Trey, you can stop this. Chase is dead. Scrub is dead. There's no reason to continue," I yelled over the cacophony of more sirens and gunfire echoing off the metal train cars.

No response. He simply avoided me.

I ran down the aisle, ducking to peer under rusting train cars and jumping between them in search of my son's Intern jacket. A few times, I spotted him passing at the end of an aisle of train tracks. The glimpses were fleeting but sent me sprinting towards him.

Periodic bursts of gunfire ricocheted around me.

Suddenly, a scrawny Shiner with more black and yellow teeth than white stumbled in front of me, shotgun over his shoulder. I'd seen Arnie in the drunk tank more often than I wanted to count. Shock caught him unawares at seeing me when he rounded the corner. He skidded to a halt. Without missing a beat, I slammed the butt of my pistol between his eyes, muttering, "Sleep it off, Arnie," as he slumped to the ground. Jamie seemed to be heading deeper into the collection of old train cars.

"Stop right there, Drummond," came a voice from some distance behind.

It was yet another voice I recognized, which wasn't unusual in this small town, but this was not from personal experience. A memory flashed to life:

"Nice shot, Deacon," Chase had said after Deacon gunned down Jamie's best friend, Donny. "I think that's the first time this little prick ever got any action." The others laughed and chortled.

"Ahh, just a little bird shot. Ain't no permanent harm," Deacon replied, sounding disappointed.

This was no innocent child. He had made his decision and acted to end the life of at least one person, probably more. I didn't have time for the budding thug, not now.

The ghost of Tommy's mother whispered in the wind, "Quickly!"

I ducked left, continuing in the direction Jamie had headed. Freight cars flashed past, but still I couldn't find him... until Deacon's voice boomed over the screams and chaos, "Drummond, I've got something of yours"

That stopped me cold. *No, Jamie, I can't be too late. I can't.* I turned and tore through the lanes of trains looking for him.

"Follow my voice, Drummond. Come get me."

Lieutenant Tullings' voice finally echoed over a bullhorn, "Drop your weapons. You're all under arrest."

I ignored his futile attempt to end the battle. He would only bring the wrath of both sides down on law enforcement. What he needed was overwhelming odds, which I doubted he could gather this quickly, or a surgical strike.

Seeing Deacon down a middle aisle, my jaw locked in place. His arm was tightened around Jamie's neck from behind, a pistol hanging in his hand as he stared back at me. He grinned and brought the gun up.

Jamie's eyes widened, but not from the gun rising to his head. As I closed the distance at a fast walk, not slowing or halting, eyes drilling into Deacon, Jamie knew what was happening. Poppa bear was on the hunt.

"There you are—" he began, but then everything happened so fast.

Jamie bolted left, momentarily opening my target—Deacon's face.

As I'd been trained over the last decade, my 9 mm came up, sighted in a split-second, and fired. A hole blossomed in Deacon's eye socket before he could finish his sentence. I fired a tight grouping of three before the body seemed to fall in slow motion.

Not waiting for me to get closer, Jamie bolted in the direction he'd been heading all along.

"Jamie?" I looked after him, but someone else caught my attention. Officer Theresa Fuller stood ten feet away, gaping. She'd seen everything. Her hand held still on her holster as if unsure what to do. I hadn't tried to negotiate with Deacon. I had just acted. There would be repercussions. It was a hostage situation. There were protocols, but in that moment I didn't care.

"It's always the quiet ones," she said, barely audible.

Holding up a finger, I told her, "Not right now," and followed Jamie, yelling his name.

He didn't slow or pause; he just followed his internal compass. One final fleeting glance showed Jamie jumping up the narrow steps of a caboose in the far back corner, second to last.

"You're too late," Tommy's mother wailed, her voice emanating from everywhere and nowhere.

Too late? How am I too late? I saved him. I saved Jamie.

Dismissing my confusion, I quickly followed and clambered up the steps two at a time, pistol ready. Inside the dark, narrow engine car, machinery gave off a low hum. One red bulb lit the entire compartment, aside from the scant rays spilling through the windshield behind Jamie. He stood erect, unmoving, looking further inside. His face was expressionless. In the middle of the room stood the man we had been looking for, the murderous Scrub, minus one hand. His hair looked like a pincushion of springs, scruffy whiskers adorned his face, but he was alive.

"Ahh," Scrub, AKA Steve Klein, crowed. "It seems you arrived at the father-son dance too late this time, Detective Drummond. No cigar for you. You know, I've looked you up. That seems to be your habit, or downfall rather. Can't keep your family safe."

"Klein," I said, pushing in front of Jamie, "you lose. There's no escape here. We're tearing apart your drug ring as we speak. It's over, and what's more, my family *is* safe."

"Spoken like a true father," he replied, grinning maniacally. He took a step forward, and his coveralls slid into the light from outside. Crimson coated them—some dried, some not. "Family is such a fluid term. You will let me go, and you may be in time to save your friend. I've heard you call him your brother at times. That makes him family, no?"

A few futile thumps echoed from the narrow hydrolysis machine running the length of one side of the caboose. They seemed sluggish, like final heartbeats. The lid didn't budge, and I noted an electronic keypad where a lock should be. Muffled screams seemed to gurgle out.

Hec?

"Tick—tick—tick—tick—*tock!* Time's running out. I'd love to sit here and chat, but I have a train to catch." He chortled.

What to do? What to do? With every passing second, chemicals were searing away Hector's flesh. I raised my pistol, stopping Klein.

"He's been in there a few minutes already, Mr. Drummond. Are you sure you want to negotiate? I know the code to save him."

The pistol began to shake in my hand. and my arm fell limply to my side. "What is it?"

"Ah-ah-ah," he chided, shaking a long, bony finger on his remaining hand. "Not until I'm out."

Fire and brimstone erupted in my eyes. This madman was torturing my partner mere feet away and withholding the code to his freedom. I started to raise my pistol again, but Jamie grabbed my arm. Holding in my anger, I spat, "Get out!" and moved to the side along with Jamie.

A second later a rifle shot resonated from just outside the engine car. The shell tore through the windshield, ripping open Klein's heart like a cruise missile. Blood spattered all over us. The crazed maniac fell to the floor inches away, and we could only watch in horrifying contradiction. Turning astonished faces to the source of the shot, I spotted a vision I never imagined I'd see. Lying atop the engine hood of the caboose behind us was Dillon McCullin's bearded face. He smiled, saluted, and slid off the side, striding away without a care in the world.

More pounding came from the machine with its motor running. We stepped over the lunatic's body and tried the lid. It didn't move.

"The lock, Dad," Jamie shouted. "Maybe I can talk to his ghost. Maybe he'll give it up."

"No time. Hec, shove against the other side if you can."

"But, Dad, if it doesn't work—"

"It'll work." Aiming from inches away, I unloaded two bullets into the lock itself. The lid clicked, and I pulled it open, dreading what I'd find.

Inside, a chemical stew bubbled. An arm reached out and then a head, but there was little left to call human. Skin and hair seemed to slough off, falling into the bloody mix. Only red and black patches of humanity remained, a mass of muscles, sinew, and char. Hec's halfway decomposed head pleaded, "Help me."

Fighting down disgust and nausea, I swung into action. Jamie put one of Hector's arms around his shoulders while I took the other, pulling him free of the chemical bath and lowering him to his knees in the red light of the room. The concoction burned my skin, and Jamie and I both tore off our jackets to wipe away the residue. I made to do the same for Hector, but after the first wipe, he let out a guttural scream that seemed to pierce the entire world.

"I c-can't clean it off without doing more harm than good," I explained, uncertain what to do. Our feeble training in poisoning cases usually said to give people milk or water. Would that make the situation worse?

Hector slumped, allowing a groan to escape but remaining on his knees. Just then Paige pounded up the steps and into the engine car. Her hand immediately covered her mouth as she saw Scrub's body, then Hector wavering, looking as though animals had ravaged him for days. After a shocked intake of breath, she stumbled backward, knocking over whatever mess of cans and wrappers the lunatic had left sitting around. "Oh God," she moaned, "who is that?"

Looking into her eyes, I could feel tears welling in my own. "H... Hector," I blurted.

Her eyes grew to saucers. She jumped off the train and vomited.

"Alex," Hector rasped. A large hole had appeared in one cheek as the remaining chemicals continued eating away. Half his teeth were missing and his eyes had burst, leaving only bloody sockets. "K-kill me."

The tears flowed freely then. I shook my head.

"P-please, Alex."

As I looked down on my partner—my best friend—tears streaming down my cheeks, I could barely think. However, I had seen brutality, spoken with victims, and watched their recoveries. Hector was too far gone and in immense pain. The best thing for him was a bullet, but bringing yourself to do that for a friend is a task I wish on no one. Raising my gun to his forehead, I tried. My finger wouldn't respond. Wouldn't act. Wouldn't obey. The trigger wouldn't pull.

Blood ran down what was left of Hector's face like gruesome tears.

"I c-can't, buddy. I c-can't." I turned away, ashamed. Paige stepped back inside wiping her mouth. Our gazes met after she took in the scene. My inner turmoil, my shame and sorrow, were reflected in her eyes. We held each other's gaze, conversing silently until Jamie's quiet voice interrupted my thoughts.

"See ya soon, Uncle Hec. I love you."

A gunshot rang through the small train car, and I swiveled in time to see my partner's decomposing body slump backwards to the grated floor. In the red light, smoke streamed from the 9 mm in Jamie's hand, one I didn't recognize. Then it clattered to the floor. Jamie turned, slid past without a word, and stepped off the train. Paige and I looked at one another in shock and horror.

The events following that moment flowed in a fog. Paige panicked and went after Jamie, who was casually walking along the abandoned train tracks, away from the trains and the depot. I picked up the discarded gun. I had to get rid of it. I knew that. It couldn't be traced to him... I couldn't allow it. Mercy killings weren't legal in any form in Virginia. But there was no avoiding the connection between the bullet and this gun. If they checked his hands for gunpowder residue, that would end any hope at a life outside a cell.

The decision was made before I knew what I was doing. Using my tattered jacket, I wiped away Jamie's prints and intentionally replaced them with my own, gripping the gun hard. Then I stumbled out of the railcar.

Lieutenant Tullings, Theresa, and other officers were heading our way in a flood, following the gunfire. It was only then I realized that for the last few minutes the gunplay that had resounded moments before had died to nothing.

I later learned Tullings had called in the entire force, on and off duty. Some of the Reds and shiners were in custody. Others had escaped.

When Lieutenant Tullings charged up to me, I handed him the gun, which he slipped into an evidence bag. Remembering Deacon's well-deserved execution, I unholstered my personal firearm and handed that one over too.

"You up for talking?" he asked. "There are a lot of questions that need answered."

I shook my head. "Not now." I was still moving in a daze, but a second thought brought me up short. Instead of turning away, I stopped and said, "I killed Deacon Smotes and Hector

Martinez." More tears threatened to flow at the wave of memory that returned.

Some officers held their breaths at the admission. Others growled, ready to take retribution, but Tullings nodded and motioned with a lowered hand. The disgruntled sounds dwindled. "We have too many bodies. More explanation is needed, Drummond."

"It'll come, but not now," I replied, pulling my shield off my belt, I let it fall to the gravel below. "Not now." Turning, I went to Paige and Jamie, who stood holding one another fifty yards away, embracing over the loss of a loved one.

Chapter 23

Family

March 16th, 2012

I GAVE LIEUTENANT TULLINGS my account of what happened the next morning. Many people demanded that I be brought in, but he was patient. I wasn't going anywhere, and he knew it. When I arrived at the precinct, I was a disheveled mess. But I had come prepared. Paige and I agreed on a story, and we stuck to it.

I had pulled the trigger. I had done what I should have done in the first place. So far as everyone knew, I was the murderer, the traitor, the turncoat. I had killed Hector Martinez, my partner—my brother. Charges were pending, but I was released on my own recognizance. I was officially relieved of duty without pay, which I had expected, and stripped of my pension. A murder confession will do that to your career.

During an open investigation, the stories are normally hidden, held under wraps until the case is closed. That didn't happen. Everyone knew my story within hours of my leaving. As soon as I walked down the front steps of the Tranquil Heights Police Department, word went out. Over the days since, some people came to my home to express their condolences, emotional people who understood what I was going through—or thought they did. But my shame was worse. I was a father, a husband, and a friend. I had failed in all of those duties.

Surprisingly, Jamie seemed to be coping well. His understanding of death far exceeded my own. It probably helped that he could see the victims. They weren't shadows or voices. They existed in the beyond, and he could speak with them. However, his innocent smile had yet to return. For the first time outside of just looks, Jamie reminded me of myself at his age—the troubled youth with jumbled thoughts whirling behind his eyes. After losing his best friend and Hec, I feared he would retreat from the world, but instead he grasped a new one. His visits to the cemetery I'd come to know so well as a teenager became more frequent. He was grieving and healing.

Paige was a different case. She took watching Jamie kill Hector pretty hard, but she coped. It helped that Dillon McCullin was still walking free, so she set to work analyzing evidence from Cameron's brutal murder. She started leaving for work before I even got up and coming home late into the night. Her ER shifts were set aside until she could nail him for murder. If there was anything there, she would find it and Dillon would go away for the rest of his life.

A combined funeral was held for all four officers lost in the shootout at *La Grand Depot*, as it became known. The bastardized attempt at a Spanish name was clearly a tribute to Hector. The church was packed to the rafters; many of the attendants glaring at me. A sermon was given in words I didn't understand. Everyone listened in rapt attention, but I only had eyes for the one solitary closed casket up front and center, sheltered in wreaths and flowers, an American flag lying overtop. What was left of Hector lay at peace—Jamie had said as much—but my shame hung on me like a slick, oily cloak. It weighed down every move and thought I made.

Afterward, we trudged out to escort the dead to their final resting spot. What hurt worse than losing my job was when Tullings informed me that I would not be a pallbearer. It hit home then.

Watching six other men in blue take hold of Hector's casket and walk it out, my disgust at my own inaction grew. If I'd killed him, as he begged me to do, I could stand proud in the knowledge that I'd granted his final wish. No matter the looks or the late-night threats over the phone, I could stand it. Now, each one was another nail in my coffin of shame. Jamie had to pick up the pieces when I'd failed, and Paige had watched it happen.

After I'd watched Hector and three others lowered six feet under, I wandered out into the cemetery I'd come to know and love since I was thirteen. Hands in my pockets, fedora pulled low as I stared at my feet, I meandered through lines of gravestones, down and up hilly aisles, past the fountain with the sandstone rock façade, toward the towering pine tree at the foot of my father's grave. Before I got there, Jamie's sneakered feet came into view.

"Hey, son," I said, my gaze rising. "How are you holdin' up?"

The stern look he returned held more emotion and anger than I expected, but after a second it made sense. Jamie had endured a tremendous amount, and he had crossed a line that could never been uncrossed. He still suffered.

"I came to a conclusion," he said. The words came out stale and emotionless, his anger bubbling just beneath the surface.

I nodded and waited.

He didn't respond.

"What is it?"

"That's just it," he spewed. "You don't give a damn about anyone but yourself, do you? You don't even know what's wrong."

I could tell he was angry, but this accusation caught me unaware. "I don't know what you're talking about, but I certainly care."

"Look at me!" Jamie shouted.

"I am," I said, exhausted and still confused.

"No," Jamie contradicted, "you're staring at me. Don't stare. Don't assume. Look at me. See *me*."

With the gears clicking into place like a rusting clockwork orange, which is about how my mind felt after the events of the week, I finally understood. Taking a moment to look him over, a small smile lifted the edges of my lips. Jaimie wasn't depressed, constantly considering what he had lost. He wasn't just my son, the teenager always asking to take out the car. He wasn't the boy I was striving to raise into a man who valued respect and hard work. He *was* that man. He'd been able to do something I couldn't, an act I failed to do and regretted every second. He wasn't a reflection of my errors, my shame. He was a reflection of me and Paige, our pursuits, our unconditional love. I may have failed once, but there was a lifetime of love between us.

"I see you, Jamie." I closed the distance. Unfolding a decrepit Fluffy from across my arm, I slipped it over his shoulders and then took hold of one. Leaning forward and gazing into his eyes, I whispered, "I see you, Jamie. I truly do. Thank you for reminding me."

His dark eyes were almost black. We looked into each other in that moment, discovering the steam engine driving each of us, the will to live and struggle on, the power to right wrongs. He was the man I'd hoped he would become. The duster didn't fit quite right, but he would fill out in time.

"I love you, Jamie. I always will. You did the right thing."

He nodded and mumbled, "That's what Uncle Hec says, too."

"You did what I couldn't." Clapping him on the shoulder, I pulled him in for a hug. He didn't resist, but his body was tense at first, slackening as I enveloped him.

A sniffle echoed between us and when we pulled apart, a solitary tear streamed down his cheek. "I know," he mumbled. "He's pretty broken up though. Misses Delilah."

My lips pressed together. "I know. I'll try and talk to her."

As the wind picked up in the trees, I could've sworn I heard Hector say, "That'll be somethin' to see."

Jamie smiled and I did too. "Yes it will," I mumbled as reality and doubt set in. His wife still thought I'd killed Hector, and I couldn't change that. "Yes it will."

Taking a moment to clear my thoughts, I asked Jamie, "You mind goin' home with your mom? I've gotta stop off and see Dad for a few minutes. It's been a while."

Jamie nodded. "He's waiting for you."

I chuckled, turned, and headed for the pine tree with the bark worn smooth on one side of its trunk, the solitary friend who kept me company for so many years while I sat at the foot of my father's grave, the place Terry Drummond awaited me—our place.

Chapter 24

Apologies

March 16th, 2012

THE FEW STEPS up to the porch of the Martinez family home felt heavy. My footsteps echoed off the green, paint-flecked boards. Even the weight of the bouquet of white stargazer lilies behind my back seemed to increase with each inch of altitude I gained. The home was cozy, a large weeping willow shrouding the front lawn surrounded by scattered pine trees. Hector's brown cruiser, *The Ocho*, no longer sat in the driveway in front of the garage like I was accustomed to. Yet another reminder of his passing, as though I needed one. The two-story house had a sense of loneliness, its dark, faux shutters adding to the impression. It took a moment to raise my hand at the door.

I'd been rehearsing in the Subaru the whole way over. The mechanics had fixed everything but couldn't quite get the seals right. My thoughts fought over the wind noise filtering into the cabin. I just couldn't decide what to say or how to say it. "I'm sorry" always played a part, but that wasn't enough—not nearly enough.

But should I tell her the truth about Jamie?

Part of me wanted to, to redirect her hatred away because I cared so much for both her and Hector, but it wouldn't be right to put that blame on Jamie. Not right for Hector or Jamie. My son had done so much, endured so much, gone beyond what I could do to help Hec. Hector was as good as any uncle that Jamie could have, blood or no blood. He had given Jamie the gun and taught him to use it when they went out to the firing range, all without my knowledge. It had been the right thing to do. I couldn't fault him for that. It had enabled Jamie to step in when I faltered.

Man up! I told myself.

Jamie had done Hector a service. They both knew it, even if in the eyes of the law and the family it didn't seem so. Delilah wouldn't understand, not now, maybe never. However, some day she might. If that day ever came, I would let her in on the honest truth, how Jamie had saved Hec and her both from immense suffering and anguish. From a slow and torturous death for Hector followed by tons of hospital bills that would have devastated her future financially, all for nothing. More importantly, it was what Hector had wanted. This way gave him peace and an honorable death in the eyes of the department and his family. They wouldn't have to watch his dissolved, decrepit body fall apart while he lay in the hospital, drugged up on morphine and in so much pain that his only solace was death.

With my confidence returned, I knocked.

A caramel-skinned woman with dreadlocks answered, her face distorted and swollen from crying. However, the anger peering out of her brown eyes answered my silent question. She hated me.

I started with the one phrase I knew was appropriate, "I'm sorry."

"The hell you're sorry!" she spat back. "You go and kill my husband and now you come back to say, 'I'm sorry'?" she mimicked sarcastically. "I've half a mind to beat you black-and-blue, but that would be too good for you, Alex Drummond. Losin' your shield's the least you deserve."

Holding a hand up to slow her verbal assault, I said, "Please let me explain, Delilah."

She came to a stuttering stop, waiting. However, her eyes brooked no nonsense.

In my line of work, Hector and I had made numerous house calls to deliver unsavory news, from imprisonment to death announcements, but this was far different. Uncertain what to do next, I revealed the flowers, an awkward smile plastered to my face as though they would somehow make this easier.

"Oh no, you didn't!" she shouted, stepping back and trying to slam the door, as though touching them would make Hector's death more real.

I slid the tip of my boot just inside the door, and it came to an abrupt halt, her hand still pressing it closed in her fury. "You don't have to take the flowers. I can't imagine how hard this is for you, and if you need to blame someone, by all means blame me. Please, just let me say my piece. Just listen for two minutes," I pleaded.

Her extended arm relaxed a minute later, and she slumped against the door, her face visible through the crack as her forehead rested against the inner wall. A sob escaped her lips.

"There's nothin' I can say that will make what I did right," I began, "but I did it for Hector. He wanted…" I cleared my throat as the memory of his scratchy words echoed through my mind. "He begged me to do it."

Tears streamed down Delilah's cheeks. She knew it had been bad. I had identified the body before other officers could even approach her about it. The funeral had been a closed casket because no amount of makeup could have hidden the horrendous damage the Alkaline Hydrolysis system had wreaked on Hector's skin and body. She hadn't seen him since he left that morning for work.

Thinking of Jamie, I added, "Only a true friend—family—could have made that call. I'll suffer the consequences for it, and you can hate me for the rest of our lives. I understand. It's fine. I took him from you, but just know that I had no real choice. I'll miss that man till my dying day. Hec was my friend, my brother, and nothin' will ever change that."

Turning with downcast eyes, I let the door shut and set the flowers on the porch. There was nothing more to be said. Delilah was in mourning; the love of her life gone without a final good-bye. Hector had taken a small part of all of us with him when he departed this Earth.

About the Author

Weston Kincade writes fantasy, paranormal, and horror novels that stretch the boundaries of imagination, and often genres. His current series include the A Life of Death trilogy and the Priors. Weston's short stories have been published in Alucard Press' "50 Shades of Slay," Kevin J. Kennedy's bestselling "Christmas Horror" and "Easter Horror," and other anthologies. He is a member of the Horror Writer's Association (HWA) and helps invest in future writers while teaching English. In his spare time Weston enjoys spending time with his wife and Maine Coon cat, Hermes, who talks so much he must speak for the Gods.

For up-to-date promotions and information on new releases, sign up for the latest news here: https://kincadefiction.blogspot.com.

As a special bonus, the first three stories in *Strange Circumstances*, a short story collection I co-wrote, are included below so carry on. Happy reading!

Tempt fate. Destroy destiny. Demand retribution.

If you like delightfully dark diversions from reality, stories strange and wonderful that leave you begging for more, Strange Circumstances is the collection for you. The future is a gamble. Care to place a bet on yours?

Sign up to read Strange Circumstances FREE today.

http://strangecircumstances.gr8.com

Strange Circumstances

A Magic Short Fiction Collection

BY

WESTON KINCADE,

DAVID CHRISLEY,

AND

MARSHALL J. STEPHENS

(Excerpt)

Part One - Short Stories:

The question of fate goes back beyond written record, and everyone finds themselves considering mortality at times. But few people are actually challenged to discover the extents to which fate and their own desires can take them. How far does your sanity stretch?

These stories are an attempt to open your eyes and minds to the possibilities, however unlikely, that even you might wind up on the long end of a short chain or playing a hand of cards with death, your life hanging in the balance. Explore the unknown in the upcoming stories, and above all, enjoy the ride.

Undetermined Fate

The darkness parted and my mind whirled back to life. *What happened? Where the hell am I?*

A man's deep, sinuous voice chuckled. "Welcome to Limbo, Travis. Care to make a wager?" His voice was calm but confident, and his tone held experience.

Wager, what do I have to bet? In answer to my unspoken question, three octagonal chips glowed blue atop a black, marble table. Faint swirls of gray were embedded in the tabletop and reflected the light, but not far. An inky fog dimmed everything within six inches, and an aching chill seeped through my jeans from the matching bench. Picking up one of the chips, a silver lightning bolt gleamed fiercely across its face.

The sound of fabric sweeping over the polished marble filtered through the air, and an arm extended from the man's direction. His body was a black silhouette in the misty existence, but his visible hand was dark, almost chocolate, with well-manicured fingers. A silver band adorned his thumb, and a stamped hourglass was etched onto the ring's surface. It sprang to life once his hand stopped, and the glass rotated before my eyes. Miniscule grains of silver sand began their journey south. He paused a moment, allowing me to take it all in. Beneath his fingers were three sparkling cards, face down, with scroll work reminiscent of Greek artistry. His hand was mere inches away and revealed a white sleeve that stopped at his forearm. The cloth flowed from him with enough room to encompass a bowling ball, and an identical golden pattern stitched its way around the edge.

When the man withdrew, I slid the cards from the table. They were more like tarot than the playing cards I'd grown accustomed to. Memories flashed before me, revealing the disparity; many nights spent at Atlantic City casinos. The cards depicted pantomiming jesters and glistened in stark contrast to the shadowed world I'd appeared in. One pleaded to me with waving arms as though beckoning me forward. On the second, the jester fled with eyes cast back over his shoulder, while the third was absent of movement. The archaic comedian instead stood with arms crossed and feet spread wide as though exercising. However, his face was set in consternation with eyes that bored into mine. I shuddered, then slid the card's gleaming outline behind the others and looked away.

Something dimly lit the edges of my new world with gray morning rays. Dark shapes were silhouetted at the edge of my murky vision, much like the man who dealt the cards. Shadowed columns were spaced every couple feet around the small area. It was as though we were at the center of an ancient Greek courtyard, but the air held death in its permeating silence. The atmosphere was completed by the dank smell of stagnation. I reached out to touch the moving shapes, but felt nothing more than dense condensation.

"Come on, make a bet," urged a tinny voice to my right. "I ain't got all night."

"Why, you have all the time imaginable, Everett," replied the white-robed man. There was a hint of laughter in his serene voice, as though he knew the punch line to a comedy we were unknowingly acting out. Everett's figure folded his arms with a harrumph.

"I'll bet this," I muttered, trying to find my voice. The mist muffled its vacant echo, as though no walls were near enough for comfort. I slid the chip to the center of the table with feigned confidence.

"That's one favor wagered," added the older man like a lackluster sports announcer. "Passion, yes, you won't need that favor anymore. So what did you do with this Passion? Just one instance from your life?"

Favor? I wondered, but the thought was fleeting. *What is this?* My mind jogged through the dark recesses within, but came up empty. I stuttered over something to say before seizing an idea. "Y-y-yes, once, I cared for a –"

"You lie!" The dark man interrupted. "You never cared for anything more than yourself."

My mouth hung wide. He was right. I could barely remember my past, but the certainty of his words was irrefutable. Before I could utter a response, he swept the glowing chit off the table and into a bag. It clattered against others in a growing collection. His silhouetted face turned to a long-haired, slender form to my left and resumed his earlier calm.

"And what will you wager, Lauren?"

A feminine voice with breathy undertones rasped, "What favor do you ask of me?"

What happened to her?

I couldn't take my eyes from her slim outline. So far as I could tell, she appeared to be at her peak. She was fit and had a frame that would have put any Bond movie-intro to shame. Something clicked in the back of my mind like a switch.

A woman much like her sat bound and gagged before me, but in vivid detail; a checkered, blue bandana was tied around her head, holding her mouth open like a horse's bit. It matched the ribbon in her brunette hair. My fingers encircled the soft flesh of her neck. Her eyes widened into pleading orbs. Thick, red blood flowed from where the jugular had been severed and streamed over my fingers.

Did I do that? I couldn't remember, and no answer came. Instead, the smell and sight became strangely alluring... intoxicating even. It was a feeling I could drown in.

"Whichever," the elderly man answered with a wave of his hand, pulling me from the vision. "It won't matter. You will use every favor you've earned in life."

I peered down at my two remaining chips, or favors, as he called them. My heart began beating like a speed-infused bass drum. "Wait! What about me?"

The old man continued as though he hadn't heard. I screamed for him to wait, but he only crooked a finger in my direction. The deathly mist collected around me, obscuring my vision, and absorbed my words.

"Then, here is my Dedication," she whispered and slid a chip infused with a silver swirl across the table.

A low chuckle came from our Dealer then. "You are most certainly dedicated, but perhaps if it were Loyalty instead, you wouldn't be here."

He picked up the favor and flipped it into the air toward his bag. I couldn't take my eyes from the spinning coin; its whirling flight seemed to take an eternity. It expanded in my vision and I closed my eyes to break the link. I opened them onto a scene I couldn't control.

A young woman's hands diligently copied notes, my eyes (no, it was her eyes) strayed up to the professor. Each time, I could feel a blush rising in her cheeks. Her hand had a wedding ring on it, as did his. They didn't match. The scene blurred, and I found myself in an office, my inbox piled high. A man's voice broke in behind me, "You are such a hard worker, but you don't have to be." Something else was added to my inbox, a wrapped condom dropped on the pile. I watched as his broad shoulders and silver hair disappeared into the office at the end of the hall. I picked up the condom and followed.

The scene changed again, this time to a club.

It was dark and smoky. Latex-clad servers weaved between groups of customers. I marveled at the number of suits rubbing

elbows with the denizens of a world I thought only existed in movies.
I didn't particularly like the man whose arm I was holding, but he
was the most familiar thing there. I clung to him like a buoy in
stormy seas. A girl has to do whatever it takes to get ahead in the
corporate world, and while I "worked" late, my husband sat at home
spending my paycheck. I loved him, but he lacked ambition. In the
back of the club, we were welcomed to a table by a man that looked
very familiar, but I couldn't place him. Mid-thirties, broad-
shouldered, short but built well. An intense leer beamed from behind
clear, blue eyes. He and my boss shook hands, "Travis, it's so good to
see you again. I'd like you to meet Lauren."

The vision faltered. That was me. I began to shake. I wanted to
vomit. I didn't remember that, but she did. The coin finished its
slow arc and joined the others.

"Are you all right, Travis? It is just a game after all. That is what
you always used to tell everyone." The dark man's words twisted
in my gut.

"Can we please just get on with this? I have other things to do,
and more important people to do them with." Everett's voice was
almost pleading. He seemed on the verge of tears. I wondered what
he saw as Lauren's dedication took its slow journey through the
darkening mist. He was still hard to make out. He looked slender
and tall, but his clothing was dark and drew his lines out into the
shadows. He slouched in on himself, minimizing what was
probably an impressive six-foot-plus height. I studied him, hoping
to get some insight into whom he might be. With Lauren I got that

image, but with him it just gave me a headache. Or, more accurately, I felt something press into the back of my skull. I reached back to find nothing, but every time I looked at him, the pressure returned. He scared me more than this place, the fog, and the living cards in my hand.

"Of course we can, Everett," The Dealer intoned. "We're waiting on your bet. What will you wager?"

He looked down at his cards and paled a bit more in the dim light. "I have only one favor to bet with, so it must be my Patience."

"Everyone in then?" The Dealer asked. I heard the familiar flip, flip as The Dealer's card came off the deck and onto the table. The Dealer put it down with such force that a puff of air from beneath pushed aside the mist so that its face was clear.

It was a boy sitting on the floor with a top. The look on his face was radiant with delight.

From one side, Everett drew in a breath that even the most rookie poker player would know. It meant that he liked what he saw. No sound came from Lauren, no hint of her take on the situation.

"Choose," The Dealer said.

"How does this work?" I asked. "What are the rules?"

The Dealer said, "That's not how it works here. You have to learn as you go. But don't worry just yet. It is Everett's turn. Watch and learn for once, Travis."

My cheeks burned like they did in Catholic school.

Catholic School. I went to Catholic school! Joy came with the memory, joy at the fact that I remembered something, anything. It faded as soon as I realized that it helped me not one bit.

Everett threw down a card from the two in front of him with a snort of contempt. Lauren did the same, though she had three cards, the same as I did. I lifted up mine and guessed. I chose the one looking over his shoulder. It felt like the cautious bet.

As I pushed it forward, I felt it stick to the table like it had been put there with superglue.

The dealer passed his hands over the cards we played. The table vibrated, and I felt like I was at the top of a roller coaster.

"Now," The Dealer said. "We reveal."

The cards flipped over without anyone touching them, slamming onto the table like a gavel on the judge's bench.

Everett said, "Gotcha."

I looked at his card and found it was a figure with beckoning arms, like mine, except where I had a jester, Everett's card bore a king in a tarnished crown and tattered robes.

The dealer said, "The Future against Joy?"

"I'll be happy to get out of here, won't I?" asked Everett.

The Dealer said, "Maybe so. Maybe not. No matter. You win."

Everett sat back. I could feel the smugness rolling off of him. Maybe a lucky streak was what made the damn mist around us.

"Now you, Travis."

"Failure," The Dealer said flatly. "You have no innocent Joy in your past."

"What?" I said in confusion. Before the word was past my lips, I felt the bottom drop out from under me.

Another dream. I was in the back of a car... no, a limousine. The taste of high-quality gin was on my lips. Someone leaned up against me, and we laughed, nearly spilling our drinks. It was a woman with a familiar, unforgettable figure, and she was drinking champagne. I knew it was her third, and the first two went down in under three minutes.

Her weight against my arm was a welcome thing. I could see down her blouse, but not enough. We weren't alone, but I paid little attention to the other person in the compartment. I wanted this woman like a schoolboy wants ice cream. And for some reason, I knew I'd likely have her.

"Another round," someone said. The there and here mixed and I didn't know if they were talking about the game or booze. I wanted to go back to the scene in the car. I wanted to feel like she was making me feel. I wanted simply to want something that much again.

But I couldn't. The knowledge filled me from the front of my skull to my gut. I might never feel that again if I didn't win this damn game.

I felt the bench under me and looked around the table, still unable to make out anything clearly that wasn't the cards. I felt hollow.

I looked over at Lauren's card. It was the past. I hadn't heard whether that meant she won or lost.

The Dealer held up something, and the mists parted so I could see it. It was a die. There were images on the side of it in place of the dots, and as he rolled it across his fingertips, I could see that there were hexagons, rectangles, and two other figures that I couldn't make out.

"The roll," he said and let the die fall to the table.

Octagon.

"Winners receive a Favor," The Dealer said. "Losers forfeit an additional Favor."

The cards we had played all went up in little flashes of blue flame. I heard Everett chuckle, a cruel and malicious sound.

"The past?" he said. "Dumbass. You can't win back the past."

I was seriously starting to hate that guy.

I looked down and saw that my chips had been reduced to one chip. I started to ask The Dealer, "What gives?" but he already had something to say. "You lost Independence. My choice. They weren't doing you much good anyway."

I felt cold to my toes.

"Don't worry, Travis," The Dealer said. "You've got one more Favor: Cruelty. It's done you well in the past, hasn't it?"

I said, "Cruelty is a favor?"

"For a priest, no. For a butcher, yes," the old man's voice intoned. "You were no priest. Now, place your bets. This next round could be important for you."

I bit my tongue and slid my last chip forward.

Everett said, "Let's go with Cunning this time." He flipped the chip he'd won last round at The Dealer. I looked at it, trying to peer into it intentionally this time. It worked.

I watched as a woman made out with me on a couch. It was the woman from the car, I knew. She was even more tipsy, and viewing the scene in the third person, I wanted her as myself and as the man whose eyes I was borrowing. But as the latter of the two, I knew she was doing a job. She was the bait, the kind a high roller would go for, window dressing for a game with the highest of stakes.

My eyes looked toward me and said, "So how long till your girl shows up with the other boys?"

I heard Everett's voice lie, saying, "About an hour. You've got time. Let me give you kids some space."

I sneered, left the room, and waited for the girl to slip a mickey into the other Travis's drink.

I was back at the card table as soon as the doors closed. The transition was instantaneous, and it was Lauren's turn to bet.

The Dealer asked, "What'll it be?"

"Remorse," Lauren replied.

She looked down at her chips; she had five left. I didn't know if that was good or bad for me. The only thing I could do was play the game.

The Dealer flipped his card. This time it revealed a man on one knee accepting a crown on his head, his eyes downcast.

I looked at my cards. The still one felt wrong. If over-the-shoulder was the Past and the other moving one was the future, then the still one was probably the Present. And my Present right then didn't feel much like I was being crowned. I played the Future.

Everett smacked down the present. Lauren played the Future, her card like mine but with an innocent maiden in place of the jester. The table's faint light illuminated her hands as she played the card, slender and graceful like the rest of her. It didn't take a photographic memory to tell me it was the same Lauren I'd been with on the couch, the one who tried to drug me.

The details were coming back like a dream that I didn't want to remember.

The Dealer said to Everett, "You fail."

"But I'm winning!" he said.

"No," The Dealer said. "You're not. You've never accepted anything with Humility."

I looked over at Everett. The mist seemed to part before his fear. His eyes widened with panic. But he was searching for a way to win.

The Dealer ignored him and said, "Travis, you win a hand. You too, Lauren. Well done. And now... the die."

I watched it tumble onto the table and clatter to a conclusion. Octagon.

"A Favor again," The Dealer said. "That means you're out, Everett."

Everett paled, as though the mists wanted us to see the failure. Then he was gone, drawn back into the shadows before he could scream. If I'd blinked, I'd have missed it.

I looked down at my chips. I was back to a set of three. She had six. We both had one card left, the Present.

"Place your bets," The Dealer said.

I said, "Passion."

Lauren rasped, "Regret, one more time."

The Dealer asked her, "Haven't you had enough?"

Lauren leaned forward. The light cast long shadows across her face, revealing beauty and contempt. She snapped, "Just deal."

The Dealer replied, "So be it."

Lauren slid the chip over. In it, I again saw things as they once were.

At least this time I was an earlier version of myself. *I sniffed the gin and tonic in my hand, then looked back at the door the men disappeared through. Lauren's pulse quickened under my hand. She'd botched it. I shook my head and lunged forward. The struggle was brief, and soon I had Lauren's wrists tied to the chair.*

I moaned and grunted as I bound and gagged her body, making a good show of it. Anyone waiting to rob me at the door would be convinced that all they'd have to do is wait for the afterglow, and I'd be easy pickins.

Lauren screamed against the gag when I pulled the nickel-plated revolver from the holster on my ankle. She fought against the phone cord binding her wrists, her eyes following me as I hid. I screamed, "Oh god, oh god," as though I were close to the end and it was about to be someone's payday.

Everett burst in, gun drawn. When he saw Lauren tied up, he stopped and looked to his side, where I stood with my pistol leveled, less than ten feet away. But it was too late.

Lauren's wrists slipped free. She jumped in the middle, her cry of "Wait!" swallowed by a pair of gunshots. One sped over her shoulder and caught me in the chest as Everett maneuvered to use her as a shield. The other punched through Lauren's belly, out the back, and into Everett's side.

I opened my eyes.

"There's not room for all three of you tonight," The Dealer said. "Do you understand the stakes now?"

"Oh yeah. I get it."

"Then let's play," The Dealer continued.

His card was a man standing on a cliff, raising a fist to the world and screaming. I threw down my card. Lauren did likewise.

"Defiance," The Dealer said. "The Present certainly holds that for both of you."

The die came up on a rectangle this time. "You get back a card. Choose, the Past or the Future?"

"I didn't think you could get the Past back," I interrupted.

"Everett said that," The Dealer replied. "Was he ever running the game, though?"

"I guess not. I'll take it." I looked at Lauren, enjoying the game at last. The mist had parted, and I could see her clearly now. Her face was stained with tears. She had five chips again to my two. And she didn't look happy to be ahead.

She mumbled, "I'll take the Future."

"All right," The Dealer said. The cards appeared. "Bets?"

My gaze lingered on Lauren. Her horror and anguish flowed off her in waves. It was like I was still in her head. Her husband would never remember her as they met, only as she was found. Her last act was to protect a man who disgusted her, but who she didn't think should die.

The fun of the game seemed to plummet through an invisible hole, leaving the room cold and desolate.

Turning to The Dealer, I said, "Let's make this interesting. Winner take all."

"Should she agree...?" The Dealer responded, as though the idea were certainly an interesting one.

"I agree," Lauren interjected. "Let's get this over with. I'm tired of playing your game."

"So be it," The Dealer said. The tumblers to a lock I couldn't see fell into place.

The card came up with a picture of a newborn. Life.

Lauren started to cry.

The Dealer looked at me and said, "So... the past."

I said, "Yeah."

"In order for her to win, you have to lose. You can't both win."

"I know," I muttered solemnly.

"So," he said. "Do you understand the rules now?"

"Yeah," I answered.

"And did you win?" he asked.

"No."

"What?" Lauren shouted. "What does that mean?"

"It means I forgive you." My chips slid across the table, merging with hers. My remaining card disappeared in a puff of smoke. The eight chips came together in a ring. The Dealer reached out and took it, then threw it between us. It hung in the air for a moment and stretched to become a door.

I looked at Lauren, her face confused but the spark of hope back in her eyes. "Go. I'll settle up here. Good game."

She stood and said, "I'm sorry."

"I know. Go," I continued, ushering her toward the door.

She stepped through and away the door went.

It was just me and The Dealer now. He regarded his ring. Only a few grains remained in the upper part of the hourglass.

"So you lost," he said. "You agreed that life was in her future, not yours."

"I did."

"One problem," The Dealer replied. "To lose means you had to be wrong."

"Is that how it works?"

"Yes." The table cracked. His ring cracked. Suddenly, it was like I was falling, the columns and marble table flew past, the room spun, and air whooshed past my ears. Then, I gasped as someone yelled, "Clear!"

Tubes streamed out of my nose and arms. When I pried my eyes open, I glimpsed them wheeling Lauren out on a stretcher.

She looked back at me before disappearing through the door. A paramedic was zipping Everett's body up in a black body bag.

I wasn't sure what fate had in store for me from here on. But I was certain of one thing. I'd just broken even.

Roots

The train car shuddered and the wheels squealed, interrupting Adrianna as she pecked at her laptop keyboard. The great beast trundling over the rails couldn't stop on a dime, and she watched as the moonlit trees outside her window slowed. Groans escaped the mouths of the occupants around her, and a frizzy-haired woman in front of Adrianna panicked, twisting in her seat in an effort to match the chaos nested on her head.

"Wha-what was that?" the woman stammered searching the passenger car for the demon that had to be descending on them.

Adrianna sighed. "Just the brakes. I'm sure it's nothin'."

But was it? Trains didn't stop like that for raccoons or even cows: at least not that she knew of. A calm, bass voice echoed from the speakers overhead. "Passengers of train 30, we've made an emergency stop, but there is nothing to fear. We will soon be back on course. Again, I apologize for our earlier two-hour delay. At this time, it doesn't appear that we will be any later, but we'll keep you posted. Please return to your seats and get some rest."

The speaker clicked off, and muttering instantly flooded the passenger car. The attempt to assuage their fears had piqued Adrianna's curiosity, and it seemed she wasn't alone. Before long, most of the train's occupants resumed their earlier tasks: pecking at mp3-players and computers, resting, or reading books and e-readers. They were too engrossed in their own lives to let the temporary delay distract them. The frazzled woman was the only other occupant that seemed even mildly concerned.

"What do you think happened?" she whispered, peering through the headrests in front of Adrianna. "Do you think it's terrorists?"

"Oh, God! Get real, lady," snapped a young man in khaki shorts and a T-shirt after removing his earbuds. Adrianna hadn't heard him say a word since they left, but now she wished he'd kept his mouth shut. "Look," he continued, "we aren't even in Toledo anymore. We're out in God's country now, where the mountain folk'll introduce themselves by saying, 'You gotta purdy mouth'. Terrorists would run screaming if they saw this place. There's no way this is an attack." He snubbed the frantic woman with an upraised nose and put his earbuds back in, refusing to look anywhere but out the window.

The woman's hair shook as she huddled into her seat.

Thanks for nothin'! Adrianna wanted to scream. *Can't you tell she's scared?* He wouldn't have heard anyway, with the drum and guitar solos screaming so loudly she could discern the band from two seats away. *ZZ Top... even jerks can have good taste.* She'd been thankful that no one had booked the seat between them, but now she was having second thoughts. Anyone would've been better than the sobbing woman and this insolent prick. She had to get out of there. Adrianna slapped her laptop shut and rose.

"Ma'am, please take your seat," warned a uniformed woman from the end of the train car.

Adrianna glanced back at the two seated around her and the bald man with the squared jaw sitting next to the frantic woman. He seemed to be the only one in their section also attempting escape, but rather into a magazine held mere inches from his face. Her mind raced, searching for an excuse. "I-I have to go to the bathroom. I can't wait."

Before the train employee could say more, Adrianna dashed past and into the next florescent-lit car. It was much the same as hers, and she continued down the aisle past kids, college students like herself, and people waiting to return to their lives. The next one was the same, but as she reached the last passenger car, the door opened into darkness blacker than the world outside. The chatter of people died as the door sealed behind her. No moon shone through the car windows… in fact, there seemed to be none in the closed room. But as her eyes adjusted, a subtle, jagged line of green glowed in the center of the room, trekking up to eye level.

What in the world? Adrianna stepped closer. Something crunched beneath her tennis shoe and she looked for the source, but the bare scar of light didn't reach her feet. Taking a deep breath, she neared the glow, suppressing her imagination at each crunch underfoot. As she approached, the light cast an eerie glow on the floor of the car, but what she found made no sense. Dead leaves and twigs littered the ground as though she'd stepped deep into the heart of a forest.

That's not supposed to be here. Her eyes returned to the base of the light. It was coming from something. Kneeling down, she ran a hand over the enormous roots running between her feet. The scar of glowing light was seeping from inside a huge tree. Her hand and eyes climbed the rough texture until they came upon a slick surface, slightly curved. Adrianna looked closer, but leaped back as the outline of a fireman's helmet was illuminated by the growing glow. The gruesome scar branched and grew at her touch, defining the curves of a man's face below the helmet. His body and uniform were encased in the tree as though it had grown around him. Adrianna touched his cheek with gentle fingers. The breath she'd been holding hissed past her lips. His skin was cold, but still tender. At the front of his burnished, red helmet stood a large number seven, bordered by the words 'Insurance' and 'FDNY' above and below.

Where did this come from, and how did the tree grow around him so quickly?

Before she could voice the question, a queer voice croaked from the other side of the tree, "That man's been here for the last hundred years, but you, my dear, are new."

Adrianna's head swiveled left and right like the frazzled woman's had earlier, but in this darkness there was nothing to see beyond the outlined man and leafless tree. "Where am I? How'd I get here?"

"Here?" repeated the guttural voice. "You're still on train 30, the express from Toledo to DC."

"But... it can't be. Did you stop the train?"

"Stop... start, the train's movement means nothing to us."

"Us?" asked Adrianna.

"Yes," a croaking voice behind her said. Adrianna felt a puff of cold breath on the back of her neck with each word. "We are many. Legion. We live in the space between breaths and on the side of the door you cannot see. We vacation in your nightmares and fill our pantry with the thoughts that you had just a second ago, but then blink and forget."

"Stop," the voice from the impossible tree said. "We need not offer our full honorifics here, my brother. Be more kind to our guest."

A wicked and menacing chuckle came from the one behind her. "As you wish."

Adrianna felt her feet lift and warm furs curve around her legs and back, a chair made of some living and breathing thing supporting her in space. She could feel it rise and fall, feel a heartbeat against her back.

The second voice was circling her now. Adrianna could see him move, though couldn't make out the details of his form. She asked, "Is there something I can do for you? Because if not, I'd really like to stop having this acid trip and get back to my seat."

Dozens of tiny voices tittered and jeered in the darkness. It became very hard to control her breathing.

"Your mind is your own," the first voice said. "You're just not asking the right questions."

"What questions do I need to ask?" Adrianna replied.

"We cannot tell you."

"Then why did you bring me here?"

"Ah," the second voice said. "She found one. Took her long enough."

The voice behind the tree interjected, "That's enough of that. Now, girl, what makes you assume we brought you here? You were the one who walked and you were the one who arrived. Why do you think you did not choose your own course?"

"Because…" she began. But she realized she didn't have any follow up to that.

"Dark," the second voice said. "Rich."

"What?" Adrianna asked. She'd lost track of him, though his footfalls were heavy. Her eyes had begun to adjust to the pitch darkness. More shapes were appearing in the tree. There was a man in a suit higher in the limbs; she had mistaken his outstretched arms for branches. Just above him was a woman, her hair now like straw, shaking gently.

"Your name," the second one said, "Adrianna. That's what it means."

"Good to know," she muttered. She was ashamed at how frightened it sounded. "Who the hell are you?"

"And another," the voice from behind the tree said. "We're teachers, merchants that deal in wisdom, present among many cultures in many times."

"Sounds good." A nervous smile came to her lips.

The second one asked, "Really? Wisdom comes at a price. That's why so few have it, you know. We don't give it away for free."

"Is that why I'm here?" Adrianna was trying not to let the fear crack in her voice. This would all make sense soon, she was sure of it. "You're going to teach me some of this terrible wisdom?"

"And at last," the first voice, the voice in the tree, said. "You've asked the best question. You're here because you wanted to be. And we will teach you, but only time will tell if it's wisdom."

"I… I didn't want to come here," Adrianna protested.

There was a hand on either side of her living seat. She could see the sharp nails at the ends of the furry fingers. Heavy breaths tickled her ear; puffs of air that she was sure were making their way past sharp fangs.

The second one hissed, "Yes, you did. We do that which we wish, even when we don't think we have a choice. A man jumping out of a burning building might not want to fall and go splat, but he wants to avoid burning more. And you soon will have a choice."

"Did they get a choice?" she asked, pointing at the tree.

"They did," the voice in the tree replied. "The same as you now have."

"This tree is 'THE' tree of legend. You Christians call it the Tree of Knowledge. The Norse called it Yggdrasil. It is Samoyed and axis mundi. And we are the Greeks' Kallikantzaroi, though we tend the tree, not saw at it the way we were portrayed in those times." The hissing voice stopped for a moment. After a long breath that seemed to stretch for days, he continued. "Every so often, someone is born in possession of something the Tree is missing. We watch them grow. If that thing is still a part of them by the time they are mature enough for the choice, we find them. In you is something rich and dark to be added to the Tree."

The first voice interjected, "The choice is... do you add yourself to the Tree and help guide humanity in its cosmic journey? Or, do you deny us and wake up in your train seat believing what you will of this encounter?"

"A life forever in the Tree or my life..." Adrianna mused. "There is always another choice. I am familiar with these stories. There must be a way to guide humanity, add to the Tree, and still live my life."

"In all these centuries, you are the first to ask. You can challenge me for a seed." The owner of the second hissing voice dropped from the branches to bow before her. A small, gnarled creature, he looked as though he were half sculpted from lumps of mismatched clay. "If you win, you remember everything and get a seed to plant near your heart so that it may guide you, and you may teach it. If you lose, you become part of the Tree. Not as they are, but buried in the roots so that your strength of will can nourish the Tree as your soul adds to its purpose."

"Has no one before gotten a seed?"

"There have been those that were so bright at birth that they were given a seed. They were visionaries, the best at what they chose to do." Voice one's tone changed and became melancholy. "It has been many generations since we have found a child worthy of one."

"What is the challenge?"

"You said you know the stories. The test is always a riddle challenge. And by rule, the challenge begins. What falls without breaking and breaks without falling?" There was a crooked smirk on the goblin's face as he let fly with the first riddle.

"Night and Day. But I didn't accept," Adrianna protested.

Voice one whispered, "You didn't have to. You laid the challenge."

"Alright. How many sides does a circle have?"

"Two. Inside and outside. Name three consecutive days without using the words Sunday, Monday, Tuesday, Wednesday, Thursday, Friday, or Saturday."

"Yesterday, Today, and Tomorrow. How many months have 28 days?"

"All of them. How far can a man walk into the woods?" The smirk became a full-fledged smile on the imp's face.

"Halfway, the other half he's walking out. A mother has seven children, half of them are boys. How is this possible?"

"They are all boys. Think of words ending in –gry. In the English language there are three of them. 'Angry' and 'Hungry' are two. What is the third word?" He straightened up, eyes glowing with obvious confidence in his superiority.

Adrianna shook her head. "You told it wrong. Most people do. The way you told it has no answer, as there are five words in

English that end in –gry. It's just that three of them aren't used anymore. The riddle is supposed to go… Think of words that end in –gry. 'Angry' and 'Hungry' are two of them. In the English language there are three words. What's the third?"

Voice quivering, the little man replied, "That one has no answer either. We will throw them both out."

"But mine has an answer, 'Language'. The rest of it is misdirection. The riddle is 'In the English language there are three words. What is the third?' The: one. English: two. Language: three."

The creature stopped, bowed, and held out a seed. "Plant it well."

"I will." Adrianna tipped back her head and swallowed the seed. On the way back to her seat, the train started again. New hope for the day took root in her breast along with a small sapling of the 'Tree'.

Falling

There's a sharp ping of metal snapping, and then John's stomach lurches into his throat. If that isn't enough to tell him he is falling, the roar of wind rushing past his ears confirms it. That most deafening of white noises is impossible to disguise if you've ever been skydiving. The falling isn't John's issue. He can't see. He's certain there is no blindfold, and there isn't the pain he would associate with losing his eyes. So, what did she do to him?

John's been falling a very long time… an impossibly long time. HALO jumps don't take hours. Falling doesn't leave time for reflection. He has time for reflection. Who is he, really? How did he get here? How does he get out? Something about the first question frightens him. Not ready for that sort of introspection, John moves to the second.

The badge said Ian Masters, as did the smooth, looping signature in the log book. The security was tight, but he was well prepared. His lockpicks were Kevlar; his boot knife was ceramic. His smart-phone was far smarter than any agency would anticipate. His team was good. They had buried a code breaker and a satellite uplink in his phone; that way even if he couldn't get out, the information could. Industrial espionage is a very profitable career, and he had exceeded the life-expectancy of a spy by at least a decade. This would be his last job. Never mind that he had said that after the last three. The silver creeping in at his temples and the amount of time needed for recovery after the last job convinced him that it was time to retire.

John shakes his head. *That's not relevant.* What happened after he got past security?

Ian was early for his meeting and was left to wait in the public areas of the Dawbry Corp tower. The large, open area was littered with propaganda and awards meant to breed goodwill in visitors regardless of what had led them there. The news had been harping on unproven claims that Dawbry was poisoning the land, causing hideous mutations. Families were clogging the phone lines looking for spouses and fathers that went to work one day and never came home. The agency wanted an inside view of the tower, and Ian was the best; good enough to know that in the age of computers, the skeletons in the closet were easiest found at the servers, not the offices. The servers had incredible net-based security. One of the agency hackers was sent to a psych-ward after trying to crack it. But the physical security was usually very lax. The alarm on the fire door was easy to disable. The lock on the basement was complex, but Ian was better. There wasn't any human security down there, and to his surprise, Ian didn't see any automated security either. He found an access point to the server and connected his phone. It would take some time, so he decided to look around. Near the back of the basement was something putrid.

It smelled like a mixture of a slaughterhouse and a sewer. The source of the stench was a large tube coming from the back of one of the servers and going into the floor.

Click. No time for further investigation, someone was there. A sultry woman's voice called out, "It's time for your meeting, Mr. Masters."

The panic came instantly. Ian locked it down as fast. How could she know he was in this room? No one had seen him. There'd been no cameras.

Wait... he'd *seen* no cameras. None were on the layout he'd gotten from his contact. None of that meant they weren't there. *Stupid, old man.*

"My employer is eager to meet you," said the woman, "but he won't tolerate any dawdling. Leave your phone and let it do whatever it needs to. You can get it on your way out."

Ian ran through the possibilities. If this was a bluff, there would be security. He'd hear them. They wouldn't be polite. They'd be enumerating which of his major organs they were going to pierce with bullets. So she was probably telling the truth.

Don't pause. Act. Pausing gets you killed. Jump through the window. Worry about the landing in the air. Again age--wisdom some might say--convinced him otherwise.

Ian didn't say a word, but came out from his hiding space. The woman was dressed in a suit: grey, severe, just enough slit in the skirt to let you know that she was a distraction. Her expression was pleasant but unreadable. She stood waiting, hands in front of her, clasped palm to palm.

Ian stepped up and gestured. She smiled, nodded, and led the way.

Where a blank, concrete wall had been, there was now an opening to an elevator. She stood and let him enter first, then positioned herself like a proper distraction should, bent over in front of him to press the lower of the two unmarked buttons.

Ian kept his eyes up, off her impossibly toned ass. *Stay sharp. Look for the angle.* This had to be an interview. It wouldn't be the first time that the original job had just been a test, a smokescreen for the real deal. *Fine. Agree to the terms. Do the work. Go along with whatever they ask until you can get your depth. Once you understand what's going on, take the control back.*

It was always about control. They had it for the moment. That moment wouldn't last.

He laughed thinking about that moment. He's anything but in control now. Maybe he never was. Maybe his whole life was just a series of illusions, a set of dominos that he thought he could stop when he wanted to. Espionage is the business of lies; why did he ever think he knew the truth?

Stupid, old man.

The fall will kill him if he actually hits the ground. Stupid... Stupid. What got him here? He hadn't leapt out the window. What came later?

The doors slid open, and Ian was surprised to find a hallway chiseled from stone stretching so far he thought the corridor might span the earth's width. Yellow, phosphorescent lights were staggered the length of it. Striations in the rock followed him in waves. The woman led him down its length, passing under light after light. She walked with a knowing stride, elegant and confident in her form-fitting skirt. It was hypnotic and graceful, like she belonged in the sea, swaying back and forth. The woman glanced over her shoulder, and a knowing grin touched her lips before she turned away.

Ian tore his gaze from the woman's toned rear. *Jesus, keep your focus,* he reminded himself. *I must be getting old. She knows what she's doing and I've been around the block enough to know better.* Ian felt for his cell phone, but only found the holster. The reminder that he was out of touch and alone shattered the façade. *I've gotta get through this.*

The hall sloped, and they passed deeper into the earth where water began cascading down the carved sides, seeping from various levels of striated rock beds. Small, grated drains on the floor edges dispersed the water to some place unknown. *Aren't we too deep to be in the water table?* He'd never been much for geology, but he'd brushed up when the contractors drilled the wells for his ranch house in Oregon.

The woman didn't slow, and Ian resumed his pace. The walls began to glisten beneath the thin waterfalls, the rock beneath reflecting the light in shades of blue and purple. The thin sheen of water had grown to envelop the entirety of both sides and now shimmered like nothing he'd seen before.

Ian coughed into a balled fist, then asked, "Hey, lady, you mentioned an employer. Are we gonna meet any time soon, or should I have packed some leftovers?"

She stopped walking and turned to meet his gaze. "Hungry, are you?" She licked her lips as though savoring a memory, then turned back down the hall. "It isn't far." Her heels splashed in the thin sheet of water now flowing across the hall.

Ian had no choice, as much as he hated it. There was no way out. He followed her farther until she stopped, bit her finger, and pressed its bloody end against a flattened panel the size of a fist. It blended into its surroundings under the glistening water. A doorway slid in and she passed under the sheet of liquid without hesitation. Ian passed through after her, drenching himself. When he emerged on the other side, he was surprised to find the woman standing next to an obese man in archaic, royal garb flowing with deep purples and greens. Unlike any monarchy he knew of, this man wore an ornate kilt and green cloak. Other than that, he was bare-chested and hairless, seated in a stone chair with more ornate carvings than anything Ian had seen before. A stern face and bulbous nose peered down at him with an inner fury. Ian ran a hand over his forehead and through his hair, clearing the water from his vision.

Wait, what about her? He looked from one to the other. Neither seemed to have been touched by the water. No other doors or panels appeared around the chiseled, stone room. The water flowed here, as it had in the hall, but neither of them seemed bothered by it. Looking between the two, he noticed something he hadn't seen before. They shared the same deep-purple eyes and a hungry glare.

How could I have missed that? A vision of her well-formed rear entered his thoughts. *Stupid, old man!*

Ian's heart skipped a beat, and he glanced nervously at the walls: no windows anywhere. He turned to retreat and found a muscle-bound man blocking his way. The black suit and sunglasses seemed out of place, but it was apparent what the man's function was. The door swung shut after his silent entrance, sealing Ian in like a rat in the sewer. The only differences were the flickering colors and the luminescent lights above. Even the nauseating smell returned in this room.

The absence of light seemed permanent, and the cold wind slapping his face was damp, not like the air he'd felt at altitude. *Where am I?*

"Where you are, is in my audience chamber." The voice was deep and powerful. His words lapped on the back of his teeth like tidal waves on the shore.

I know I've never heard that voice before, and yet it feels familiar. Wait, did I ask that out loud before? I'm sure I didn't. How did...

"How isn't important right now. Are you going to introduce yourself? I grow bored of this interview already."

Regain your composure, old man. "My name is Ian Masters. I apologize for my rudeness. This is all just so surreal. How would you prefer to be addressed, Sir?"

"You may refer to me as Your Highness," the large man replied. The woman leaned in and whispered into his ear, then he continued. "So, Mr. Masters is it?" His voice carried a deep, cold hatred at the utterance of the name. "Why give me such an obvious lie? You were caught in the basement uplinking Dawbry's mainframe with whoever your benefactors are. You accepted going deep into the bowels of the earth for an interview. And, more impressively, you reacted to my presence with only a brief moment of panic. You are no EPA investigator." He leaned closer and the combination of fish, brine, and brimstone wafted on his breath. "Who are you really?"

"Your Highness's observations are astute." *Got to think quickly, I need an old, verifiable ID.* "The name is Daniel Simmons. I'm a private investigator. The locals hired me to get info for the case they're bringing against Dawbry."

The woman smiled, almost seeming to purr. "John, who are you really working for? We will get the information from you, but I promise it will be much more fun if you cooperate."

I think that's my name, but how does she know it?

"I don't know who you think I am, but you're sadly mistaken. My name is Dan." The lie didn't even sound convincing to Ian...

John; he still wasn't certain who he was. His voice cracked as panic started to sink in. "M-M-Maybe we could get some coffee when this is over, but I think I should be leaving." Before he could turn, two large, cold hands grabbed his shoulders from behind.

"Take him to my office... by Your Highness's leave, of course," added the attractive woman in a voice that had lost all sense of compassion.

"Do what you must, Arielle. I'll expect your report soon."

Unable to do more than protest, the goliath shoved Ian through the wall of water. By the time his eyes cleared, he was alone in a room with Arielle. Seaweed wraps entangled his arms, holding him firmly to a small stool

How the hell did I get here? It was as though the minutes faded into hours, leaving him with less than a memory.

The room was featureless, and for all Ian knew, he could be inside an egg. Stark, white walls seemed to flow in an oval. The only furniture, other than the stool, was a low table that Arielle sat perched atop, legs crossed as though the world could crumble around her, and she wouldn't bat an eyelash. Her smile was gone, vanished like so many unexplainable things. Everything that was once sultry had become predatory. She was a shark and Ian, a minnow. For the first time in many years, a trickle of nervous sweat rolled down Ian's temple.

Get a grip. There's a way out. There always is.

"Who do you work for," asked Arielle, wasting no time on simple chit-chat.

"You seem like you can read my mind," Ian retorted. "You tell me." *I don't believe the words I'm saying. It's an expression of speech,* he reminded himself. *But it's one that fits.*

"I would," she replied. "But you're a strong man, John. You have so many thoughts in your head and you can't keep them all in that basket of a brain. I'm only catching the ones that trickle over the brim. But the ones you've got floating down at the bottom... no, can't reach those."

Arielle slid from the table to stand in front of Ian, peering into his eyes. *How did I miss those sunken cheeks? The glint in her eyes that says she could gut me with one hand and talk on the phone to her mother with the other? The incisors that would make Dracula jealous? What have you gotten yourself into, old man?*

Arielle dragged her hand over the table as she took a step forward. The scrape echoed in the small room until her hand fell on a knife. Lifting it up, she admired her reflection for a moment. The blade itself was thin, nothing like the one in John's boot. His was meant to make horrid punctures that refuse to stop bleeding. Hers was made to peel back the most delicate of flesh with minimum trauma, a fillet knife.

I really don't like where this is going. But I still have the knife in my boot. That hideaway sheath was the best investment I ever made. It's not over yet, not till the pig's roasted, party goers are stuffed to the brim, and the fat lady can't sing another note.

Arielle lazily regarded the edge of her shiny tool. "I wanted to reward you, John. I wanted you to tell me everything your mercenary heart had to say, and I wanted to give you warm, soft, and wet gratitude in return. Now, I have to play with things you were never meant to see outside your body. It isn't what I intended, but we all have our jobs to do, unless you tell me, right now, who… do… you… work… for?"

Ian struggled to come up with something, anything, and finally resorted to the truth, hoping it would buy some time. "I don't know. I worked through intermediaries. They just called it the 'agency'. The money was good, so I didn't ask for more."

Arielle stopped just past the table. *Closer, but not close enough, yet.* Cocking her head to the side, she gave him an unreadable look. In those fleeting moments, Ian guessed what she was thinking; something to do with which part of him would look best minus some skin.

"I believe you," she said after a moment's pause. "But you're going to have to tell me more."

Time to switch tactics. "I don't have to tell you jack," he spat. "I'm going to end up bait in the river, and you know it. There's not a damn reason I should make this easier for you."

With a twist of his ankle, Ian tested the straps as though struggling to break free. The wraps tying his legs to the chair were tight, but slick. Aware of what needed to be done, his last chance at survival, he waited for the proper moment.

She stepped toward him in slow, graceful strides. The knife flashed and Ian was instantly bleeding from both cheeks before he could blink.

Stepping back to the table, Arielle picked up a small vial. She popped the stopper off with a thumb, then flung it into his face. The cuts lit up like neon, and pain coursed through his veins.

Over his hissing screams, she yelled, "Reason enough for you?"

Ian gritted his teeth and managed, "Nope. Need a better one."

Laughter erupted from the woman like a bubbling furnace: another uncomfortable sound. *That's not good. I want her mad, not amused.*

"Oh, this is going to be a long, entertaining night isn't it," she said through her mirth.

"Does that mean I get a lap dance?" asked Ian. Writhing in his chair, he loosened the binding around his good leg.

"No, but you do get this."

Arielle flew at him like lightning and her fist slammed into Ian's gut like a well-manicured Volkswagen.

Blood flew from his mouth, spattering the white room, and was closely followed by, "Please, miss, may I have another?"

The purple-eyed woman granted his wish. Ian rolled with it and stifled a smile as his leg almost slipped free of the slimy bonds.

"Wanna go for the bonus round, sweetheart?" asked Ian. His voice was patronizing, but the anguish stretched across his face told another story. He couldn't take another shot, and he knew it.

Arielle screamed and lunged at him. *This one's going to shatter my pancreas,* Ian thought with certainty, *but I have other plans.* His leg pulled up and out of the bindings. Pushing away from her, he rolled to the floor, compressed like a spring waiting for the right moment. Realizing her punch landed on nothing but air, she turned her momentum and fell on Ian like a tiger pursuing its dinner. Ian slid his free calf against the still-bound foot, catching the heel of his shoe and the pommel of his boot knife. With an instantaneous jerk, the blade ejected itself through the bottom of the sheath and four inches past his boot sole.

A widening of her eyes revealed her astonishment as Ian thrust his bladed foot into her chest. Seconds seemed like painful minutes as Arielle's quivering form weighed on Ian's foot. But eventually, her wide-eyed stare darkened, and her quivering form went limp.

I don't have much time. They've got to be watching. Pushing her back with his free leg, the blade tugged at what was left of the sheath but stayed dangling from his ankle. The years hadn't yet stolen his flexibility, so Ian pulled his ankle up to his left hand and began slicing at the remaining bonds. The first restraint was awkward to cut, but the others rapidly disappeared with just a single stroke *At least two minutes have passed. The guards will be here any moment.*

The walls appeared smooth. The spot behind Ian should have had a door, but he couldn't discern one. Peering around him, he scanned the table in the hopes of finding a button or control; something that would give him a viable egress from this prison.

The only things he found were more implements of torture, a host of tools: pointy, hooked, and sharp. There were three syringes, each one filled with an ochre fluid. Thinking quickly, Ian grabbed one and slid it into his pocket.

It might be evidence of what they produce here. I know it's a long shot, but it's a spot above where I stand now, which is empty handed.

Minute four passed, and Ian began to panic. That's when he heard the scraping.

Turning in place, a nightmare appeared before him with horrible, feral claws and teeth. Arielle was moving when she should have been nothing more than grub fertilizer.

Ian backed into the wall. *I can't believe it. This can't be real.*

She screamed and lurched for the table, her face now more beast than beauty. She grabbed one of the other two syringes and jabbed it into her own neck. Ian's stomach turned a somersault as the bleeding wound in her chest began to bubble with yellow froth and seal itself.

His composure broke. Turning in place, Ian slammed his shoulder into the wall. It gave, but only a little. In panic, he slammed into it again and the wall gave way like tearing through chicken skin. Through the wall, Ian fell to the floor of another unknown room with walls like the previous.

Oh, man. I'm not just one room away from where I met His Twisted Majesty. How long was I out? It could take ages to escape this place.

Peering around him, Ian spotted stairs going up. Glancing over his shoulder, he spotted Arielle getting to her feet and looking at him through the tattered wall with a much more substantial knife in her hand than the boot knife in his.

He scrambled to his feet and ran without a thought more. His lungs burned as he topped the fourth flight of stairs at full sprint.

A Klaxon sound echoed above, saying "The prisoner has escaped."

With no time to rest, Ian tried the two doors that appeared before him, but behind each one a horde of boots and shouts warned him away. From two floors below, Arielle bellowed, "He's here!"

Up's the only way left.

Rounding the stairs, he chanced on a door that looked normal enough, with no sounds behind it. Ian pushed through to find normal-looking office doors lining both sides of the hall. Ian tried the first, but it barely jiggled. Pulling a wire and card from his pocket, he paused to try to pick one, but paused too long.

The hiss of an opening door alerted him to the vicious bitch's approach, her blade out in front, leading the way to him. He deflected it by reflex, but not fast enough. Rather than sliding to the side and innocently avoiding his tender bits, it impaled his spleen.

Ian counterstruck automatically. Her neck gave way to the edge of his knife with a sickening gurgle, and her eyes died a second time that night.

But what if she comes back? Ian wondered. Unwilling to take the chance, his knife struck out a dozen more times as he yelled, "Stay dead."

As his thrumming heart slowed, the pain in his side returned. He felt where her knife had momentarily embedded itself in his side, and his hand came away coated with warm blood... his blood. Boots echoed up the stairs, mere feet away, and from somewhere else on the floor came the ping of an elevator opening.

This isn't how I want to spend my last moments. Ian's mind flashed back to the syringe. *Don't think, old man, just do.* The needle stung like pissed-off fire as it sunk into Ian's neck. He pushed the plunger and instantly his skin tried to crawl off his bones. Nausea engulfed him, but overshadowing that was a feeling of pure strength.

Boot heels smacking on tile forced Ian up. No time to question it further, Ian leaped at the first door and bashed it open. An empty office greeted him with a large open window and a window washer's scaffolding outside. *It's a jump, but I can make it. I'm sure of it.*

Bullets smacked the doorframe and all questions fled. He had no choice. He ran headlong for the window and everything slowed down. His senses became heightened with the adrenaline rush. Bullets whizzed past him, and Ian counted thirteen motes of dust. His senses were so aware he could feel every hair on his body, every thread of the clothes touching his skin.

As his feet left the windowsill for the second jump, his thoughts turned back to his flight. He landed on the platform with a hard thump, and as the scaffolding swayed, he held the knife away from his body. The last thing he needed was to become a human pincushion, his life ended suddenly on his own knife.

Bullets pinged off the frame as he hit the controls. In the sunlight the sky was so bright, he could barely see. *There's a lever on this contraption. It'll make the thing descend faster; if I can just find it...* His hands flew over the controls in a millisecond. It wasn't hard to find. Time was so stretched that every second seemed like an intermission.

As another barrage of bullets thundered around Ian, he felt the lever under his hand. *No time like the present,* he thought with a laugh and pulled. The bullets flew around Ian like a hailstorm. Even in his enhanced state, all sense of direction eluded him, and the brightness turned to black.

Bullets slammed into his flesh, one... two... three. The wind whipped at him from below, reminding him that he was falling. *Is that good or bad?* he wondered, unable to connect the dots that led him to that moment. Bullets clanged on the cable holding the platform up. A distinct twang sent a shudder through the scaffolding and the platform upended.

Oh, that's when the falling started. Good to know.

A voice echoes through the void. "It's falling, plummeting."

"I know I'm falling dammit...! Wait, who the hell's that?" asks John, but the urgent voice continues without hearing him.

"The N.S. isn't enough. Push fluids!"

Light speckles John's vision.

"Get his damned clothes off, and get me four units of O-negative, stat. He's bleeding out."

Something jerks at John's suit pants, and as they're cut away, air greets his exposed body. The wind rushing past has calmed, merging with the hum and beep of machines clustered around him. His vision slowly returns and the spots disappear. Gravity still pulls at him, though, rushing toward his head in his awkward position. His sneakers perch above him on the tilted table and beyond that, a stark, white ceiling.

"Who is he?" asks an older nurse with gray-tinged hair from across the room.

"God knows, but he's lucky to be alive. Where is that O.R. team? Get Doctor Ralin on the phone."

"On it," squeaks a slim man with a five-o'clock shadow and green scrubs. The others ignore him as he mutters into the phone.

Applying pressure to a compress on his side, the nurse mumbles, "That fall should've killed him. I think landing on the scaffold might have saved his life."

A fragile blonde outfitted in more green scrubs interrupts. "Should his innards be foaming like that?"

John tries to fight gravity and leans forward. A groan escapes his lips. "A-a-am I still falling?" The effort triggers a bloody cough.

"Enough, Irene. We'll have it tested," answers the deep voice that broke through the darkness. The man grips John's rising shoulders and forces him back down. A square of white covers his mouth and nose. As their eyes meet, a shiver runs through the patient. The doctor's purple eyes peer down, weighing John like a scale, but to what end?

Oh, no. Not again.

"Don't try to say too much. You're not falling. The ground took care of that. Do you know your name?" asks the man in a soothing voice.

Ian... John... Dan... Paul... Sam... and a dozen more names filter through John's hazy brain. *Which is mine?*

"N-n-no," he mutters in a staggered breath.

Thank you for reading. I hope you enjoyed the excerpt. You can get your copy of *Strange Circumstances* on Amazon.

Tempt fate. Destroy destiny. Demand retribution.

If you like delightfully dark diversions from reality, stories strange and wonderful that leave you begging for more, Strange Circumstances is the collection for you. The future is a gamble. Care to place a bet on yours?

Sign up to read Strange Circumstances FREE today.

http://strangecircumstances.gr8.com

Made in the USA
Coppell, TX
20 July 2020